Quest for New England

Book One

Rising from the Ruins

Anna Chant

To the memory of victims of war, of every race, every colour, every creed and every time

Prologue: October 14th 1066

The cries of the wounded slashed his ears, the clash of weaponry continued relentlessly on. The wyvern on the standard above him fluttered bravely and hopelessly. It was obvious he was about to die. His shield was in splinters. Only his mail shirt and sword stood between him and the axe of the man of before him. As the man raised it, he took a deep breath, the peculiar battle stench of blood, sweat and horse dung scorching his nostrils, terrified it would be his last.

With all the strength of a desperate man, he blocked the blow but the weight of the axe sent vibrations up his arms. Fatally his sweaty hand lost its grip on the sword, just for an instant, but an instant was all it took for it to slip from his grasp. He scrambled for it, knowing the axe would strike him before he could reach it.

But as he waited for the blow to fall, a man came from behind him. A man quick enough to get between him and the axe, quick enough to push a spear in the direction of the foe but not quick enough to drive it in, before the axe fell, biting into his neck.

He had heard many a desperate cry that day but none more than the one his rescuer gave as he collapsed to the ground. With his sword now back in his grasp, he forced it at the foe, thrusting it in before he had time to raise his axe again, pushing it deeply. Another cry rent the air but this one brought him only satisfaction.

Forgetting the foe he had slain, he bent over his rescuer, seeing under the helmet, blue eyes filled with despair...

Part One: January – February 1073

Chapter one

Oswyth placed a pillow behind the old man's back. "There, Grandfather. Is that better?"

"Thank you, my child." Raedwulf patted her shoulder with a trembling hand. "Come, let us dine."

Oswyth took her place on the dais next to her grandfather, pouring a horn full of ale just as he liked her to do. She smiled out at the churls who had given service that day, taking their own places at tables and the thralls sitting on the floor. They ate with a forced merriment, one they had maintained every night for more than six years. Oswyth had dim recollections of lively nights in the hall as a child when music filled the space and laughter rang out. Back in the days of King Edward and even those brief months of King Harold's reign, there had been no need for such forced cheer. She swallowed the lump in her throat that came every time she thought of the battle which had robbed her of her father and England of its king, leaving only a tyrant to rule in his place.

She noticed her grandfather was eating little, simply crumbling some bread between his fingers. Oswyth shivered. He was her only family. Her mother had been brought to childbed just weeks after hearing of the death of her father. But any hope this event would restore joy to their household had been swiftly dashed as both she and the boy she carried, perished.

"Grandfather, this pork is very fine. You know Lent will be upon us soon. You should enjoy it while you still can."

Raedwulf started as if disturbed from his thoughts. He smiled at his granddaughter, taking a bite of the meat. "You are right, my dear. This is truly fine." He ate the rest of the slice and gestured to one of the thralls to cut him another piece.

Oswyth smiled but she was not fooled. It was doubtful he had even tasted it. She knew what worried her grandfather. As her grandfather's sole heir, she had, like many another English orphan, been betrothed soon after the battle which brought the Norman duke to the throne of England. Her intended husband, one of the new king's men. She shivered again, remembering him as a towering man, who had laughed loudly and patted her on the head, making a derisive comment in his own tongue to his companion. The look of despair on Raedwulf's face had deepened as she had pledged herself to marry the man. As she was at that point just ten years of age, the wedding had not been solemnised and less than two years later the man was dead.

Raedwulf had kept quiet, maintaining his own lands and not giving any trouble to the conquering duke. Every night he went down on his knees and prayed they had been forgotten. His lands were fine but not extensive and the pretender king had his hands full with rebellion. Raedwulf's own single act of rebellion was to make cautious overtures to other Englishmen, desperate to see his only granddaughter married to one of their own kind but to no avail. The rebellions had taken their toll and those who survived were unwilling to antagonise their new lords by seeking marriage with such an heiress. Although she had recently turned seventeen, Oswyth was still unwed.

They had not yet finished their meal when a man was ushered through the door, dressed in dark dusty clothes. His hood fell back to reveal the short hair so beloved by their conquerors. He strode up to the dais bobbing his head in a curt bow to Raedwulf. Oswyth ground her teeth at so little courtesy. Her grandfather deserved better.

"Greetings, Thegn Raedwulf. I am here on behalf of the noble Turstin Fitz Rolf."

Raedwulf's knuckles whitened as he clutched his knife but nothing else betrayed his consternation at the name of the man who held so much of the surrounding lands. "Greetings," he replied. "Have you travelled far? Please, sit yourself and take some ale."

"I will deliver my message first, if I may," the man replied.

Raedwulf nodded.

"The good lord, Turstin Fitz Rolf will be in these parts in the next days. He intends to pay a visit to your lands."

A smirk flickered across the messenger's face at the fearful murmurs whispering through the hall. Everyone knew what this meant. It was likely the lands would be not be Raedwulf's for much longer. It seemed his obedience was not to be rewarded.

Raedwulf gave no sign of the distress Oswyth knew he would be feeling. "I shall be glad to welcome him."

"He will be accompanied by his son, Ralf Fitz Turstin. An excellent young man," the messenger continued with a long look at Oswyth. Her fury deepened at the lascivious glint in his eye.

Raedwulf inclined his head. "I thank you for your message. Please, refresh yourself. I trust you will rest by my hearth this night. In the morning return to your lord and assure him a welcome will be ready for him whenever he chooses to arrive."

Oswyth looked down at the table, not knowing how her grandfather could sound so calm. She wanted to shout and shriek, hurl the jug of ale over the man's head and stab him with the knife she held, to do anything rather than bid the hated Normans and their servants welcome in their hall.

She tried to finish her meal but the food stuck in her throat. Setting down her knife, she looked around the hall and saw even the forced cheerfulness had dimmed. The people quickly scraped their trenchers, none of them meeting her gaze. Several murmured excuses, slinking away to pretend to sleep in the corners of the hall.

∞∞∞∞

After the meal she and her grandfather withdrew to their private space behind the hall. It was not where they normally slept in winter, preferring to join the rest of the household around the hearth. But it was a place they could talk without being overheard.

Swathing herself in blankets, Oswyth shivered. An anxious glance at her grandfather showed him to be lost in thought, his brow creased into deep furrows. This new burden seemed to have aged him even further. She huddled closer, wrapping the folds of the blanket over them both as she tried to bring him some comfort.

"My child, their intentions are obvious," Raedwulf said at last, putting a thin arm around her shoulders. "You are to be married to this Ralf and he will take my lands."

Oswyth nodded, trying to smile. "Perhaps it will not be so bad. At least we will stay here. They would not turf you off the lands, would they?"

Her voice died away as she imagined her grandfather forced from his dwelling the day after her wedding. Tears filled her eyes. If the bastard duke had not conquered the land, all would have been well. Her wedding would have been a joyful occasion, perhaps with her father still alive to choose her husband and she did not doubt he would have chosen wisely. This marriage would be so different. All too clearly she could imagine the day of forced merriment when their people would have to pretend to celebrate. When she too would have to appear content with the arrangement. For her grandfather to have to give her in such a marriage would surely hasten his end and then she would be all alone with her Norman husband.

Raedwulf gave a faint smile and patted her hand. "I am too old to be any threat. I doubt they would force me away."

"Then it will not be so bad." Oswyth blinked back her tears

with an effort. "One day my son, your great-grandson, will inherit these lands."

Again her voice trailed away. She wished to name her first-born son, Raedwulf for her grandfather and father, who too had born that name, but it would not be allowed. Her sons would be expected to bear names such as William or Robert. Or Ralf and Turstin.

"This is not what I want for you," Raedwulf said quietly, tears springing to his own eyes. "It would not be what your dear father, may God have mercy on his soul, would want either."

"No, it would not," Oswyth replied. "But what can I do? I could enter a convent but then they will take the lands anyway. They are greedy these Normans. They have so much but still they take more. They will not rest until the English have nothing to call their own."

"I know." Raedwulf pulled his granddaughter into his arms, holding her tightly. Oswyth was clinging back, determined not to add to his worries by weeping, when he suddenly straightened himself, a smile flickering on his face. "My child, when they come, take to your bed. Pretend you are suffering a severe sickness, so they will not enter."

"What good will that do? It just puts off the inevitable. I cannot keep to my bed for the rest of my life, can I? At some point I must recover and then they will come." Oswyth's voice shook as the hopelessness of her fate sank in. "There is no escaping this, Grandfather. I will be wed."

"It gives us a little time." Raedwulf smiled at his frightened granddaughter. "As soon as that Norman departs in the morn, I shall send off my own messenger."

"Where to?"

"To one man who may be willing to help us."

Chapter two

Siward sat bolt upright in his bed, the sweat on his body chilling him on that winter's night. The nightmare had struck him again. For more than six years it had plagued him, as again he looked into the blue eyes of the dying man who had saved his life. It wasn't the first man he had seen die and he had seen many another perish since, yet that was the one he could never forget.

He pulled a blanket around his shivering shoulders, his thoughts dragged back to the battle near Hastings. He had helped the man from the field, lying him by the back lines. As he had removed his helmet, he recognised him as Raedwulf, son of Thegn Raedwulf, a well-respected landowner from Somerset. With the blood flowing from the wound in his neck, he had known it was hopeless. Although he was needed in the fight, he was unwilling to allow the man to die alone and even as a priest knelt beside him, he had not left.

He had hoped the priest's final blessing would bring the man some peace, but he had remained agitated. Although almost too weak to move, his eyes had darted frantically around, eventually meeting Siward's.

"Oswyth," he whispered. "My sweet child, may God be with her. My wife, my poor wife, my father. What will become of them? Oh, sweet little Oswyth."

Siward had leant closer to him, praying the dying man could hear him. "Do not concern yourself for them. If I survive this battle, I shall render them any service I can."

He had no idea if the words were understood but the despair had faded from the blue eyes with the life fading shortly after. As the man breathed his last, Siward had risen to his feet, taking the man's shield to replace his own useless one. Resolutely he returned to the fight. To the brutal defeat.

In the darkness the faces of those he had seen die swarmed around him, desperation in every eye. His heart pounding so hard he could scarcely breathe, Siward lit a candle, knowing the night was over for him. The flickering light drove away the tormented faces, illuminating only the cloths hanging the walls of his bed chamber.

He knew why he had suffered the dream that night. The previous day he had received a message from Thegn Raedwulf, begging him to come.

"You once promised you would aid me in any way you could," the message had stated. "If you are a man of your word, come to us as soon as you can."

Siward well remembered the day he had made that promise. It was shortly before Christmas six years previously, when, in spite of his efforts to convince the Witan to the contrary, the nobles had submitted to William the Bastard. He had known he could either join them or return home. Unable to face the man's crowning, he had left London, hoping that even though the south and east of the realm had submitted, there might still be some heart in the west. He had taken a circuitous route, breaking his journey at Thegn Raedwulf's residence to return the shield. He thought perhaps the man had a son who might one day proudly bear it in honour of his dead father, but when he arrived he found death had proceeded him. The man's wife was dead and so too was the only son he would sire.

As he entered the hall, he was aware of the grief hanging tangibly in it, shrouding the bright tapestries of what had once been a scene of merriment. Dressed in dark clothes, Thegn Raedwulf had received him with solemn courtesy. As he held the position of eorl, Siward far outranked the thegn, but he had bowed low before him, avoiding his eyes as he described the heroism of his son.

He had not immediately noticed the child standing behind the old man, a grey clad, fair haired girl of no more than ten years. He had not noticed her until she launched herself forward, beating her fists against him.

"My father is dead because of you," she had shrieked. "This is your fault. How could you drop your sword? My father should be alive. He would have won the battle. He would have defeated the invaders."

He could easily have held her at a distance but instead he had stood still, allowing her to hit him, accepting it as the punishment he deserved from every grieving mother, widow and orphan in the land. He had failed to defend his country and now it was in the hands of its conqueror.

Thegn Raedwulf had pulled the girl away, gesturing to one of the maid servants to take her from the hall. His gaze had followed the weeping child before looking resolutely at Raedwulf, half expecting a similar tirade from him. But the man had come forward and embraced him. The two had wept together, allowing their tears to mingle for the death of a fine man, for the loss of England.

"But this is not the end," he said at last. "The Bastard can have himself crowned but the fight will go on. We will resist. Soon we will drive him from England."

"I pray you do," Raedwulf replied. "I do not mind for myself. It is for young men like you, that England must go on."

"I will not rest until I have freed Englishmen from the Norman rule, I swear it. And if you ever need my help, send word to me. If it is in my power, I will serve you as a tribute to your fine son."

Lying back against the pillows, Siward gave a grim smile. When he had spoken those words, he had no idea how hard it would be. Far from toppling the Bastard, he had watched the man's grip grow ever stronger. As he had hoped, the West had risen but that hope was dashed when the revolt was swiftly suppressed. Then, bolstered by support from the King of Denmark, the North had rebelled.

Tears came to Siward's eyes as he reflected on the tragedy which hit the North. Whole villages burnt to the ground. Many thousands of men, women and children slain or starved. Never had he thought one man could be responsible for the deaths of so many innocents, their only crime to want their land returned.

Siward had not been in the north that winter, his remaining lands in that region having been already stripped from him and he had no wish to ever return. The area north of York was said to be a wasteland, haunted only by the despairing ghosts of those who perished. It was clear to him that the Norman duke was no mere man, but a demon sent from hell to destroy them.

There had been one ray of salvation. A mighty man, Hereward by name, had risen. A man who appeared strong enough to take on the Bastard pretender. Siward, like many another English noblemen, had ridden with his men to join him at Ely, certain they could hold that land and from that bleak island, England would rise again.

It was an Englishman, a monk, who had betrayed them, telling the Bastard's army how to reach them. Siward had barely escaped alive, somehow escaping with his men through the fens. Afterwards he heard he had only escaped because so many of the Bastard's men had drowned when their own causeway had collapsed. But the brief surge of joy that the very land itself was rising against the invaders was thwarted as he learnt the fate of many of his friends and kin. The lucky ones had died in the struggle while the less fortunate now languished in captivity. Yet Siward could not bring himself to blame the one who had betrayed them. He could understand the East fearing the same fate as the North. So many had now capitulated, the situation seemed impossible. Siward had vowed not to give up the struggle but he was fast losing hope, certain he would fail everyone who asked for his aid. As he feared he would now fail Thegn Raedwulf, the father of the man who had sacrificed himself to save him.

He shifted his shivering body under the covers, staring at the candle, wondering what to do. He was tempted to reply that he was unable to help, firmly blotting out the memory of the man's dying eyes. But the echo of his voice came to whisper in his ear, speaking again his final words.

"My sweet child, may God be with her. My wife, my poor wife, my father. What will become of them? Oh, sweet little Oswyth."

The anguished tone of the whisper made him hesitate. If he refused, he would fail that man all over again. By the time dawn broke and he could leave his bed, Siward had made his decision. He dressed in a riding tunic over thick, woollen breeches.

"Pack me some spare clothes and some victuals for a journey," he commanded one his thralls. He smiled at his surprised mother. "There is a good Englishman who has need of me and if it is in my power to aid him, I will do it."

Chapter three

Oswyth lay before the hearth, swathed in blankets. She was far too hot but she supposed the sweat dripping from her brow might be a good thing when the wretched Turstin Fitz Rolf arrived. She was glad not to have to greet those men although she still had no idea how this delay would help. Despite her constant pestering, her grandfather had refused to explain who he was contacting or what this man could do.

"He has arrived," a man at the door called.

"Play your part, my child," Raedwulf muttered, moving towards the door.

She kept her eyelids half lowered, but turned her head to gain a good view of the two men entering.

"Greetings, Thegn Raedwulf. I am Turstin Fitz Rolf. I present my son, Ralf," the older of the two said. He was a tall man with dark red hair, somewhat scanty at the front. The man with him looked to be around twenty-five years but with the same red hair, he strongly resembled his father.

"Greetings, my lord," Raedwulf replied in a weary tone. "I bid you welcome but must caution you to enter at your peril. We have been struck by a most grievous sickness."

Oswyth gave a muffled cough although neither of the men payed any attention.

"Well, the day is a fine one for this season," Turstin commented in strongly accented English. "We shall talk outside. Do you at least have some ale for us?"

"Of course," Raedwulf replied, gesturing to one of the thralls to bring a jug and some cups.

"The thralls and churls here, are they obedient?" Turstin asked.

"They have always served me well," Raedwulf replied.

"Excellent. My son and I will take a look at your lands while we are here. I trust there is no objection to that."

"None at all," Raedwulf said. "But may I ask the reason for your interest?"

Remembering she was supposed to be seriously ill, Oswyth coughed again and let out a low moan. The maidservant kneeling beside her also played her part well, muttering some soothing words and wiping the sweat from her brow.

Turstin exchanged glances with his son and laughed. "I am sure you are no fool, my friend. You know that just because you held these lands during the reigns of the previous kings does not mean that will continue. The noble King William bestows lands only on loyal men."

"But I have caused him no trouble," Raedwulf cried, his voice crackling. "I am an old man. Can he not at least let me die in my own home?"

Oswyth moaned again, the sound all the more genuine at her grandfather mentioning his death. She could see how frail he had become and her grief at the thought of losing him, mingled with a bitter fear of what would happen to her after he died.

Ralf laughed again. "Do not fear, my friend. We are not the monsters you Englishmen seem to think we are. Naturally you shall remain here."

"We are familiar with your situation," Turstin said. "You have a granddaughter who is unwed. My son too is unwed. They shall be joined and my son will be your heir."

"Yes, I have a granddaughter." Raedwulf's voice broke. "For now, I do."

"What do you mean?" Turstin demanded.

"I have told you. We have a grievous sickness in the house. Two thralls have already succumbed. And last night my precious Oswyth took ill. Pray for her, I beg you."

There was a long silence. "That is unfortunate," Turstin said. "Well, we shall take a look at your lands in any case."

Ralf shook his head, frowning. "I wished to see the girl. We know nothing about her. I trust she has no deformity or other such matter which would render a marriage distasteful."

"My sweet Oswyth is the most beautiful of maidens," Raedwulf said. "But she lies grievously ill. I must counsel you not to approach her."

"Do not be a fool, Raedwulf. We shall not linger but let Ralf see the girl. Of course we will pray she recovers."

"It would certainly be unfortunate if she dies," Ralf muttered.

"It makes no difference, my boy. If she lives, she will wed you and you will inherit these lands. If she dies, well, he has no other heir and upon his death, the lands can be bestowed upon you in any case."

"That is true."

Oswyth cried out as if in pain, furious at the two men so calmly discussing her death. A fine husband he would be. With her eyes closed, she was aware of footsteps coming closer and gave a cough, using the excuse to bring her hand to her mouth, pushing in some mushed bread. She half opened her eyes to see the two men staring down at her. There was little in their appearance to disgust her but her skin crawled with nothing false about the shudder coursing through her body.

"Well, she is pretty enough," Ralf said. "I hope she will recover. I am sure she will be an acceptable wife."

Oswyth's rage rose. He should consider himself highly fortunate to gain her as his wife and to inherit her grandfather's lands. If there was one certainty in her mind, it was that he was not an acceptable husband.

"Is she also accomplished and hardworking?" Ralf continued.

"She is the dearest, sweetest girl," Raedwulf said in a sad tone. "She works tirelessly for my comfort, asking nothing in return. I beg you to be good to her."

"If she is an amenable, obedient wife, she shall have no cause to complain of me," Ralf said tersely. "I will expect her to converse in my language. If she does not already speak it, find a priest to start instructing her as soon as she recovers."

For Oswyth this was the last straw. She coughed again, retching on the bread in her mouth. Jerking forward she took great pleasure in pretending to vomit, spitting the mush over his well-made shoes. That was what she thought of him and his language.

Ralf yelped in disgust, stepping sharply away from her as she slumped back with a moan. The maidservant gently wiped her mouth, exclaiming over the sickness.

"I fear she grows worse, my lord," she said.

"My poor child." Raedwulf shook his head. "My poor, poor child."

Ralf and Turstin strode from the hall, Ralf still complaining at the mess. "We shall ride around your lands before we depart," Turstin called. "I hope the girl recovers. If she dies, send us word. Otherwise we shall return in two weeks and trust she will be well enough to be wed. A good day to you."

A silence fell on the hall and Oswyth lay still, not daring to rise from her bed or even betray any glee at her actions until she could be certain it was safe. She had no idea what they had achieved by this deception but it had been satisfying all the same.

"They are away, my lord," the man at the door stated.

With a sigh of relief, Oswyth sat up, throwing back the blankets. "God be praised," she muttered, letting her smile out at last.

Raedwulf glanced at her. "Really, my child, was there any need for that? It is not how we treat a guest in our residence."

"It is how I treat that one," Oswyth retorted. "And you are proud of me. Do not deny it, Grandfather."

A ripple of laughter went round the hall and Raedwulf's mouth twitched. He did not deny her words.

"Oh, my dear child. You have your father's great spirit. You deserve so much better than that man."

"I know. To marry him…" Oswyth's voice trembled at the thought of a life with him, managing the household to his specifications with no thought to their customs and submitting to his desires in the bedchamber. "But I am sure it will not be so bad." She made her voice determinedly cheerful, not wishing to distress her grandfather. "You will still be with me. Your home will remain yours."

"Yes, so great spirited," Raedwulf said. "Do not fear, my child. I have a plan. We have two weeks, do we not?"

"But what can happen in the next two weeks?" Oswyth asked. "You spoke of one who can help us? Who is he?"

"Just wait, my child." A satisfied smile spread over Raedwulf's face. "A lot can change in two weeks. And I received a message yesterday. We shall have another guest in the next few days, a far finer one than the two we just received."

Chapter four

Siward dismounted his horse, handing it to a boy for stabling. It was dusk, the sun setting behind the largest of the buildings which was evidently the hall. Pushing his dark hair back from his eyes, he smiled. It was good to see a building still in the old style. The castles springing up everywhere were magnificent and Siward knew if they had such buildings, their position would be so much stronger but he missed the simplicity of these English halls.

An old man hobbled from the doorway. Siward nodded at him, taking a moment to recognise him as Thegn Raedwulf. The last time he had seen him, he had been a man past his prime but still vigorous and upright. The previous years had taken more of a toll than they should.

"Eorl Siward of Gloucester, greetings and welcome," Raedwulf called.

Siward strode towards him and took his hands. "Thank you. It is a long time since any called me that. I held the title only briefly after my father died before the Bastard came. Please, use my name. It is good to see you again, my friend."

"And I thank you for coming so quickly. Come inside. This day is a cold one for riding."

"Your message spoke of needing my aid. How can I be of assistance?" Siward asked as they entered the hall, the heat from the central hearth providing a welcome relief from the frosty night.

"We shall speak more on that later. First you must dine."

Siward looked around, surprised at the extent of the welcome laid out for him. The hall was lit by brightly burning torches, illuminating tables decked in fine foods. At the dais an attractive young woman waited. Two fair plaits fell almost to her waist but the smile of welcome curving her lips was fading. Siward recognised her instantly. The six years had changed her even more than they had changed Raedwulf but the hostility in her eyes was exactly the same as when she was a child.

Raedwulf beamed. "Do you remember my granddaughter, Oswyth?"

"Of course." As he bowed, Siward reflected he was not likely to forget the heartbroken child who had railed against him. "Greetings, Lady Oswyth."

She gave a curt nod. The years had taught her some restraint as she did not fly at him with her fists but he suspected she still wanted to.

"Is this the guest you spoke of, Grandfather?" Oswyth asked.

"It is, my child. Fill his cup. He has had a cold ride."

Oswyth forced her lips into a smile. "Of course." She handed him a cup. "I bid you welcome, Eorl Siward."

Siward gave an uncertain smile. When her grandfather had used his erstwhile title, he had taken it as a compliment but on the lips of Oswyth, it sounded more of a taunt, yet another reminder of everything he had lost. For her to launch another attack might have been preferable over the discomfort of this forced welcome. With relief he took the seat his host indicated on the dais, glad Raedwulf would be sat between him and Oswyth. He hoped he would not need to make too much conversation with her as he waited impatiently to find out why he had been invited.

"How are you faring, my friend?" Raedwulf asked. "Is there any news on when our true king, Edgar, will return?"

Siward sent a startled glance around the hall and Raedwulf chuckled. "Oh, do not fear. Everyone here is true to King Edgar."

"Yes," Oswyth put in. "We have no traitors in our household."

Siward flushed, guessing she was referring to the man who had betrayed them at Ely. He would have liked to have snapped that the traitor monk was no acquaintance of his, but out of consideration for his host, he was determined not to let the girl rile him. He gave a pleasant smile. "You are fortunate but even so, I urge you to be cautious."

Raedwulf shook his head. "I am too old for the Norman pretenders to concern themselves."

"I would not be so sure. I have seen old men dragged from their homes and left to starve in ditches as their dwellings were set ablaze."

Raedwulf's hand trembled and Oswyth clutched it. She narrowed her eyes, her fury at seeing her grandfather so upset echoed in the sharp edge to her tone. "Like we said, our people are true."

Siward flushed again, wishing the night was over. He hoped the matter Raedwulf needed assistance with was of a trivial nature so he could leave at daybreak. "Of course. Forgive me if I make matters seem too bleak. I have seen such terrors, I see threats everywhere. I spoke merely out of concern."

Raedwulf patted his hand. "I know, my boy. It is sad indeed we must always be so wary. Once a man's dwelling was a place he could be easy. But truly, I do not think you need to fear here. I keep a small household. So, tell us of King Edgar."

"He is still in Flanders."

"Still? He has been there for two years now."

Siward took a mouthful of ale. "I know. But I cannot blame him. The consequences of his last attempt to take the throne were..." He took another mouthful, determined not to let the memories take over.

"You mean when your rebellion failed?" Oswyth asked.

Siward gritted his teeth, angered by the impertinence of his hostess. Raedwulf too darted a reproving look at her. "I believe the failure was on the part of King Sweyn of Denmark, my child. If he had remained true to our cause..."

"The gold the Bastard flung at him was a temptation he could not resist." Siward shook his head sadly, the images of death encroaching in spite of his efforts. They included men who had served his family for generations. He had tried to save them but in most cases his efforts had not been enough.

"How many died?" Raedwulf asked quietly. "I heard rumours but they were too terrible to believe."

"Believe," Siward said. "Thousands of men slain. Tens of thousands more from starvation, their wives and children too. Perhaps more than a hundred thousand dead in all, their dwellings burnt to the ground, their livestock killed and crops spoiled. Never did I expect to witness such cruelty."

"What sort of monster is this Norman?" Oswyth cried. "Does he care nothing for his soul? Does he even have one?"

Oswyth and Siward's eyes met for the first time in a genuine connection. Raedwulf gave a satisfied smile but it lasted only an instant as Oswyth's eyes dropped.

"It is an evil one, Lady Oswyth. He is the most ruthless of men. He will stand no opposition."

"Then you are brave indeed to keep opposing him, is he not, my child?" Raedwulf put in.

Oswyth's polite nod did little to conceal her true feelings and Siward could tell she considered him the abject failure he was.

"I do not know if I am a brave man or a foolish one," Siward replied. "I only know I shall never swear loyalty to that man. I would sooner die."

As the meal came to an end, Raedwulf withdrew with his guest to their chamber. It would be placed at his disposal during his stay, although it was assumed, with the weather so cold, he would choose to sleep with everyone else in the hall. Oswyth followed them, impatient to learn more of her grandfather's plan. She was shocked he had invited Siward there. The man who was responsible for her father's death was one man she never wished to see and it hardly seemed likely that he could help them. She would like to completely ignore their guest, but as she glanced at Raedwulf, the pleasure in his expression as he smiled at Siward, melted her heart. It was good he could for once enjoy himself and presumably the visit would not be a long one.

In the chill of the chamber, Oswyth pulled her cloak tightly around herself, noticing how Siward was doing the same as they both waited to hear why Raedwulf had wanted so urgently to see him.

"We had a visitor recently," Raedwulf began. "A Norman baron informing us that Oswyth is to marry his son."

Siward gave a sympathetic smile. "It is inevitable, I'm afraid. Your granddaughter will be a significant heiress upon your death. But at least your line will continue to dwell here on your lands. Who is the man?"

"The Norman baron is Turstin Fitz Rolf. His son is a man named Ralf."

Siward grimaced, having his own reasons for disliking Turstin. "I do not care for Turstin at all. But I have heard nothing ill of his son. She could do worse."

"But I cannot bear that my sweet Oswyth should be wed to a Norman. She is all I have left. I wanted better for her."

"I know you do but truly I advise you not to fight this. It will be very much the worse for you and your granddaughter if you do. It has been the fate of many an Englishwoman and all they can do is bear it bravely."

"I do not want it to be Oswyth's fate. That is why I asked you here. I believe you can help us."

Siward raised his eyebrows. "What can I do?"

Raedwulf took his hand. "I know we have not met in the last six years but even so, I have kept myself informed. You are not yet wed."

Chapter five

"**B**ut Grandfather," Oswyth protested. She realised she had been foolish not to see this plan. But Siward had been a man at Hastings, albeit a young one as he appeared to be no older than his mid-twenties now. She had assumed he had a wife and children at home. Inwardly she screamed her objections. The man whose foolishness had cost her father his life was the last man she wished to marry.

"Hush, my child." Raedwulf looked sharply at Siward. "Well, am I right?"

Siward too appeared stunned. "Well, yes, it is true that I am unwed but…"

"Then, I beg you, wed my granddaughter. Save her from the marriage which has been proposed."

"I…" Siward stopped, glancing at Oswyth. She stared back, her eyes narrowed.

"My lands, all possessions I have will be hers. She will be a wealthy bride. And is she not pretty?"

Siward swallowed, sending another swift glance at Oswyth. "Truly you honour me," he said. "And the fair Lady Oswyth would be a blessing for any man. But there is a reason why I have remained unwed. Before the Normans came, I was, as I am sure you know, a considerable landowner with extensive lands near Gloucester as well as several smaller estates dotted around the realm. But over the years these have dwindled. With each rebellion my lands have been confiscated and bestowed upon the companions of the Norman pretender. All I have now is my

Gloucester estate and even that is much diminished."

"I know this," Raedwulf said.

"Then you know what a poor prospect I am as a husband. I can offer no guarantees of being able to provide for a wife. Indeed the likelihood is that all I will offer is the chance to become an impoverished widow. And if I were to sire a child… well, what sort of life would that child have? I suspect I will have no lands to leave him. He would be born to a realm under conquest, despised for his traditions and with little hope for advancement. That is not what I want for my child. I have resolved not to marry until I have rid the country of these Normans and my lands are restored."

Oswyth sighed with relief as she seized on the way out of her grandfather's plan. "He speaks the truth. Do not press him."

"Nonsense," Raedwulf said. "He speaks nonsense. He has good Saxon blood in his veins. That is something fine to offer any woman. As for lands, he still has some lands and he shall have mine. You have heard him, my child. He will continue to rebel against these Normans. When a king of the true line reigns again, all his lands will be restored. It is simply a matter of time."

"But we do not know how long it will take," Siward said. "Or whether I will still be alive to see such a day."

"But my granddaughter does not have time," Raedwulf begged. "They will return in just ten days to force her into marriage. You alone can save her from this."

There was a long silence during which Oswyth clenched her fists. It was almost impossible to restrain herself from uttering the words she wished to speak.

"Please." Raedwulf looked into Siward's eyes, his gaze intense and desperate. "I know your lands are much dwindled but you will have mine and everything on them. I would be glad to know it is a good Englishman who takes them."

"Even if I did wed Lady Oswyth, I do not think the Normans would let me keep your lands. If they have already come, they will be eager for them indeed. I am sorry but I suspect it will not be an Englishman to preside here after you are gone, no matter how your granddaughter weds."

Raedwulf waved his hand. "It is Oswyth who is the most important. I do not want this soulless Norman blood tainting my line. I am begging you to wed my granddaughter. You once promised you would do anything to aid us. More than six years have passed and this is the first time I am asking it. I do not doubt it will also be the last."

A lump came to Oswyth's throat as she recognised afresh how frail her grandfather had become. He had not been eating normally for some time. Soon her only family and her sole protector would be gone.

Siward wet his lips. "Truly you honour me. I wish I could be worthy of the fair Lady Oswyth." He looked from Raedwulf's pleading eyes to Oswyth's cold ones. "I beg you allow me time to consider this offer. I shall give you my decision in the morning."

Raedwulf nodded. "That is fair enough. Do you wish to sleep in here or join us in the hall?"

It was cold but Siward replied, "I think I shall stay here so I have the quiet to think."

Raedwulf nodded again, putting an arm around Oswyth. "Then I shall bid you goodnight."

Oswyth barely waited for her grandfather to shut the door before she rounded on him. "I do not want to marry that man."

"He is a good Englishman of Saxon stock. I would be delighted to see you marry a man such as him."

"Father might still be alive if it were not for his foolishness," Oswyth replied, tears filling her eyes as she thought of the father whose memory she so desperately kept in her heart. "Please do not make me marry him."

"It is either him or the Norman," Raedwulf replied. "Please do not make me give you to one of them."

"What about a convent? Can I not devote myself to God?"

"Is that truly a life you long for? Because I think it not one you are suited to."

"It no longer matters what life we are suited to," Oswyth said bitterly.

"I know. I shall not force you to marry Lord Siward but when Ralf Fitz Turstin returns, he will force you into marriage. Please, my child, do not dismiss this prospect. It is the one hope I have left that I can see you wed to one of our own kind."

In the cold chamber Siward knew he would get little sleep. He remained dressed, wrapping blankets around his legs, wishing he had not come. The desperate expression in the old man's eyes had been hard to bear. They were so like those other eyes, the ones haunting his nightmares. How could he marry the girl? There were no advantages in it for him. She would bring him nothing since he knew the Normans would confiscate her lands. And she hated him. He gave a grim smile as he realised there was something she would bring him – grief.

Yet how could he not? Two sets of dying eyes had now looked at him, consumed with fear for her future. Two men who he had pledged he would do anything in his power to aid. This was in his power.

He forced himself to think of Oswyth without emotion. Delicate features, clear blue eyes and that long fair hair. Yes, he supposed Raedwulf was right to call her pretty although the hostility in her eyes made it hard for him to share that opinion. Now he had seen twenty-four years, his mother was longing for him to wed and with her beauty and status, Oswyth was, in many ways, an ideal wife for him. Except she hated him and with good reason. She would bring him no advantages and he would bring none to her. All he had brought anyone in the past years was misery. He did not know how he could marry her, knowing he would fail her as he had failed England. But if he didn't marry her, he would be failing her father and grandfather.

He still hadn't made his mind up as he left the chamber the

next morning but the decision was made as he looked upon his host in the bright winter sunlight streaming through the open door. His face was paler and his figure frailer than he had realised. The man was clearly dying and then Oswyth would have no one. He might fail her as her husband but he would definitely fail her if he left her to her fate.

He strode over, taking a seat next to Raedwulf and murmuring a thanks to the thrall who filled his cup. He pulled a ring from his finger and held it out to Oswyth.

"I will be honoured if Lady Oswyth will be my wife."

Oswyth clenched her fists, furious with this offer. She had hoped he would refuse so he would be the one to disappoint her grandfather. He stared back, his blue eyes betraying nothing of what he was thinking. Oswyth caught her breath, his good looks driving away all other thought for an instant. She blinked, recovering herself. He might be handsome but he was also the man who had emerged unscathed from the battle which killed her father.

She looked again at her grandfather, her heart breaking at the pleading expression in his eyes. This was not how his last years should have been. He should have been presiding over a merry hall, fussed over by his daughter-in-law and supported by his son with laughter and jests. She should have had a brood of siblings to join her around him, eager to hear his tales of old. But all this had been snatched from him and now he had just one wish left. She could not refuse it.

She took the ring. "I will be honoured to accept."

Raedwulf's face lit up, lightening the hearts of both Oswyth and Siward. He pulled off his own ring. "Give your betrothed this, my child. None of yours will fit him."

Gravely she handed it to him and just as solemnly he slipped it over his finger. Raedwulf enclosed their hands in his own. "I know this is not what either of you have expected but I think you two will deal very well together. I am certain you will be happy."

Fortunately he did not wait for a reply as he addressed the

curious people in the hall. "Prepare a feast for this very day. We shall make merry. My sweet Oswyth and Eorl Siward of Gloucester are to be wed."

Chapter six

Oswyth was taken into the chamber where a thrall pulled from a chest her finest clothes. She shivered in her linen under-dress as the kirtles were presented for her approval.

"That one," she said as they held up one in a deep blue which she had edged around the neck and hem in a fine scarlet thread. Raedwulf had once commented on how it suited her and, although she cared nothing for impressing her betrothed, she wished to look her best for her grandfather.

She stood still as the women tightened the lacing, staring down at the betrothal ring on her finger, shaken by how fast events were moving. At this time of the previous day she would not have given Siward even a moment's consideration. With an effort she forced her mind blank, knowing it was best not to think too deeply on the marriage. The thought of how much time she would have to spend with a man she had no wish to even look at, was hard without dwelling on the intimacies it would involve.

"I shall see if she is ready." Her grandfather's voice came from just outside the door.

She did not look at the door as it opened but kept herself still while the woman combed her hair into a golden cloak, muttering compliments as she did so. As the woman stepped back, admiring her work, she could feel her grandfather's eyes upon her and muttered a prayer that he was pleased.

"You look lovely, my child," Raedwulf said.

Oswyth glanced shyly at him, her heart lifting slightly at the pride and joy in his face. It was a long time since he had looked so pleased and she knew he regarded this day a victory as he kept what he prized most, free from the Normans.

"Thank you, Grandfather."

"I wish your dear father and mother could see you this day. They would be so proud."

The resentment flooded back. It was bitter to know the reason why her father was not present, was waiting for her in the hall. She wondered what manner of a man her father would have chosen for her if he had lived. "I wish they were here too. I still miss them so much."

"I know you do, my child. As do I. But truly, I think they would be pleased if they were here today."

Oswyth did not voice her thoughts on that, simply murmuring, "I hope so."

Raedwulf picked up her cloak of a fine dark wool and draped it around her shoulders. She pulled it tighter, grateful for the warmth, but before the women could fasten it, he took something from his pouch, pressing it into her hand. It was a bronze disk coated in gold and set with more than a hundred fragments of garnet in a circular pattern. Oswyth stared at it, astounded by the beauty of the twisted gold engraving, whirling around the pure white shells in the centre.

"Oh, Grandfather. This is beautiful."

"Your father gave it to your mother on their wedding day. I have been saving it for yours."

Tears welled up in Oswyth's eyes, spilling over to roll down her cheeks. With a laugh she wiped at them. "Now look what you have done. You have made me cry. This will not do."

Raedwulf smiled, taking the brooch from her hand and using it to fasten her cloak. "No, it will not. This day is a joyful one. Come, your betrothed is waiting."

Maintaining her smile, Oswyth took her grandfather's arm and they left the chamber. The hall was full as everyone had been summoned to witness the nuptials but she saw Siward straight away, standing in the doorway. He too had changed and his fine red tunic made a dramatic contrast with the hair brushing his broad shoulders. He was certainly handsome but Oswyth took no pleasure in this. All she could see was her father, tall and upright, his fair hair tied back for travelling, standing on the same spot, giving her a last kiss before he rode away to serve his king, never to return.

Siward too was feeling glum as Oswyth left the chamber. He knew most men would be delighted to see such beauty approach them on their wedding day but he could not enjoy it. A wedding should be a happy occasion, full of hope for the future, but all he knew was death and defeat. It seemed impossible to him that this marriage could end in anything other than disaster. Undoubtedly he would fail the two men he had pledged to aid all over again, just as he had failed his king and failed England.

As Oswyth and Raedwulf drew near, he stretched out his hands. Oswyth placed her cold hands in his, letting them lie there limply, while Raedwulf stood beside his priest, nodding encouragingly at Siward.

"I, Siward of Gloucester, do take you, Lady Oswyth, daughter of Raedwulf as my wife with the permission of your grandfather, the noble Thegn Raedwulf. I pledge myself to you until death parts us."

"Say the words, my child," Raedwulf whispered to Oswyth.

With a smile which was obviously false, Oswyth looked at Siward. She had intended to do her best but the sound of her father's name on Siward's lips was too much. "I, Oswyth, daughter of Raedwulf do take you, Lord Siward of Gloucester as my husband until death parts us, with the blessings of my grandfather, the noble Thegn Raedwulf." To her surprise her voice rang clearly. She had expected it to sound as miserable as she felt.

"Present the swords," the priest commanded.

Siward drew his sword and handed it to Oswyth. "I bestow upon you this sword so you may keep it safe for the son I pray we are blessed with." His cheeks burned. That sword had not been present at many victories. It was a poor legacy to leave a son.

It was no easier for Oswyth and her hand shook as she passed her father's sword to Siward. Her cheeks stung as the man who had caused his death, pushed it into his sheath. "I present this sword to you so you may defend me and any children we are blessed with." In her own mind she finished the declaration with the words "and I hope you manage that defence better than any defence you have managed so far."

"Then you are wed," the priest said and Raedwulf beamed, ignoring the discomfort of them both.

There was an expectant rustle among the watchers and with a sinking heart, Siward realised everyone was expecting him to kiss his bride. He took a step towards her, brushing his lips against hers. The hostility narrowing her gaze was so strong he had expected to find her lips hard and unyielding. The softness of them was surprising. But any pleasure he felt, vanished as he pulled away, seeing the hatred in her eyes as strong as ever.

They looked at each other for an instant, Oswyth fighting the urge to childishly wipe away the feel of his mouth from hers. Reminding herself of the joy this day was bringing her grandfather, she managed a smile.

Despite the reluctance of both bride and groom, the feast was the merriest occasion Oswyth could remember in that hall for many years. The laughter rang out as the people freely displayed their glee at thwarting one of the plans of the Norman invaders. To Oswyth's joy her grandfather too was in good spirits, eating more than she had seen in a long time and raising no objection as she filled his cup to the brim with rich wine.

There was music too as a musician strummed soft strings, singing an old tale of love and heroism. The people smiled, forgetting the current plight of England as they relived the days of the great kings of their past.

With the shadows lengthening outside, they lit more lights, brightening the merry scene. Oswyth caught her breath, seeing the smiles on the faces of the people as they looked at her. She knew it would soon be time for her to withdraw to the chamber, where she would be alone with her husband.

Nervously she sipped again at her cup as she wondered what would happen. Siward was a stranger. He felt nothing for her. A lump rose in her throat and she gulped more wine to prevent the fear bursting from her. In the chamber she would have to submit to him, allow him to force her open. And soon she would no doubt become with child, the child of the man responsible for the death of her father.

One of the women had come forward and she knew there was no escape. Determined that none should know how afraid she was, she smiled at everyone and bade them a goodnight. Siward glanced up but the reassuring smile he had meant to direct, slipped at the arrogant tilt of her head, her expression still unyielding. He nodded and returned to staring into his drink, wondering what he was supposed to do with such a cold-hearted bride.

∞∞∞

In the chamber the woman helped Oswyth into a nightgown and combed her hair afresh.

"There, you look beautiful," she said. "Your husband will not believe his good fortune."

Oswyth's haughty manner had slipped with every stroke of the comb. "I am afraid," she whispered.

"Of course you are, my love," the woman said cheerfully. "Every bride is. But you won't need to be. Such a kind man, as Lord Siward is. Handsome and strong."

"But…"

"Oh, I know. No matter what words I say, you will not be reassured. But your husband will show you soon enough that you do not need to be afraid." The woman planted a hearty kiss on her cheek. "At least you are not with that Norman. I did not like the look of him at all."

Oswyth muttered a few prayers as she was left alone, wondering if she could be more anxious, waiting for the Norman husband intended for her. A burst of raucous laughter from outside startled her from her prayers and she clutched the blankets around her as the door opened and Siward came in.

Chapter seven

Siward said nothing as he sat on the edge of the bed to remove his shoes. Weariness had struck him and he longed for sleep. Certainly the hatred so obvious in Oswyth's blue eyes did nothing to tempt him to want anything else. He tugged off his tunic and breeches, until only his linen undershirt was left. Oswyth sucked in a sharp breath as he pulled back the covers beside her and sat down. She tensed her body, determined to display no reaction as he touched her. Still he had not spoken and it was hard to keep her face expressionless. She wondered if he could hear the rapid thud of her heart.

He bent down to the floor, where he had dropped his belt and removed a sharp knife. Oswyth stared at him, her heart racing faster than ever as she wondered what he wanted with it. Nothing in what she had heard of the marriage bed had led her to think a knife would be needed, although various terrifying possibilities raced through her mind.

Siward looked at it for an instant before pulling the point lightly over the tip of his thumb, grimacing at the slight pain as the blood welled. Oswyth watched from wide eyes as he reached under the covers, rubbing his thumb over the blanket beside her thigh.

"What are you doing?" She was startled out of her cold disdain.

Siward glanced at her. "I trust that will convince everyone I have taken your maidenhood."

Oswyth's mouth dropped open. "Are we not going to…"

"No."

"But… why?" This was the last thing Oswyth had expected.

"I do not want to and nor do you. What is the point?" Siward got up and pulled back the covers at the other end of the bed. He got in and Oswyth felt his legs against hers. Impatiently she shifted over.

"Our marriage will not be a true one."

"Exactly." Siward gave a joyless smile. "But your grandfather will think it is and that is all that matters. We will maintain the act as long as he lives."

"What then?"

"You can enter a convent if you wish. Or marry a Norman for all I care."

"I do not want to marry a Norman," Oswyth cried.

"Be silent," Siward hissed, glancing at the door which separated them from the merry-makers. The noise was still lively so he trusted no one would hear them.

"My grandfather thought he was marrying me to a man of honour. But you are just waiting for your opportunity to be rid of me. I see now the value of your promises."

Siward shot forward at that, grabbing her by the shoulders and thrusting her back against the pillows. "I am a man of honour. I will not go back on my word to your grandfather. You will remain my wife and under my protection for as long as you wish. I am giving you the choice. I have none."

Oswyth gaped up at him, frightened at the fury in his eyes. Instantly regretting such force, he relaxed his grip and sat back again.

"But while you retain the title of my wife," he continued. "I expect you to treat me with respect."

Ashamed of the fear she had shown, Oswyth sat up very straight and folded her arms. "You are the man responsible for the death of my father. You have a long way to go before you earn my respect."

She expected him to be angry again but a ripple crossed his face and he pressed his lips tightly together. "Go to sleep, Oswyth," he said at last. "I have no wish to talk further with you this night.

∞∞∞

He blew out the candle, glad she would no longer see his face. Why did she have to mention her father? His eyes were the last thing he wanted to think about especially now he was in bed with his daughter. But as he lay in the darkness, he could think of nothing else. An echo entered his ears as again he heard the dying man's words about his sweet Oswyth. Sweet. That was the last word he would use to describe her, although probably he was being unfair. Back then she would have been sweet, a happy, carefree child. Probably she would have remained sweet as she grew up under the firm but loving guidance of her parents. Without them and only a grieving old man to indulge her... Siward sighed. He could not blame Raedwulf. No doubt indulging his granddaughter was the only pleasure he had left.

The wetness of the pillow made him realise his tears were escaping. He wiped at them, overwhelmed by weariness once again. Doing his best to push his new wife from his mind, he soon drifted into an uneasy sleep.

∞∞∞

It was harder for Oswyth to sleep. Although, like Siward, she had slept little the night before, it was no easier that night. She was very aware of Siward's legs next to hers, his foot brushing her hip. She shifted herself to the edge of the bed, almost hanging off it. She tugged at the covers, but weighed down by Siward, she could not stretch them that far. Shivering in the chill of the winter night, she wished she could return to the hall to lie by the fire.

Eventually she must have slept because she was woken by

short whimpers as Siward thrashed from side to side. It ended as he let out a low groan.

"No...." he called out. His body jerked and he lay still.

Oswyth sighed, irritated at being disturbed when she was sure she had only just got to sleep. She turned over, wondering why it was so hard. She slept easily enough in the hall surrounded by all their people.

At the other end of the bed Siward lay tensely, the tears wetting his cheeks once again. He would give anything to be free of the dream. That night it had been worse than ever. As he looked beneath the man's helmet he had seen, as he always did, the pain and despair in his eyes. But that night there was something more. Blame. They had looked accusingly at him, telling him as clearly as if he could speak, how he had failed his king and his country. Silently he cursed the presence of his wife. With her there he could not do what he usually did which was to light a candle, and weep freely into his pillow. All he could do was stare into the darkness, reminding himself that the agonised faces looming over him were not real. He was even more afraid to shut his eyes in case the dream came to claim him once again.

"Did you sleep well?" Siward asked as they dressed the next morning, more because he found the silence too awkward than because he really cared.

Oswyth paused in the act of wrapping her hair. "No. You disturbed me by crying out in your sleep like a small child."

Siward reddened, causing Oswyth a flicker of guilt. She could hardly condemn a man for what happened to him in his sleep, even if she suspected this was further evidence of his cowardice. He fastened his belt tightly and strode over, gripping her by the arm. "Now you listen to me. Your grandfather is old and he has suffered. Do not display your disgust of me so freely once we are out there. Pretend to be happy. Is that clear?"

Oswyth wrenched her arm away. "I do not need advice from you on how to treat my grandfather."

They finished their preparations for the day in an icy silence. Siward only glanced at her again to see her covering her head with a veil.

"Are you ready?"

She nodded tersely, hating the weight of the arm he had draped around her shoulders. Hoping the radiant smile on her face did not appear as ghastly as it felt, they left the chamber. There was a warm murmur of greeting from everyone in the hall and Siward gave what appeared to be a cheerful smile.

Oswyth saw her grandfather looking anxiously at her and she left Siward's side to hurry to him. She knelt beside him, taking his hand with a smile. "You were right, Grandfather. He is truly a fine man."

"Did I choose well?"

"Yes, you did."

Raedwulf beamed, looking up at Siward. "You will always look after my granddaughter?"

Siward placed his hand on Raedwulf's shoulder. "I will. Do not be concerned for her. I regard it truly a privilege to have her as my wife."

Raedwulf looked close to tears as he hugged Oswyth. "I knew you two would deal well together. You will be happy."

"When will you be departing?" Raedwulf asked that night.

Both Oswyth and Siward were startled. "I am not leaving you, Grandfather," Oswyth cried.

"You have a husband now, my child. Your first duty is to him."

"I do not care. I am not leaving you." She shot a look at Siward, the affectionate act she had been maintaining all day slipping easily from her features. "Do not try to make me."

"I have no intention of making you," Siward replied with a

warning look. "I agree. Naturally we will not leave your grand-father unprotected."

"Turstin Fitz Rolf will return soon. It could be dangerous. I want Oswyth away from here," Raedwulf insisted.

"That is why we cannot leave you," Siward said. "In happier times, I would certainly be making plans to take my new wife to my own lands. But in times such as this, I cannot. Unless…"

"There is no unless," Oswyth snapped. "I am not leaving my grandfather."

"And I am not asking you to," Siward replied, putting his hand in an apparently affectionate manner on her shoulder, but squeezing it tightly. "I was wondering if he would come with us."

Oswyth brightened. "Yes, will you, Grandfather?"

"I will not leave my lands," Raedwulf replied. "I was born here. I shall die here."

"Then I will not leave you unless I can be assured you are safe." Siward looked at Oswyth. "But perhaps I should have you conveyed to my lands, out of harm's way."

Oswyth pushed back her chair sharply. "I am not leaving my grandfather. I do not know how many times I have to say it."

As she swept away from them, Raedwulf sighed. "She is wilful. I hope you are not finding her too trying."

Siward wholeheartedly agreed with him but he smiled to allay the old man's concerns. "She is certainly spirited, but I do not mind that. There is precious little spirit left in the English these days. It is good to see some that has not been quashed."

As he spoke those words, he realised they were true. He would admire Oswyth's spirit if it had not been so frequently directed in malice at him.

Raedwulf patted his arm. "To keep Oswyth safe, I would leave my lands and come with you. But I do not think I would survive the journey. I am dying, my boy."

"I suspected as much." Siward gripped his hand, his smile sympathetic. "Does Oswyth know?"

Raedwulf gave a sad smile. "I do not know. She knows something is amiss. I see her watching me."

"Perhaps she cannot face her knowledge," Siward suggested, thinking he could not blame her. "Do not demand she leaves you. You are all the family she has left."

"She has you now," Raedwulf said.

"I am not much more than a stranger to her at present." Siward glanced around the hall, noticing the sparse numbers of thralls and churls present, the bulk of them well past their prime. "I think it would be best if I sent for some additional men. I may no longer officially hold the title of Eorl, but in the Shire of Gloucester, those who oppose the Bastard do not care for that. I have many I can call on. That way both you and Oswyth can be defended if necessary."

Raedwulf nodded. "But as soon as I am gone, take Oswyth from here. Take everything you can so the Normans do not get their hands on it, although I think I must accept that they will take the lands. At least until you succeed in driving these conquerors away."

Chapter eight

Reluctantly Oswyth was impressed by how swiftly Siward acted. Within a few days well-armed men set up camp on their land. When she took jugs of ale out to them, she noted the bulging muscles of the men sat around blazing fires, their weapons lying almost casually beside them. The numbers were vast and Oswyth's spirits rose. If Turstin and his son caused any trouble, it would be more than mushed bread to be hurled at them.

With great pride, Raedwulf had regaled that tale to Siward and he was further impressed by his wife's spirit.

"I wish I had seen that," he said with a smile at Oswyth, which for once was genuine.

On the day Turstin and Ralf were expected, men were sent to keep watch. They returned saying that the entourage with the two Normans was adequate but not impressive. They certainly did not look prepared for a fight.

"Why should they be?" Raedwulf commented. "They think me a helpless old man, ready to bestow his granddaughter in matrimony. This is not what they will be expecting."

Quickly Siward brought his men to gather around the hall. "This is a small battle, but it is a worthy one," he addressed them. "Today we defend the rights of this good Englishman, Thegn Raedwulf, to arrange the marriage of his granddaughter to his own preferences and to keep the lands he has worked all his life like his father and grandfather before him. There can be no nobler cause than this. In the name of the blessed Saint Edmund, we will defend this land. My men, are we ready for this?"

The deafening roar of the men left no one in any doubt they were more than ready, they were eager to see Norman blood spilt to defend that piece of land.

Raedwulf hobbled to the door of the hall, pride overwhelming the frailty of his face. Oswyth stood beside them, looking at her husband. He too was prepared for a fight with a sword hanging at his belt. He had taken back his own sword, saying it would be best for him to have one he was familiar with. Oswyth had simply smiled and nodded, secretly glad he was not using her father's. Over his tunic he wore a mail shirt and although his head was uncovered, his helmet was under his arm. Momentarily a flicker of pride flared in her at how strong and handsome he looked, before the memory resurfaced of another armed man, also strong and handsome, standing in that doorway, bidding everyone farewell in the confidence he would soon return.

"Just as soon as we have sorted those Danes, my little Oswyth," her father had said, patting her on the head.

Resolutely Oswyth drove the thought from her mind, turning her attention to the archers, their quivers full of sharp points and the long row of men armed with spears and axes. The men Siward had brought had been joined by Raedwulf's own men. Even those who bore no arms were there, with the scythes and shovels more commonly used to work the land resting over their shoulders. She forgot all other emotion as she rejoiced in the courage all were showing.

"We shall keep them away," Raedwulf said, looking at the men.

"For today at least." Siward gave a sideways glance at Oswyth. He knew there was no chance of keeping the Normans away permanently. If they wanted those lands, they would take them. But what he could buy with this show of strength was time. Time to allow Raedwulf to die in peace in his own hall. He wondered if Oswyth realised that was the aim.

Oswyth's smile was bright, her eyes sparkling with excitement. Her thoughts were well away from her grandfather's impending death. She was wondering if this might be the start of something bigger. Perhaps from their lands the fight would begin to take back all England.

"Shall I have a chair brought out for you, Grandfather?" Oswyth asked.

"No, my child. I shall stand before my hall, defending it to the last."

Oswyth looked down to see he had buckled on his own sword. He whispered a few words in the ear of one of the thralls. The man scurried away, returning swiftly with a shield. Siward recognised it immediately. It was the one which had belonged to Oswyth's father and that he had taken for his own use at Hastings. Sweat trickled down his neck as he took some deep breaths he hoped no one would notice, trying to force the memory away.

Fortunately Oswyth's attention was elsewhere. "You cannot fight," she exclaimed.

Raedwulf gave a laugh which turned into a cough. "No, my child, I shall not fight. I am sure to be nothing more than a nuisance to Siward and these fine men if I did. But until the fight starts, I shall stand armed before my hall."

Siward managed a smile, putting an arm around him. "You shall indeed and I suspect there will be no fight this day. I think it likely you will still be standing before this hall as they slink away, cheated of both bride and lands."

"A retreating Norman. That is certainly a sight I would like to see," Raedwulf said with a smile.

Siward glanced at Oswyth, wondering if her manner was softening towards him. Her eyes seemed to have lost some of the hostility although there was still no warmth in her wary gaze. "Oswyth, if there is any fighting you and your grandfather must go inside and bolt the door, along with any other women and those unable to fight."

Oswyth sent him a scornful glance, making him feel stupid for his instruction. He guessed she wanted to make some scathing comment, but she contented herself with speaking in a curt tone. "I know what I have to do."

"Excellent," Siward said, his hopes that she was softening towards him rapidly dashed. "Then we are ready."

Raedwulf was standing before his hall, his head high and his back straighter than any had seen in a long time with Oswyth on one side of him and Siward on the other as Turstin and Ralf approached. As the scouts had reported, there were nowhere near the numbers of men that they had. Nor were any armed more than was normal for a journey and their raiment was festive rather than martial. They were prepared for a nuptial celebration not a battle. The Normans looked startled by the numbers of men gathered before the hall, but said nothing. They dismounted and strode forward with the air of ones who already owned the lands.

"Greetings, Thegn Raedwulf," Turstin said.

"Greetings, Lord Turstin," Raedwulf replied calmly, not moving from the doorway.

"I trust your granddaughter is much recovered."

Raedwulf gestured at Oswyth. "She is indeed in excellent health."

Ralf and Turstin glanced at her briefly before both returned for a second look. Oswyth smiled at them, delighted to see their uncertainty as they realised she was already wearing the veil of a married woman.

Ralf frowned. "We are here for the nuptials."

Raedwulf stood straighter than ever. "You are too late. My granddaughter is already wed."

Turstin's face darkened. "How dare you arrange such a thing? What fool would agree to marry her, knowing she has been promised to another?"

Siward stepped forward. "I have the honour of the fair Lady Oswyth as my wife."

Turstin's eyes narrowed. "Siward of Gloucester. I might have guessed. Whenever there is trouble, you always seem to be present. Yet never are you there when we triumph to face the King's justice. The continual runaway."

Siward said nothing, staring back at the man. Many of the lands taken from him, including a portion of his Gloucester estate, had been given to Turstin and he hated him with a hatred he reserved for few men.

"Since I have so many of your lands, it will be no hardship to take more from you. And your life with it," Turstin continued. "The King will be delighted to hear you are gone."

He took a step towards Siward, his hand curling around his sword. As Oswyth drew a sharp breath, clasping her grandfather's arm in preparation to withdraw inside, Siward's hand flew to his sword. But before he could draw it, every man present surged towards them, their own weapons at the ready.

Turstin paused, stepping back. He gave a grim smile at the realisation he would not bring Siward down that day.

"The girl was promised to me," Ralf complained.

Turstin gave a dismissive gesture. "Who would want such a sickly bride?"

Ralf stared at her. "She does not look sickly to me."

Oswyth smiled sweetly, delighted to see the realisation that he had been tricked, sweep across Ralf's face. She looked at him, holding his gaze for a moment and then glanced meaningfully at his shoes, a smirk spreading clearly across her features. She smiled at him again, defiantly displaying her glee for all to see.

Ralf scowled. "It is as well for her that she is not my wife. I would have spared no efforts in taming her."

Almost Siward laughed at that comment, his admiration for Oswyth's spirit flaring once again. But his amusement faded as he thought of what Ralf might mean by those words. Oswyth was such an innocent. She had been a much loved daughter, her grandfather doted on her. She had no idea of what a man could do to break her spirit. For the first time he was truly glad he had married her. In making sure she never would find out, he could repay the debt he owed her father.

Turstin shrugged. "The girl is unimportant. It is the lands we want. You fool," he spat at Raedwulf. "If she had married my son, you could have remained here. We would have let you preside over these lands until the end. But now we will take them."

Again the people raised their weapons, edging towards the Norman entourage.

"You will not," Raedwulf said. "You will depart my lands and you will not return."

Turstin scowled, gesturing to his companions to turn back. "You have not heard the last of this. I shall return with more men. And then it will be you who is cast out with nothing more than the clothes on your back."

Siward stepped forward but Raedwulf placed his hand on his arm. Leaning on it, he moved towards Turstin. "Go," he shouted, his voice stronger than Oswyth had heard in a long time. "Get yourselves from my lands. Go from all England. The Bastard will never be my king!"

The people cheered his words as Turstin and Ralf mounted their horses with many a black look. Cheated of their fight, the people hurled dung, rotting food and even stones as the Normans rode away, the muttered curses drifting back to them a finer sound than the sweetest of tunes.

"They are gone," Oswyth cried. Forgetting her dislike of him, she sent a delighted smile in Siward's direction.

With his newfound determination to protect her, Siward smiled back. But the jubilation was short lived. Raedwulf, who was still leaning on his arm, gripped it tighter. He stumbled forward, causing Oswyth to cry out, terrified her grandfather would fall to the ground. But Siward was quick, catching him in his arms. Raedwulf's other hand had gone to his chest, a pallor sweeping his lined face.

Chapter nine

The old man barely weighed anything. Siward easily swept him up in his arms as Oswyth ran ahead, calling for blankets and hot ale.

"Lay him down here," she said, gesturing to a pallet close to the central hearth. As Siward carried out her instructions, she smoothed out her grandfather's scanty hair. "Oh, Grandfather, you should not have stood out there for so long. The day is too cool."

"Oswyth," Raedwulf whispered, his face more pallid than ever.

"Let us loosen your belt. Really, Grandfather, this sword and shield is far too heavy. Rest yourself now. You will feel more yourself soon. Will you take some ale?"

Siward could see the look in Raedwulf's eye as his lips struggled to bring forth further words. Tears came to his eyes, which he swiftly blinked back, knowing his own emotions would have to come second to Oswyth's. He laid his hand on her shoulder. "Oswyth, he is dying."

He was unsurprised when Oswyth shoved his hand away. "Do not say such words. How dare you give up on him? Oh, but that is what you do best, is it not? Give up. Go away and let me tend to my grandfather."

Misery flickered across Raedwulf's face, his limp hand lifting in a futile gesture. Siward knew they were not succeeding in the one aim he wanted to achieve and that was to set the old man's mind at ease.

"Last... Last..." Raedwulf struggled to get the words out.

A lump rose in Oswyth's throat. She could ignore Siward but

she could not ignore her grandfather as he called for Last Rites.

"Do you want the priest, Grandfather?" she asked, somehow keeping her voice steady.

"Yes," Raedwulf whispered.

Siward beckoned to the priest to come over. He and Oswyth stood back as the priest spoke the sacred words of the creed, Raedwulf mouthing the words in a whispery echo of the priest's compassionate tones. At a gesture from the priest, they retreated even further as he took the dying man's confession. A tear trickled down Oswyth's cheek as she wondered what sins her loving grandfather possibly had to confess. It was as they could see the priest was making his final blessings that Siward turned to her.

"All you can do for your grandfather now is make him comfortable." He was overwhelmed with pity at the misery in her eyes but for Raedwulf's sake, he knew he had to be firm. "That includes letting him think you are happy. Do not speak to me so insolently in his presence."

Oswyth nodded, unable to speak. She would not admit it but his arm around her shoulders was comforting as she returned to kneel beside her grandfather. She tried to smile, her heart breaking as she prepared to say farewell to her only kinsman.

"Forgive me for how I spoke," she said. "I did not wish to hear what Siward was saying although I know he was right to say it."

"Keep Oswyth safe," Raedwulf whispered.

Siward planted a kiss on the top of her head. "I am going to. I shall defend her with my life, I swear it."

"Then go."

Oswyth and Siward exchanged startled glances. "Go? We cannot go now," she cried.

"Please, go." Raedwulf forced some strength into his voice. "I shall die anyway. But you two... go. Take everything of value, take our people and leave."

Oswyth's eyes filled with tears at the thought of leaving her grandfather to die alone in an empty hall. "No, Grandfather," she wept. "Do not ask us to do this."

"Turstin will soon return," Raedwulf begged, his voice failing again. "Please, Siward. Save Oswyth."

"No," Oswyth cried. "I will not leave you like this. Siward, do not make me." Overcome with tears, she ran to the door, letting the cool air calm her.

Siward looked back at Raedwulf, understanding the fear in his eyes. "You ask too much."

"You promised… keep her safe."

"I know, but this would be too much. To leave you here to die alone, or worse, not alone but surrounded by the jeers of Turstin and his men… It would destroy her spirit. Please, Raedwulf. You have given Oswyth to me. Trust me now."

Raedwulf shut his eyes and Siward followed Oswyth to the door. "Come back and sit with your grandfather," he said. "I have some thoughts which I hope will please you both."

Oswyth wiped her eyes and did as she was instructed, kneeling down and taking her grandfather's hand. His eyes flickered open. "Farewell, my child."

Oswyth looked sharply at Siward. He took Raedwulf's other hand. "We are not yet leaving you," he said. "I know Turstin will soon return but he is not here yet. There are some matters which are keeping many of his men busy elsewhere so we will likely have a little time. Of course, we need to be prepared for his return, so we will start packing up everything of value and sending it to my lands. I shall also welcome any of the people who also want to leave."

"But Oswyth…"

"Yes, I know she is the most valuable of all. As soon as you need us no longer, I will take her away."

"They may return too soon," he whispered.

"I know. I shall have men on watch and the two fastest horses will be saddled and ready. If they return, I will take Oswyth even if you do still live. But I shall pray it will not come to that."

Oswyth stared at Siward, wishing she could say exactly what she thought, longing to rake her nails across his face for suggesting she leave her beloved grandfather.

But it was unnecessary. Siward could read her thoughts pretty well. He pulled her stiff body towards him. "Oswyth, your grandfather's last action was to send the Normans packing from his home. And it was a glorious one. Do not destroy it by letting his last sight be of you falling into their clutches. It will be hard to leave him and I swear we will do it only if necessary, but you must find the courage to do it for him."

Siward left Oswyth kneeling beside her grandfather. She was holding his hand, mopping his brow and talking to him in a soft voice. He could see the weariness on Raedwulf's face yet his expression was peaceful and he knew he was finding comfort in his granddaughter's attentions. Hoping he was doing the right thing, he instructed the thralls to start packing up everything of value. He wished it was not necessary, that Raedwulf's last sight could be of his hall in its accustomed splendour. He felt little better than a thief, bundling up Raedwulf's belongings while he still lived, forcing the dying man to witness the weaponry and tapestries removed from the walls and hear the clashing of platters as they were loaded onto a cart.

Yet when he went back to see how he was faring, he noticed what could only be described as glee in the old man's eyes. He smiled, ever impressed at such spirit. Raedwulf was glad to see all he valued removed, so that it would not be Turstin or Ralf who dined from those platters.

Oswyth too rejoiced at the peace she could see on her grandfather's face as she prayed she would not have to leave him. At every entry to the hall she started, afraid it would be a messenger telling them to flee. But each time it was only the churls returning for more of their belongings. Soon the first cart rolled from their dwelling, accompanied by a significant number of their people. As night fell, she muttered heartfelt prayers she would be able to stay with her grandfather until the end.

∞∞∞∞

Raedwulf lingered on through the night and at dawn more carts and people left, driving the livestock to Siward's lands. Siward had already given orders for a grave to be dug. He hated doing this for a man still living but he knew they needed to be ready to flee as soon as possible after Raedwulf breathed his last. With tears on his cheeks, one of the thralls prepared a coffin before he left, saying it was the last thing he could do for a man he had been proud to serve.

Siward took a jug of ale and a platter of smoked fish over to Oswyth who had not stirred from her grandfather's side all night. Raedwulf's eyes were closed and his breaths shallow. But still he lived.

"I had hoped he would be gone by now," she said, sipping at the ale. "I do not know how to bear leaving him while he still lives."

Siward hesitantly put an arm around her and it was a measure of her grief and weariness that she leant her head against him. "I do not think he will wake again."

"I know, but even so, I feel sure he knows I am here."

Siward looked down, seeing how Raedwulf's hand was curled around Oswyth's. "I think you are right. There has been no word of Turstin yet. We can linger a while longer."

By noon the last carts had left along with the last of the people, both his own men and Raedwulf's thralls. Siward headed outside, finding the silent emptiness unnerving. This had once been a bustling residence. Now it was dead, just as its master would soon be.

Inside was almost as bare. Other than some large furniture and items of low value, there was only Oswyth, her head bowed as she continued to sit beside her grandfather. A movement in the doorway, sent his hand flying to his knife but it was only the priest, a man who had decided he would remain with his church. He nodded at Siward but neither had any words.

He knelt beside Oswyth, his heart going out to her as the tears slipped slowly down her cheeks. For a moment he was certain Raedwulf had gone until he sucked in another faint breath. Still he lingered, his face whiter than any Siward had seen and his lips tinted with blue. He bowed his head in a gesture of respect for the passing of one of England's last noblemen.

Footsteps came to the door. "My lord, we have spotted a large company of men, they…"

Siward clenched his fists, gesturing to the man to be silent as Raedwulf took in another breath, even shallower if that were possible than the last. He hoped he was right to think they could linger just a little longer.

Oswyth could hardly see her grandfather through the tears. She kept hold of his hand, clutching it to her cheek. No more breaths came. She let out a sob as Siward pressed his ear to Raedwulf's chest. It did not rise and the heart was still.

"He has gone," Siward said quietly. "May God have mercy on his soul."

Oswyth put her head in her hands, complete desolation sweeping over her. Now she had no one. When a noise made her look up, she saw, to her horror, Siward dragging in the coffin.

"How can you do that already?" she cried. "He is not even cold."

Siward felt worse than ever at the pain he was causing, convinced he was failing her already. "I am sorry, but Turstin is on his way. We must be gone at all speed. If you wish to see him buried, it has to be now."

Chapter ten

I t was a bleak funeral in the fading winter light with just Oswyth, Siward and the scout to stand by the grave as the priest rapidly spoke the words of the requiem. Oswyth wept again as Siward lifted Raedwulf's body into the coffin, only drying her eyes to comb his hair and beard. As she folded his hands over his chest, a burst of pride in his noble appearance broke through her grief. But when Siward hammered down the lid, she had to turn away, knowing she would never again look on her grandfather's face.

Siward and the scout carried the coffin between them to where the hole in the dark soil waited. She listened into the quiet words passing between them, learning that Turstin and his men were still some distance away but even so, Siward told her in an apologetic tone that the requiem would have to be conducted quickly.

"I am sorry," he said. "Raedwulf deserves better."

Oswyth said nothing as she stood beside him, pale but composed, her eyes on the priest. She barely heard the words, as instead she tried to remember her beloved grandfather in happier times.

As soon as the priest had completed the requiem, Siward turned to the scout, bidding him be on his way.

"Oswyth, change into your thickest riding tunic and warmest cloak. Wear as many layers as you can be comfortable in. And hurry."

With one last look at the still open grave, Oswyth returned to the hall. Her mind was numb as she focused on fulfilling Siward's orders, so numb she did not even feel her usual resentment at how he had taken charge. She took a moment to look around her childhood home for the last time, unable to believe she was leaving.

"Hurry," Siward called.

Tears filling her eyes, she left the hall. The fire was still uselessly burning, waiting for its new masters.

"I know this is hard," Siward said. "But we must be gone."

"I cannot bear that the Normans will soon preside here, where my grandfather presided and his father before him." Oswyth was unable to stop the tears spilling over. "This is my home. I have been here my entire life."

"I know. It is cruel." Siward looked up at the hall. "Shall we set fire to it?"

Oswyth gasped. "You wish to burn down my home?"

He shrugged. "It is the only way to ensure neither Ralf nor Turstin preside in the hall your grandfather loved. It is up to you, but please, hurry."

Oswyth thought quickly and then nodded. She would likely never return. One last act of defiance against their conquerors was something she was certain her grandfather would have enjoyed.

They entered the hall for the last time, the fire no longer seeming useless, but instead a powerful weapon. Knowing there was no time to waste, Siward lit a couple of torches, handing them to Oswyth. Barely pausing for breath, he lit some more, tossing them onto the dais, guessing it would not take long for the wood to catch.

"Quickly. We must get out," he said, seizing another two flaming brands.

Outside he hurled two to the roof where the straw crackled almost instantly. "Throw yours back inside," Siward ordered.

As she did this, she noticed how the back of the hall was ablaze, smoke already obscuring the place Raedwulf had always sat. "Farewell, Grandfather," she cried, thinking this a far more fitting requiem than the one they had just held. "You will be missed, but remembered always with love."

"Was that really necessary?" the priest asked as he came to bid them farewell.

Siward glanced at Oswyth. "Yes, I think it was."

The priest gave an understanding smile. "Farewell to you both. I am glad little Oswyth will be safe."

Oswyth managed a smile, embracing the priest who so long ago had baptised her. Over the years she had heard him say mass many times, wept through the requiem he had said for her father and then, just a few weeks later, for her mother and whispered her childish confessions to receive his absolution. Only now that she was likely to never see him again, did she realise how much comfort he had offered. "It is not too late to come with us."

"I know, my daughter. But I shall not. There will be many in these parts who will now have to adjust to the new rule. I think they will have need of me."

"You are wise, Father, but if you are ever driven from this place, please know you can always seek refuge on my lands," Siward replied, helping Oswyth onto her horse. "Farewell."

The hall was ablaze as Oswyth and Siward trotted briskly away, leaving the scorching heat behind. She could hear the crackling of the flames and the crash of what she assumed were falling beams. The smoke would likely be smelt for days, keeping her grandfather's memory there a little longer. But not once did she look back. Only their shadows dancing on the ground before them, told her how brightly the flames were burning.

Siward could feel only immense relief in their departure. But this did not last long.

"Stop in the name of the King," came a shout from in front of them.

"Go faster," Siward said in a low voice, realising Oswyth was about to rein in her horse.

Swiftly he changed direction. Although the light was fast fading, he could see several men. He had no idea where they were going but that was no longer important. All that mattered was that they lost those men. Across pastures they sped with the relentless thud of hooves pounding behind them, coming ever closer.

"We need to go faster," he cried.

"I think she is going as fast as she can," Oswyth shouted back, kicking hard at her horse in spite of her words.

Siward knew it was hopeless. Their horses were laden, unable to go as fast as the men pursuing them. It took no time at all for the first men to overtake them, blocking their path to the front with further men behind them. Turstin and Ralf pushed their way through to look at them, their faces set into ugly lines of rage.

This was not the large company of men his scout had reported and Siward cursed inwardly. The burning of the hall which was no doubt acting like a beacon in the dull light, had prompted these men to ride on ahead. It didn't matter that this group was not large. He and Oswyth were hopelessly outnumbered.

He looked frantically around for some route of escape. They were surrounded. Only on one side was there a gap but as this was against a swollen river with thick woodland beginning on the other side, it would do no good.

"So, Siward of Gloucester, we meet again," Turstin said.

"The fair Lady Oswyth too," Ralf added, his eyes narrowed.

Oswyth stared defiantly back. Her heart was racing in terror and her hands so slick with sweat, she could barely grasp her reins, but she would not give those men the satisfaction of knowing that.

"You have destroyed my property," Turstin said, gesturing back at the red glow in the sky.

"An unfortunate accident," Siward replied.

"Where is Thegn Raedwulf?"

"The noble Thegn died this day. I am taking my wife to my own lands. I would be grateful if you could let us continue on our way."

"Continue on your way?" Ralf said incredulously.

Siward gestured back at the burning hall. "The lands are yours. I shall not fight you for them. Just let us continue on our way."

"You have been a nuisance to the King for too long, Siward of Gloucester," Ralf said. "He would be grateful to us for bringing you to him."

Siward said nothing. His mind scrambled as he tried desperately to think of a plan. Raedwulf had entrusted Oswyth to him and at all costs he had to save her.

"Of course there is another possibility, my son," Turstin said. "What if there was a struggle and the troublesome Siward of Gloucester was slain? His pretty young widow would have possession of his lands. She would be even more of an heiress than we expected."

Ralf's lips curled into a smile. "Pretty and wealthy. She is far too wilful, of course."

"But you would know how to deal with that," Turstin replied, sending a mocking smile in Siward's direction.

He said nothing, finding it hard to breathe as before him he saw the dying eyes of Oswyth's father, glaring at him in bitter accusation. He had failed Oswyth, just as he feared he would, by leading her straight into the hands of the people he was supposed to be protecting her from.

Ralf laughed, edging his horse closer to Oswyth's. He reached out, touching some strands of hair which had escaped their plaits. He did not quite pull on them but it was no gentle touch. She jerked her head away from him, her face in a mask of haughty disdain Siward could not help admiring, even as he tried desperately to think of a plan. Ralf laughed again. "Now then, my pretty. You will not shrink from me on our wedding night, will you?"

Siward thought he might be sick at the thought of Oswyth's wedding night with Ralf. Almost he regretted not consummating the marriage himself, so she might at least have known some tenderness. Now all she would know was the brutality of a man who would undoubtedly never forgive her for her defiance.

Although the same fears were filling Oswyth's mind, she said nothing, forcing herself to maintain her indifference.

"If she should already be with child, such a child can be handed over to the church at birth," Turstin said. "She can start bearing yours soon enough."

"It would be more convenient if she is not," Ralf replied, drawing a knife from its sheath.

Siward stared at the blade which would kill him, caring nothing for himself. His pain would be swiftly over. But Oswyth... he could hardly bear how totally he had failed her.

Oswyth found herself strangely calm. She realised where she was and a plan was formulating in her mind. If only she could communicate it in some way to Siward, but there was no time to waste. The triumphant smiles on the faces of the men as they all drew their knives told her there was not a moment to lose. At any moment she would witness Siward dragged from his horse and slaughtered.

"Siward," she said in a low voice.

Siward forced himself to look into the eyes of the wife he was failing. "I am sorry," he whispered. "Stay strong." Tears blurred his eyes as he thought of Oswyth's bright spirit which would now slowly be worn away at the hands of the man before him.

With Siward's eyes on her, Oswyth sprang into action. As the first man slid down from his horse to start towards Siward, she gave her horse a sharp kick and to Siward's horror, she plunged it directly into the river.

Chapter eleven

I t was the last thing anyone expected and for a moment all the men were stunned into stillness. But Oswyth and her horse were not swiftly swept away as Siward's first terrified thoughts had anticipated. Instead the fast flowing water barely came up to the horse's knees. Before the other men could recover from their surprise, he followed her.

"After them," Turstin shouted.

Finding himself on a narrow ford in the water, Siward kept his horse steady. He was still worried it might slip although ahead of him Oswyth's horse was already scrambling onto the bank. A splash from behind suggested the Normans had not been so fortunate and that at least one had tumbled into the river. The danger was not yet passed but a grin burst from him as he listened to their curses, knowing the men would be slowed more than ever.

He brought his horse onto the bank beside Oswyth, daring to take an instant to glance back. Three of the men were in serious difficulty, their horses almost up to their necks in the water. If they tumbled now, it was highly likely they would be dragged down by their heavy cloaks. The two men who had slipped in the shallows were struggling to lead their horses back to the opposite bank. However Turstin was edging along the same stretch he and Oswyth had crossed, although not with the same assurance and he could see he would not be long in following them onto dry land.

"Quick," he said starting his horse along the bank.

"No," Oswyth said. "This way."

Again Siward was surprised as she urged her horse into the dense trees.

"Oswyth," he called, following her. "Do not be foolish. We will be lost in here. We must go along the river bank. You took a big enough risk going into the river."

Oswyth tossed her head, not slackening her pace for an instant. "I have lived here all my life. I know every bit of these lands." She narrowed her eyes to stare at him. "I know what I am doing."

"I will not believe you have ever been in these woods after dark," Siward replied. "Don't be foolish. It is dangerous."

Oswyth shook her head. "You can go back and be killed by those men if you wish," she snapped. "But I am going on. Do not say I did not try to save your life."

"I think I might prefer to be killed by those men than lost for too long in these woods with you," Siward retorted, but he too kept going.

Grudgingly he soon had to admit Oswyth was right. In the woods the slower speed of their horses gave Turstin no advantage as obstacles to their progress lay everywhere. To his surprise he and Oswyth encountered relatively few and were able to keep up a steady pace. But from the frustrated exclamations he could hear behind him, it was evident that Turstin was not finding his way so easily. The sound of pursuit continued but it grew ever fainter. It was darker now but still Oswyth found a route which was easy to ride. Her boast at how well she knew the land proved to be well founded.

Slightly ahead of him, Oswyth smirked, unable to help feeling very pleased with herself. She said nothing until even the faint calls and rustles of their enemies had completely died away. Then she reined in her horse, glaring at Siward in the darkness.

"That is the second time a member of my family has saved your life and the second time you have endangered ours. At least I did not die as my father did."

For Siward those words were like a blow to the stomach. His knuckles whitened as he clung tighter to the reins, startling his horse. Desperately he tried to control his breathing, glad that in the darkness she could not, he hoped, see his face.

"Do not talk to me in that fashion, Oswyth," he said at last. "It is not appropriate and I will not stand for it."

"I have no wish to talk to you at all," Oswyth replied, disgusted at the waver in his voice. What sort of husband did she have who was afraid to be in woods after dark?

They rode on in silence, the trees as thick as ever and the night growing darker. Occasionally they got a glimpse of the moon, clear in the cold night but under the trees it was black. The rustling of the undergrowth often made them jump as both wondered if wolves or boar might come at them. But always it was simply the scurrying of some smaller creature and their ride through the woods passed smoothly.

Eventually the trees thinned and their way became brighter. The pathway which had led them on twists and turns through the woods emerged onto a wide track.

Oswyth reined in her horse and glanced at Siward. "This is where my knowledge ends. I do not know which direction we should take."

Siward was relieved to see the track. He had been afraid the path they were following in the woods would simply peter out and they would be left to wander aimlessly. But a track such as this one definitely led somewhere.

"Well done, Oswyth," he said. "Your knowledge certainly saved us." Hearing the false ring of jollity in his voice, he wondered why it was so hard for him to praise her when he had never found it hard to praise his men for their acts of valour. Although, of course, the men he usually led did not turn his praise into insults to be hurled back at him.

Oswyth shrugged. "So, do you know which way to go?"

Siward glanced up at the moon. "My lands lie some way to the north of your grandfather's lands. Let us head this way."

Oswyth simply nodded, turning her horse in the direction he had suggested. It was another silent stretch on a road which in the darkness had no features. Siward had no idea if they were truly heading the right way but at least they had put considerable distance between them and Turstin. He wondered if any of the men had drowned. If so, Turstin would be angrier than ever.

The soft thud of the hooves and the occasional rustle of branches was the only sound as he lost himself in his thoughts. It was a sudden jerk which brought his attention back to Oswyth, as her head slumped before swiftly righting itself.

"Oswyth? Are you falling asleep?"

"No," she snapped. In truth she was exhausted but she would show no weakness to him.

"Why didn't you tell me you needed to stop?" Siward cursed himself for not realising how tired she would be. She had spent the previous night kneeling by the side of her dying grandfather. And she was not accustomed to such long rides as this. He pulled out a skin of ale. "Drink this."

Oswyth sipped, grimacing at the taste the skin had imparted to the ale. But it did at least revive her.

Siward had been looking around. There were no settlements in sight, not that he would trust such a place in any case.

"Can you keep going for a little longer? There is nowhere here to set up a camp."

"A camp?" Oswyth exclaimed. "We are sleeping out here? In this cold?"

"I see no other option," Siward replied. "Do not worry. We are well equipped."

He found a suitable spot a short distance later on a grassy stretch with a stream running and enough trees to provide some shelter. He tethered the horses near the stream, flinging blankets over them.

"I hope you will be warm enough, old boy," he muttered, clapping his horse on its flank. He turned to Oswyth, who was already shivering. "First we need a fire. We have some firewood but we will need more. Collect as much as you can. Do not worry if it is a trifle damp. It will soon dry."

Oswyth was irritated by the order but she was too tired to protest. She did as he instructed and soon they had a small blaze going. It was a relief when she could sit close to it, warming her numbed fingers. They dined only on ale and bread, both too worn out to prepare anything better. Afterwards Siward left Oswyth dozing by the fire as he constructed a shelter from some skins he had brought and stout sticks from the nearby trees. He had never had to do this alone or in darkness. Normally his entourage would erect a proper tent for him but eventually he stood back, admiring his handiwork. It would do.

"Oswyth." He laid a hand on her shoulder and she flinched, jerking away again. "Come in here and rest yourself."

"That is where I am sleeping?" Oswyth looked in horror at the rough little shelter. "What about you?"

"I shall sleep there too," Siward replied.

"We are sharing that?" It did not look big enough for one, let alone both of them.

"Yes. We shall keep each other warm."

Oswyth shook her head. "I am not sleeping with you."

"Fine," Siward snapped. He had half frozen in his efforts to construct that shelter while she enjoyed the warmth of the fire. "I am warning you, this fire will not burn brightly for much longer. If you wish to freeze to death, that is up to you. Otherwise your only options are to snuggle with either me or the horses. The ground by the horses will be covered with dung by the morning. Oh well, at least it will keep you warm."

Feeling pleased with this retort, Siward disappeared into the shelter, hoping Oswyth wasn't quite stubborn enough to freeze to death just to spite him.

Oswyth stared at the shelter, dumbstruck at his lack of care. She looked again at the fire. Already it was not as warm as it had been. She threw another log onto it but the damp wood hissed, dimming the embers even further.

"Damn him," she muttered, following Siward into the opening of the tent.

"Take your shoes off," Siward said, not even lifting his head. "I do not want you kicking me in the night."

Oswyth ground her teeth but did as she was instructed. There was nowhere else to lie other than the tiny space between Siward and the outer covering. She squeezed in, pulling the blankets around her. He shifted slightly but his body remained curled around hers, forcing her to realise how muscular it was and warm too. She turned on her side, facing away from him even if the air was colder. It was better than having his face so close to hers.

Siward too was finding Oswyth's presence unsettling. In the loose kirtles she wore, he was rarely aware of her body, but now it was pressed against his, he could feel how slender it was and how neatly it seemed to fit into the curve of his own. If he wasn't so cold and tired, he might have enjoyed the sensation, but as her shoulders twitched a few times, he felt only irritation in how she was disturbing him.

He opened his mouth to tell her to lie still when the realisation struck him. She was crying. Of course she was. She had buried her grandfather, the man who had perhaps been more father than grandfather, that very afternoon and had been given no time to grieve. Siward bit his lip, ashamed of how he had taunted her earlier and of his resentment at her attitude. Her world had changed irrevocably in the last days.

"Oh, Oswyth," he whispered, slipping an arm around her.

Instantly Oswyth tensed. "Leave me alone. I did not want to marry you and now I wish it less than ever. Just let me sleep."

Sighing, he removed his arm, knowing all he could do for her that night was give her the peace to grieve alone.

Chapter twelve

It was a cold, uncomfortable night as despite her exhaustion, Oswyth only dozed intermittently. Upon each awakening she was struck afresh by her grandfather's death, sending the tears flowing again. As dawn broke, she lost what little warmth she had when Siward slid from the tent. She lay still, unwilling to rise and face a day which no longer held anyone she loved. But even pulling up the blankets which Siward had left did not compensate for the warmth of his body. She sat up, stretching her aching limbs. Every movement was painful but resolutely she crawled from the tent, pulling one of the blankets with her.

Outside it was even colder as a clammy mist enshrouded her face. The wet ground soaked through her tunic, forcing her to scramble to her feet in spite of the stiffness of her body. A crunching sound came from the ground nearby as the horses cropped the grass, apparently unfazed by the dismal conditions. She breathed a sigh of relief. At least they had survived the night.

Siward was kneeling on the ground before her, bent over the embers of the fire. He had added some more sticks and was blowing at the glowing wood. He glanced up as she approached.

"I was hoping to get the fire lit before you woke," he said.

Oswyth shrugged. "It doesn't matter. I wasn't asleep."

"I don't suppose you slept much." Siward cast a surreptitious glance at her. She looked dreadful. Her face was white apart from red rims around her puffy eyes, while matted clumps of hair straggled from under her hood. He longed to put an arm around her but guessing this would not be a welcome action, he contented himself with pulling out the remaining blankets from the tent and wrapping them around her shoulders.

"Thank you," Oswyth said, holding her hands over the embers of the fire.

Siward said nothing more as he continued his efforts and soon a little fire blazed merrily. He looked again at his wife. He wanted to ride quickly on that morning but he guessed she was in need of a proper meal. He pulled some smoked fish from the pack which along with bread and weak ale would have to do.

"I shall try to find us somewhere more comfortable this night," Siward said. "But we do need to be careful."

"I know," Oswyth replied, taking the bread he had skewered onto sticks and holding it over the fire. It was not the hot broth she craved but at least it would be warming.

"Do you know anything of the track we are on?" Siward asked. "I am not familiar with this part of the realm and until we find some feature I recognise, we could be headed in the wrong direction."

Oswyth frowned, trying to remember what she had been told. She had travelled little in recent years with her grandfather preferring to lie low on his lands. "I believe it comes up from the south coast and leads towards the Severn Sea."

Siward brightened. "Excellent. My lands are on the River Severn. I wonder, does this road take us close to the abbey at Glastonbury? If so, they will welcome us there."

"I think it might," Oswyth replied. "I have seen monks occasionally on this track."

"Good. Then hurry with your food. I want us to be on our way as soon as we can."

"Do you think Turstin and Ralf will still be looking for us?"

"I hope not," Siward replied. "Certainly this mist, dismal as it is, gives us an advantage. They will not wish to try their way through the forest again in this weather. But the further we are from them, the safer I will feel." He got up, reluctantly leaving the warmth of the fire. "I shall pack everything while you eat."

Oswyth barely glanced at him as she stared into the flames, sipping on her ale and forcing herself to eat the warm bread. Never had she wanted her home so much, but returning was an impossible dream. The hall her grandfather had loved was presumably now ashes and rubble, the remains picked over by the thieving Normans. Tears trickled again down her cheeks.

"Are you nearly ready?" Siward sat back beside her, startling her from her thoughts.

She looked around, surprised to see the horses so quickly packed and ready. "Siward, you said that once my grandfather died, I did not have to remain married to you. It is not a true marriage, after all."

"Yes and I stand by my word. I assume you do not want to marry one of the Normans. Do you wish to enter a convent?"

"I..." Oswyth stared into the fire. "I do not know."

Siward gave a small smile. "I do not think this is the time to make such decisions. You are exhausted and grieving. Come with me to my lands such as they are. There is no need to rush."

Oswyth nodded, draining the last of her ale. "If I did not wish to enter a convent..."

"Then you can remain as my wife. But I shall make no effort to sire a child on you until I know such a child would have prospects of land and good fortune. I do not wish any child of mine to be born into a land under conquest."

Oswyth nodded, keeping the relief off her face. To live the life of a married woman without having to share her body with her husband was highly appealing. In many ways her new life would not be so very different from her life with her grandfather.

"But, Oswyth, you do need to watch your manners with me," Siward continued. "I am making allowances for your grief but the way you speak to me is unacceptable. I expect you to show me honour and respect."

"Do you deserve my respect?" Oswyth asked.

Siward sighed, wishing he could make some progress with his wife. "As your husband, I am entitled to it. As a man, no, probably not."

Oswyth sent him a contemptuous glance, disgusted that he could admit such a thing. "Exactly."

Siward sighed again. "We still have some way to go on this journey. It will be pleasanter for us both if we can at least be civil. Please, Oswyth. Do not make it harder than it has need to be."

Oswyth shrugged. "Oh, very well."

"Good." He extended a hand to her. "Come, let us be on our way."

As Oswyth put her hand into his, he was struck by how small it was. For all her feisty spirit, she was defenceless. Again Siward was shocked by the urge to take her into his arms and not let anything hurt her. He shook his head, reflecting that if he carried out such an action, it would probably be him who ended up hurt. He gave her hand a slight squeeze, hoping to convey friendship at least as he helped her onto the horse before swinging himself into his own saddle. Their horses seemed none the worse for their cold night and trotted away easily enough.

They still rode in silence although somehow it was a more companionable one. But if the mood between them had warmed, the day did not. The mist lifted to form a dull drizzle, the wetness soaking their cloaks. Oswyth shivered in her drenched tunic, sending beads of water down her back.

Siward was anxious, wondering if he should construct a shelter for them. It was not what he wanted and unless the rain stopped, there was no chance their clothes would dry. He had used all their dry wood the night before, so lighting a fire was likely to be a thankless task. But just as he was starting to feel he would have no choice, they emerged from a wooded tract to see an unmistakable shape looming some distance ahead of them. His numbed cheeks struggled into a relieved grin.

"That is Glastonbury Tor," he said. "I have never approached it from this direction but I am sure that is it. The abbey lies at the foot."

"God be praised," Oswyth muttered.

"Can you ride on? I know it is still some way but it would be good if we could make it."

Oswyth did not think she had ever felt so cold and uncomfortable but she managed a smile. "Yes, I will make it somehow."

"Good." Siward smiled back, impressed by her lack of complaint. "Then let us push our horses a little more and soon we will be at the abbey. There we will find warm fires, hot ale and steaming bowls of potage."

For the first time since her grandfather had died, Oswyth's spirits rose. Her smile widened. "Never has that sounded so good. Let us certainly make haste."

Part Two: February 1073 – April 1074

Chapter one

They were greeted with relief as they arrived some days later on Siward's land. After leaving Glastonbury their journey had been smooth, with a good night's rest and an improvement in the weather bringing rapid progress to their ride. As they passed through familiar territory Siward had also known where they could safely rest at night, leaving no further need for sleeping on the hard ground. At length they reached the Severn Sea, following the shore as it narrowed into the river which marked the boundary of Siward's lands.

"Welcome to your new home, Oswyth," he said as they arrived before the hall. She had kept to her agreement to be cordial in her manner towards him and he hoped it was a start to an improvement in their relations.

"My son, it is good to see you," an accented voice called before Oswyth could reply.

Siward raised his hand in greeting to the man in priest's robes as he helped Oswyth from her horse. She gave a curious glance as he came towards them. He looked to be in his late thirties, although with his shorn head it was hard to be sure. However the fringe of hair remaining was dark and his face mostly unlined.

"Thank you, Father. It is good to be back."

"And bringing a wife with you. Such a happy occasion." The priest beamed.

Siward glanced at Oswyth. "This is my chaplain, Father Colman."

Oswyth extended her hand to the man. "I am happy to meet

you, Father." She was trying to work out the man's accent. The name too was unusual.

The priest smiled. "I am from Ireland, my daughter. Although I have been here fifteen years now."

Oswyth blushed, ashamed her curiosity had been so blatant. "Forgive me, Father…"

"Not at all, my child. It is natural that you are curious about your new life. But you must hurry inside. Everyone will be pleased to see you. The last man arrived yesterday. When you did not also come, there was much concern."

"I am glad everyone else arrived safely. We were almost caught," Siward said.

Oswyth concealed her resentment that Siward was not explaining how it was her quick actions which had saved them, as she smiled again at the priest, taking an immediate liking to the man. She looked up at the hall the men were leading her to. It was larger than her grandfather's had been, the wattled walls and thatched roof rising higher. Clustered around were numerous smaller buildings which would no doubt be stores and animal stalls, while beyond she could see the many dwellings of the churls who worked Siward's lands. She knew it was the last estate Siward possessed but at least it was a fair one.

"I will show you everything tomorrow, Oswyth," Siward said, following her gaze. "But for now, let us recover and rest."

Oswyth nodded, for once agreeing with her husband.

Just before they reached the doorway, Father Colman gave them a sideways glance. "My children, I trust I do not need to remind you that Lent has come upon us."

Siward gave a slight smile. "We are well aware of that, Father. We have kept chaste."

"Ah, good," Colman said, although Siward was certain he looked somewhat disappointed. "But naturally if you were to give in to temptation, I feel sure our Heavenly Father would not wish you to receive too severe a penance with you so newly wed."

Siward nodded, wryly amused by the priest's attitude. When he had returned home after the defeat at Hastings, he had wept as he confessed his failure to the priest. Like everyone here, the priest was devoted to him and he knew how much they worried over how he had changed since those terrible days. The fact he was willingly accepting a period of enforced chastity so soon after marriage to a pretty, young bride would be taken as further evidence that he was far from recovered.

Although the priest and his mother suspected nothing, he had not been completely chaste since Hastings. But his occasional encounters with women in the last six years had brought him little pleasure and no joy. Eventually he made the decision to avoid women as much as any other fleshly pleasure, considering that desire, like everything else, could wait until England had been recovered.

Oswyth had ignored the priest's insinuations and was looking around the hall with delight. It was a fine one, the walls bright with hangings. She moved closer to study them, impressed by the exquisite stitching. She wondered who had made them. Siward's mother, perhaps or his sister, if he had one. She shook her head at how little she knew about her husband. Fortunately her curiosity was quickly answered.

"Siward?" An older woman had rushed through the door. "Oh, my dearest boy, it is you."

Siward grinned, accepting his mother's embrace. "Yes, I am back."

"And with a wife? Where is she?"

Siward gestured to Oswyth, who turned away from the hanging she had been studying.

"Oswyth, this my mother, Alfgiva."

Oswyth was about to drop into a polite curtsey when warm arms were flung around her. "Oh, my dearest, dearest, child. Welcome."

"Th… thank you," she stammered, shocked by the joy lighting up the lined face of the older woman.

Siward was amused by Oswyth's bemusement, thinking it served her right for her lack of interest in him.

"Oh, you are so pretty. They all said you were. I am so pleased. I have been urging Siward for years to take a wife. You must tell me everything of yourself and your family."

"I have no family," Oswyth said, immediately feeling bad as Alfgiva's face fell.

"Oswyth's grandfather died just a few days past as I am sure the last man to arrive has told you." There was a slight edge to Siward's voice as he spoke. He guessed Oswyth, like many on first acquaintance, was completely overwhelmed by his mother. "He was her last remaining kinsman."

"Of course. Oh, you poor child. I met your grandfather and your father too on many an occasion. They were such fine men. The last time was at the crowning…"

Her voice trailed away as everyone's thoughts went to the crowning of King Harold, the man they had expected to rule the realm for many years. Siward remembered it well. The magnificent new abbey, the heads bowing in sombre respect as the body of the dead king, King Edward, was born into the building. And how the solemnity of his requiem had given way to the celebration of the new king as he received God's blessing on his reign.

"Well, that was a long time ago," Alfgiva said, determinedly cheerful. "Come, sit yourself, my child. You must need some sustenance. Siward, why have you not called for some ale for your wife? This is a poor welcome for her."

Oswyth allowed her new mother-in-law to pull her to the table, a smile breaking through her bewilderment. It was good to be made so welcome.

It was Alfgiva who showed Oswyth around the estate the next

day, taking her to stores surprisingly full, despite the winter which had not yet passed. Grudgingly she admitted that Siward was, at least, an excellent landowner.

"I am so pleased Siward is married at last," Alfgiva said suddenly. "These last few years... well, they have been difficult for us all. But you will put the smile back on his face."

Oswyth blushed, not sure what to say to this.

Alfgiva's mood turned uncharacteristically serious as she looked down at shelves full of threads and cloths. "I think I should enter a convent now."

"But why?" Oswyth exclaimed.

"It was what I wanted after my husband died but with Siward unwed, it did not seem right. I think a household is all the better for a mistress. But this household has you to see to it now."

"Oh, I wish you will not," Oswyth stammered. "My mother died so soon after my father and..."

Alfgiva looked up at that. "Of course and you are still so young. It is hard to grow up without a mother's guidance." She gave a warm smile. "Well, I shall not make any hasty decisions. But, my dear child, you are the Lady here now. You must see to matters as you judge fit."

Oswyth nodded, avoiding Alfgiva's eyes out of guilt. It seemed wrong to oust this woman from her position when it was no true marriage. "Everything is so well managed," she said. "I do not think I shall want to change much."

"Perhaps, my child." Alfgiva squeezed her hand. "But you must not mind my feelings if you do."

Oswyth gave an uncomfortable smile knowing she could not let Siward's mother enter a convent. Not when she had made no decisions yet on her own future.

∞∞∞

In the church Siward was holding his own uncomfortable conversation. As he and Oswyth had been travelling on the day they should have been shriven, he was making his belated confession to Father Colman, including his uncharitable feelings towards his wife and how he had tricked everyone into thinking the marriage had been consummated.

"My son, this means it is no true marriage."

"Is it not? It is said the noble King Edward did not consummate his marriage but I always considered the Lady Edith to be his queen."

"And look at the trouble that caused," Colman muttered. "Suppose King Edward had sired a fine son on his queen? Do you not think England would be a happier place now?"

Siward supposed it had been a poor example. Like many, he had felt sorry for the Queen, forced to remain a childless maid, although his sympathy for her had slipped as she capitulated so fully to the Bastard pretender. She had prospered in the years since his conquest while her people languished in fear. All the same, he had seen the tender care she had given the Atheling, Edgar and his sisters and he had thought it cruel of the King to deny her a child of her own. Yet now he was doing the same to Oswyth.

"Father, I will not sire a child to be raised under servitude. That is a vow I made long ago and I will not break it."

Chapter two

"**D**o you intend to remain as my wife?" Siward demanded that night. His temper was worse than ever as he had taken the opportunity of the meal that evening to present Oswyth with her morning gift, the one he should have given her the day after their wedding. It had simply been some jewellery and his cheeks had burned in shame that he had so little to give a wife. Growing up, he had always assumed he would have property to bestow. Oswyth had barely concealed her contempt as she murmured her thanks.

"I have not decided," Oswyth said airily.

"I would prefer it if you could make a decision soon. Preferably before my mother grows too attached to you."

"Do you wish to consummate the marriage?" Oswyth asked with a defiant glare.

"It is Lent," Siward snapped.

"And when Lent is over?"

"As I have told you, I will not attempt to sire an heir until I am certain he will have something worth inheriting."

Oswyth gave a cool smile. "Then I do not need to hurry my decision, do I? It is fairly obvious from your gift this night, you will never have much worth leaving."

Siward narrowed his eyes. "I may yet take the decision away from you. Your impertinence disgusts me. Even if I had all England to leave my son, I do not think I would have any desire for you."

"So, you will break your promise to my grandfather." A triumphant smile spread across her features. "Why am I not surprised? I knew your much-proclaimed honour was worthless."

A wave of hatred swept over Siward, a hatred he had never felt for any woman. He clenched his fists, knowing he should leave before he threw something at her.

"While you remain my wife," he said through gritted teeth, "I expect you to act accordingly. That means you treat me and my mother with respect. And you can see to the household management. I will have no slacking here. You have until the end of Lent to make your decision. After that it will be mine."

He turned away, restraining the urge to bash the door behind him, hoping he could manage to be polite to her in public. Not that this would satisfy his mother and Father Colman who were hoping to see some affection.

Oswyth smirked as he left her alone. In truth she liked the look of Siward's lands and the thought of presiding over his household was appealing. If only the man himself could be more appealing, the decision would be an easy one. Siward's mother was another reason for wanting to stay. Alfgiva's relentless optimism had lifted Oswyth's own spirits and in spite of her continued grief for her grandfather, she had laughed often that day.

She settled in well, enjoying her new role. Running a larger household than she was accustomed to, was a challenge but she met it eagerly, finding everyone willing to help. Even Siward complimented her, appearing genuinely impressed at her efficiency.

As Easter approached, there were many a well-meaning but lewd comment directed at them both as the household assumed they must be eagerly anticipating the end of the fast period. Oswyth ignored those comments, mostly feeling contented with her new life. Her friendship with Alfgiva had grown stronger, with the older woman easily slipping into a motherly role. Finding herself with a family again, Oswyth grieved sincerely for her grandfather but without the desperate loneliness she had feared.

Siward headed to Worcester for the Easter sermon which would take place at the cathedral, hoping to also pick up news while he was there. Knowing he could not avoid it, he asked Oswyth to accompany him. She was keen to do so, having heard much of Father Wulfstan, the Bishop of Worcester, a man who had done much for the English in the last years but who was so popular even the Bastard had not attempted to force him from his position.

It was not a long journey to the city with the ride along the river a pleasant one. The spring sunshine further lifted Oswyth's spirits, but her good humour was not shared by her husband. It was a particularly bitter moment as they passed through lands which had once been his, but were now held by none other than Turstin Fitz Rolf. It was for this reason he hated riding in that direction and avoided it as much as possible.

Siward stared glumly at the people ploughing the fields to prepare them for the sowing of seed. Knowing how much would be taken by the new Norman lords, he longed to tell them not to bother, to instead rise up against the man who claimed to be king. But after the devastation inflicted on the North, he could not even do that. Not unless there was a very good chance of success. And with King Edgar lingering overseas, there was little prospect of that. He sighed, hating feeling so helpless.

Worcester was full of people who, like them, had come for the service. Oswyth looked around with pleasure at the groups of chattering people, sensing a different mood there than anywhere else she had seen.

"The Bishop has done much to ease the tensions between

the English and the Normans, helping the people to accept the changes forced upon us and interceding for them with those who impose their rule," Siward told her. "Truly he keeps the heart in the people."

"It is good someone can," Oswyth replied.

Siward frowned but made no comment. They had struck up an uneasy truce but as Easter approached, he was convinced she was doing her best to annoy him. Occasionally he wondered if she wanted to enter a convent and was hoping to make him the one to force her, but most of the time he was convinced it was simply the natural malice of a spoilt brat.

A contemptuous shake of the head betrayed Oswyth's disgust at her husband's lack of retaliation. Her time on Siward's lands had confirmed that, while he was a good landowner, he was a poor spirited man. Evening after evening, she had watched him stare moodily into his cup, lost in his own thoughts and only emerging to top up his drink. Often she wondered why he did not simply swear loyalty to the Bastard rather than skulking on his lands, pretending to rebel.

"Siward!" came a voice as they arrived at the cathedral.

To Oswyth's annoyance, Siward did not even help her dismount as he turned towards the voice. "Frebern! I was hoping you would be here."

The two men embraced before Siward turned guiltily back to Oswyth to see a stable boy helping her from her horse. She smoothed down her tunic, looking at the man stood with Siward. He looked to be several years younger than him as well as slightly taller. He was richly dressed in a fine green tunic contrasting in an attractive fashion with the fair hair falling onto his shoulders.

"Oswyth, this is my good friend, Lord Frebern, eldest surviving son of the late Eorl of Warwick. Frebern, my wife, Lady Oswyth."

The man bowed over Oswyth's hand, murmuring a respectful greeting. But as he straightened himself, he cuffed Siward about the head. "A wife? You're a sly one. When I saw you just after

Christmastide, you mentioned nothing about taking a wife." He grinned and winked at Oswyth. "Not that I blame you at all for changing your mind."

"It is a long story," Siward said. "Her grandfather was a man named Thegn Raedwulf. I do not know if you have heard of him? He had lands in Somerset."

"Heard of him?" Frebern laughed. "Yes, I have heard of him. Everyone is talking of how with his dying breath, he defied that Norman scoundrel, Turstin, whisking his granddaughter away from the marriage they had intended. I had no idea you were involved." He smiled warmly at Oswyth. "I wish I had known your grandfather personally. He sounds like quite a man."

Oswyth smiled back, wondering if it was the youthful exuberance of this man which made Siward appear duller than ever. "Thank you. I am proud to be his granddaughter."

Frebern clapped Siward on the shoulder. "And good on you for saving one good Englishwoman from uniting her blood with the Norman scum."

Siward frowned. "Must you talk so loudly? Are you certain there are no invaders in earshot?"

As Frebern's glee collapsed into a shamefaced expression, Oswyth sent her husband a reproving look. He jumped at shadows. It was obvious there was no one other than the stable boys close enough to hear.

"Anyone can be dangerous," Siward said, correctly interpreting her look.

"Is it really a great matter if they report a few words?" Oswyth asked.

Frebern nodded, the smile on his face dimmed. "Siward is right. I should be more careful. Anything can matter. The Normans seize gladly on every excuse to take more lands from the English."

Siward nodded as the three started towards the cathedral. Keeping his voice lower than ever, he said, "Have you or Bridwin heard any news on King Edgar?"

Frebern shook his head. "Nothing new. He is still in Flanders although they say King Malcolm of Scotland is keen for him to return. He hates the Bastard since he was forced to capitulate last year. After his marriage to King Edgar's sister, it is hardly surprising he would like to see the true line restored."

"Perhaps as the sailing weather improves," Siward said thoughtfully. "Let me know if you hear anything."

"Who is Bridwin?" Oswyth enquired.

"He is a good friend of ours," Frebern replied.

"Once the Eorl of Lichfield," Siward added. "Of course he no longer has the title. So few Englishmen have kept their titles. But he is still an extensive landowner."

After the bright spring sunshine, the cathedral was cool and dim, illuminated in places by flickering candles with the faint aroma of incense wafting between the columns. A figure in white robes was coming towards them.

"That is Bishop Wulfstan," Siward muttered, bowing.

Quickly Oswyth dropped into a curtsey and as her eyes became accustomed to the gloom, she took a proper look at the man who was a hero to so many. Her first thought was that he did not look particularly heroic. His stature was small and his figure stooped. In spite of knowing how long he had been in the ecclesiastical service, Oswyth had expected a man of vigorous, youthful appearance. But as he gave a gentle smile in greeting, she realised he surpassed her expectations. His smile enveloped her, sending peace into her heart, convincing her that if she obeyed God's laws, all would be well. She smiled warmly back, no longer surprised that even the Bastard admired this man.

Siward was watching her as she did this, suddenly struck by how lovely she could appear. He thought back to her father. He had been considerably older than him and they had not been close friends but all the same, the man had been most complimentary on his leadership following the defeat of the Norwegian King Harald. Coming from a man as well respected as him, Siward, who had newly succeeded to his position, had been delighted at the comments.

If it hadn't been for Hastings, the respect the man had shown would likely have deepened. With Siward's high rank, he would have undoubtedly considered him an advantageous match for his young daughter. As he had not even been eighteen years at the time, Siward knew he would not have been ready for marriage back then, so a betrothal to a ten year old girl would have suited him well. He would have left her to grow up with the family who loved her and then, perhaps about the current time, he would have journeyed to her father to claim his bride. He imagined his arrival, the warm welcome from old Raedwulf and the proud expression of his son as they presented Oswyth, her smile of greeting perhaps just as beautiful as the one he saw her now bestow on the Bishop…

Siward shook his head, casting away the useless daydream. Hastings had happened, Oswyth's father was dead because of his own actions and the chance of Oswyth bestowing any smile on him seemed as remote as ever.

Chapter three

With Lent over, Oswyth spent a few nights lying tensely as she wondered if Siward would make the decision to keep her as his wife. But he continued to avoid her, appearing to have forgotten that he had set Easter as the deadline for her own decision. She too remained quiet over the matter, enjoying the weeks she spent in Worcester and spending many days in the peace of the cathedral praying for her grandfather's soul. It was so pleasant she wondered if she might after all be suited for a religious life, a belief which strengthened when Father Wulfstan himself praised her piety.

Siward appeared far more concerned with other matters. He and Frebern spent much time talking together and both also talked to Bishop Wulfstan, finding that he too was cautiously optimistic about the aid the King of Scots might give.

"Although that would leave us beholden to Scotland," Frebern commented. "It is not ideal."

Bishop Wulfstan nodded. "The King of Scots is not the most pious of men although Queen Margaret, good King Edgar's sister, is truly devout. She will hopefully make some much needed changes there. But we need allies and Scotland may be our best hope."

Siward shrugged. "It is obvious England alone cannot throw off the Norman invaders. We have tried and failed too many times. It is not ideal to be beholden to Scotland but compared to our current situation of rule from Normandy..."

Oswyth bent her head over her stitching to conceal the contempt on her face at Siward's words. It was no wonder England could not throw off the invaders when men such as Siward, who were supposed to be leading them, could so calmly assume there was little they could do.

"England needs time to recover from its losses," Wulfstan said. "An obligation to Scotland would be a small price to pay."

"Agreed," Siward replied. "Well, I am returning to my lands in the morning. If England is to recover, it needs to eat. For now we must put our efforts into the crops and livestock. If you hear anything from King Edgar or the King of Scots, send word. I will be ready."

"So shall I," muttered Frebern.

"And I shall continue to minister to my flock and do what I can to protect them," Wulfstan continued.

"I think you are doing more than any of us, Father," Siward said. "But be careful. Too many good English bishops have been removed. I hear there is a new bishop in Lichfield, a Norman one, of course. It is important for us all that you remain in place."

Oswyth could hardly believe her ears, her cheeks stinging in shame as she heard Siward urge caution on the bishop, the one man who seemed to be doing anything. Again she reflected that it was no wonder England was in such a state with men like Siward so resigned to defeat.

She looked from under her lashes at Frebern, his face unusually serious. As she had got to know him over the past weeks, she found herself genuinely liking him. He might still have the heart for a fight but he was young, only a couple of years older than herself. While his spirit was more than ready to take on their conquerors, he lacked experience and she knew he was looking to Siward for guidance. Oswyth shook her head. What weak spirited guidance that would be. It seemed only a matter of time before his youthful enthusiasm was dragged down to the same lethargy Siward displayed.

∞∞∞

Back on Siward's lands they were greeted with joy by Alfgiva and the rest of the household. Siward, who had not forgotten he had told Oswyth to make her decision by Easter, was aware how they watched him curiously, expecting to see some joy in the fact he could resume marital relations with his new wife. He ignored them, simply treating Oswyth with a disinterested courtesy in public, relieved to receive no worse from her.

In confession Father Colman urged him to make the marriage a true one. "My son, no one knows what the future holds for any child as yet unborn. There is no need for you to delay."

"Even if I had a fortune to leave my son, I still would not lie with that woman," Siward said, glad to have one place he need not be discreet. "Wilful, impertinent, rude…"

"My son, your uncharitable thoughts on her do you no credit."

"They are nowhere near as uncharitable as her thoughts on me," Siward muttered.

"Her thoughts lie with her own conscience and she may discuss them with me if she feels she should," Colman said with a frown. "You must see to your own soul."

Siward bowed his head, accepting the penance the priest was prescribing. He had no regrets. It was good one person in the household knew the truth.

∞∞∞

In spite of some hints from the priest, Oswyth confessed nothing out of the ordinary, considering her views on Siward to be completely justified. All the same she was glad to be back, busy with the household and spending her days companionably with Alfgiva. As the year wore on, she considered her new life pleasant enough.

She and Siward saw little of each other. He was busy managing the crops and livestock or hunting in the forests nearby. When she rode over the lands, she admired the fields of waving wheat and barley. It looked as if the harvest would be a good one and she had to admit that Siward's management of the land was excellent. In a time of peace, when his failings would not be so evident, he would probably have been a tolerable husband.

Siward's hopes of King Edgar's return waned as the months went on with no word. And as the summer came, he disgusted Oswyth by commenting that he now hoped it would not happen that year so he could concentrate his men on the harvest.

When the men started cutting the wheat, the women were just as busy preserving the summer fruits. Oswyth was trying to avoid Alfgiva's probing questions on the state of her marriage, when a group of men entered. The women looked up from their task, surprised to receive a visit. But the curiosity swiftly turned to dismay as they realised the visitors were Normans, while Oswyth stifled a cry when she recognised the leader of the men. It was her erstwhile betrothed, Ralf Fitz Turstin.

With her head high, Oswyth got up to greet them, her face deliberately free from a smile. "Greetings. How may we assist you?"

Ralf nodded, giving no sign of recognising her. "Greetings, my lady. We seek Siward of Gloucester. Is he present?"

"He is, naturally, busy with the harvest, as all good men are at this time of year," she replied, leaving no doubt in the men's minds that she did not consider them good men.

"We are here on the King's business. It is imperative that we speak with Siward of Gloucester this day."

Oswyth exchanged a look with Alfgiva, seeing the anxiety on her mother-in-law's face. She wondered if Ralf was there to seek his arrest, but there was little she could do. "Please be seated." She gestured at the benches lining the table. "I shall send a message to Lord Siward informing him you are here." As she spoke, she glanced at one of the churls, who gave a nod and swiftly left the hall.

"Thank you, my lady. Perhaps we could take some ale." The men sat down, Ralf even resting his feet on the table.

Oswyth shuddered, afraid these men were there to take the lands from Siward, leaving them destitute. Certainly they seemed intent on making themselves very much at home. Determined not to be cowed, she poured into earthenware cups, the ale which was kept for the thralls. The men stared at the cups with a frown, but drank, even Ralf for the moment making no further comment.

"And some food," he called, just as she was thinking she had successfully put him in his place. "Try to make it better quality than this ale."

Oswyth was about to snap back that she was not their servant when Alfgiva intervened, setting down some bread sweetened with plums.

"Do not antagonise them, my child," she muttered. "Not until we know what they want with Siward."

When the message was delivered, Siward returned to the hall in a panic. This was how he had lost each of his lands so far, with a visit from the Bastard's men. In the beginning he had tried to fight, desperately defending his lands. It had taken several of his men to die before he realised how ineffective that was.

However as he entered, trying to appear unconcerned, he was heartened to see a small group of men sat at the table. That did not suggest they were out to dispossess him that day.

"Greetings," he said, his confidence faltering as he recognised Ralf. He forced a cheerful tone into his voice. "How can I assist you this day?"

Oswyth hurried forward with a fine cup of horn edged in silver, placing it before her husband. Personally she considered Siward no more worthy of such a fine cup than Ralf, but that was not the point she wished to make to those men.

Siward nodded his thanks, his startled gaze going to the rough earthenware of the men's cups. Swiftly he raised his own cup to his lips to hide his smile. It was at such moments that he considered his marriage to Oswyth worthwhile.

"We are here to make arrangements for you to pay your tributes to the King," Ralf said.

"They are not due yet," Siward replied. "We have only just begun our harvest. Naturally he will get his dues in the autumn."

He hated sending anything to the Bastard but since the failure of Hereward at Ely, he had learnt the wisdom of not drawing attention to himself, understanding it would be necessary to keep all men fresh, ready for when the true king returned.

Ralf's careful indifference broke into a distinct smirk and Siward's heart sank. Of course. That year he had drawn attention to himself by his marriage to Oswyth, the burning of the hall and his claim to her inheritance. The fact he had made little attempt to hold on to her lands was irrelevant. He clenched his fist under the table as he waited to hear his punishment.

Ralf tossed a script onto the table and Siward gestured for Father Colman to come forward. As a boy, his father had insisted on his studies. Although he had never excelled, it was likely he would be able to read it himself but he knew it was imperative there should be no misunderstandings.

Colman picked it up, his expression similarly fearful. "I, William, by the Grace of God, King of England and Duke of Normandy do demand from my loyal servant, Siward of Gloucester, the following items."

There was a long pause as the priest ran his eyes down the list, his colour fading. Fear built in the pit of Siward's stomach. "Please read on, Father," he said, shocked by the calmness of his voice.

He was aware of the gaze of Oswyth and his mother as they too dreaded what was to come. And as Colman read, it was clear with each item on the list that they had been right to fear.

Chapter four

There was a long silence as Colman finished reading. Oswyth stared at the poor quality ale she had served to them, realising they might all be drinking that over the winter.

Siward banged his fist on the table. "This is unacceptable. It is far too much for lands of this size."

"This is what the King has judged to be fair," Ralf replied.

"Fair? How are my people supposed to eat if he takes all this?" Siward gestured at the list Colman still held.

"That, Siward of Gloucester, is not our concern. We just wish to make sure the King receives what he is entitled to."

"I cannot send all this," Siward said. "You are telling me to let my people starve. As a lord, I cannot agree to it. My first duty has to be to them. My priest will draw up a fairer agreement. I am happy to send more than last year but this is too much."

"The King's orders are for there to be no negotiations. You must send what he has ordered."

Siward leant forward, his gaze needle sharp. "What if I do not?"

Oswyth stared at him, suddenly seeing a new side to her husband. She wanted to cheer, proud to see him stand up to the Normans. With baited breath she waited for Ralf to retaliate.

Ralf gave a bland smile, his eyes sweeping insolently over him. "The King will not be happy if you do not. I am sure you know what will happen if you fail the King."

To Oswyth's disgust, Siward's shoulders slumped. "What if I

cannot? You are asking the impossible."

"These are fine lands, Siward of Gloucester. A good landowner should be able to produce enough to give the King his dues. Shall we inform the King you are not capable?"

"No."

Ralf's smile widened. "You see, Siward of Gloucester, you hold these lands only because of the King's great generosity. He trusts you to manage them appropriately. If you cannot, he will have to appoint some man more capable."

Siward gritted his teeth, furious at Ralf's words. He had inherited the lands from his father. It had nothing to do with this pretender king. "I am capable."

"I hope so." Ralf drained what was left in his cup, tossing it to the ground. The cup splintered as the Normans sniggered. "Certainly you do not seem capable if that is the best ale your grains can produce. It is foul. Or perhaps your womenfolk are not skilled enough to brew it." He glanced at Oswyth, a triumphant gleam in his eye. "It seems you did not gain such a prize after all. It would not please me to have such a slattern for a wife."

Oswyth ground her teeth, her gaze going to her husband in the hope he might defend her. But Siward was no longer in the mood to enjoy her actions. "I find it quite palatable but we shall endeavour to give you better if we are to ever have the pleasure of receiving you here again."

"So, I can confirm to the King that he will receive everything he expects?"

Siward's shoulders sank lower. "Yes, he will receive it."

"Excellent. Well, we will be on our way. A good day to you." Ralf nodded at Oswyth and Alfgiva. "Thank you for your hospitality, my ladies, such as it was."

There was silence as the men left the hall, only broken by the crackling of the fire burning merrily, unaware of the horror consuming the people. Out in the courtyard they could hear the Normans still joking with each other as they mounted their horses. As the laughter got more distant, Siward looked up with a sigh.

"Give me that." He snatched the script from Colman, looking through it himself, hoping he had misunderstood something and it was not as bad as he feared. But there was to be no respite. The Bastard was demanding almost everything. There would be precious little left for themselves.

"Can we manage?" Alfgiva asked, taking a seat beside Siward and laying her hand over his.

Siward's lips curved into a stiff smile. "We shall have to. You heard the men. If I do not, I shall lose these lands."

"You did not even fight it," Oswyth said, also sitting. "The Bastard's demands are unreasonable and he knows it. You should have refused."

"Refusing would not have helped. What the Bastard wants, he takes." Siward frowned at Oswyth. "That was a foolish trick you played with the ale."

"It was better than they deserved," Oswyth retorted.

"That's as maybe but it is not how we treat guests here. Do not do it again." Siward was ashamed of his words as Oswyth flushed. He was not angry at her but he needed to vent his displeasure at someone, so had chosen this slip of a girl. He shook his head as he studied the list again, disgusted by what he had become.

"Well, that may be all we have to serve guests in future," Oswyth snapped, getting to her feet.

Siward kicked back his chair with no further words, stalking from the hall. Oswyth stared at the heaps of the wool they had been intending to spin later that day. She wondered which of the fine threads she had already spun would be wending their way toward the wardrobe of the King or members of his entourage.

"Do not take his words to heart, my child." Alfgiva put an arm around her. "This is a grave blow."

"I do not understand why he just accepts it," Oswyth said, giving a bewildered shake of the head.

"What can he do?"

"I do not know but there must be something." Her wish to

start spinning faded even further. She pushed Alfgiva's arm away as she left the hall in search of Siward.

∞∞∞∞

She did not have to go far before she found him looking over the fields, tears in his eyes. Earlier that day he had been so proud of how well the crops had grown, confident of a rich bounty that year. But instead his people would work themselves to the bone for nothing.

"Siward!"

Siward turned with a sigh. The last person he had any energy for that day was his wife. "I have much to do."

"You cannot let them do this to us," she cried.

"There is nothing I can do. If I do not meet their demands, I shall lose my lands."

Oswyth stamped her foot in a childish action which irritated him more than ever. "Well, I cannot stand for it. I have made a decision. I am ready to enter a convent."

"Do not be foolish."

"I am not being foolish. I am still a maid. Our marriage is no true marriage, is it? I will not tolerate being wed to a man who is so weak."

Siward narrowed his eyes, rather wishing he could agree to her demands. The relief of no longer being saddled with so harsh a wife would be immense. "Too bad," he snapped. "I told you to make your decision by Easter. That, in case you have not noticed, is long past."

"I do not care. We do not have a true marriage so I will go."

"You will not. Convents expect to be well endowed."

"I can endow a convent well. I have all the contents from my grandfather's household, not to mention the jewels you bestowed upon me. I am entitled to keep those, am I not? A convent would be glad to accept me."

Siward shook his head. "You really are that selfish, aren't you?

Listen, Oswyth, I am counting on the produce we brought from your grandfather to sustain us and the additional possessions will be useful in bartering for food if necessary. With those to supplement the harvest, I can meet my dues to the Bastard and still feed my people over the winter."

"You expect my property to go in tribute to the Bastard?"

"Yes, since the tribute I am facing is only so heavy because of my marriage to you." He gave a harsh laugh. "I should have left you to marry that Ralf Fitz Turstin. It would have served you right. You heard him. There would have been no little tricks like the one you just pulled with the ale if you were wed to him."

"I do not want to stay married to you," Oswyth shrieked.

"And I do not want to stay married to you," Siward replied. "But we are stuck with each other."

"I cannot do it," Oswyth cried. "I am ashamed to be married to a man as weak as you, a man who meekly gives in to such demands."

"I do not care how you feel. You are married to me and you will not speak to me in this fashion."

"My father gave his life to save yours. He died beneath the axe of a Norman so you could live. And this is how you repay his sacrifice? By becoming a snivelling failure who allows the Normans to act as they will."

Siward's heart thudded in his ears, his face turning white. He pressed his lips tightly together to stop a despairing sob from escaping, no longer able to even see the angry face of his wife. Instead floating before his eyes was the shadowy face of a man, a man in agony, a man whose life was bleeding from him because of what he had done.

"Stop," cried Alfgiva.

They both turned sharply. The tears rolling down his mother's cheeks forced Siward to steady his breathing. Oswyth took a step towards her, her hands outstretched but as she went to slip an arm around her mother-in-law, she stepped away.

"No, Oswyth. I heard everything you said. Do not touch me."

Chapter five

Oswyth flushed. Never had she heard Alfgiva speak so fiercely. She looked from her mother-in-law, flinching at the hardness in her tear filled eyes, back to Siward, his face still pale and drawn. Stammering an excuse, she fled back to the hall.

"Mother-" Siward started to say.

"Oh, Siward, my dearest boy." As she folded him in her arms, Siward clung tightly to her for a moment, ashamed of his need to do so. He could imagine what Oswyth would say about a grown man, a warrior so desperate for his mother's embrace.

"Truly I am fine, Mother," Siward said, pulling away from her at last.

Alfgiva shook her head, her disbelief obvious in her expression. "That girl. How can she say such words? Oh, I could see matters were not good between you but I had no idea it was as bad as this."

"She is not usually so forthright." Siward wondered why he was defending her. "She was upset this day."

"The news from the Norman pretender has upset us all," Alfgiva said. "We do not mouth such cruelties as she has done."

"I know."

"Is it true what she said? Is she still a maid?"

Siward nodded.

"Oh, my dear boy, why did you marry her?"

He gave a wry smile. "I have often asked myself that. Her grandfather begged me to do it. I knew she had a stubborn streak but I assumed she would become more amenable."

"And as a result of this, you now have the invaders eying up the only property you have left and the winter we face is a bleak one."

"I thought it was the right thing to do. But, yes, you are right, Mother. It is simply my latest failure. I do not know why you do not also despise me."

Alfgiva hugged him again. "Do not speak like that, Siward. You are no failure. You are a good, true Englishman. You married her to save her from a forced marriage to that loathsome man. It was an honourable action. She is the failure for not appreciating it."

Siward shrugged. "Perhaps."

"But if she is a maid, why not send her to a convent? It is no true marriage. I know you speak of needing her dower property but I would rather starve this winter than subject you to such a spiteful, malicious little..."

"Oh, Mother." Siward shook his head, amused in spite of himself. His mother's battling spirit was in full flow. "You may wish to starve but I do not and I am sure most of the others here would also prefer to live through this winter."

"I suppose so."

"Please do not quarrel with Oswyth over this."

"You cannot expect me to listen to such words as she spoke of you and say nothing," Alfgiva exclaimed.

"Please, Mother. These next months are going to be hard enough without having to be in the midst of a quarrel between you and Oswyth. You seemed to have developed a true bond with her. In spite of everything, I was pleased about that."

"That was before I realised her sweet mannerisms are all an act. I have no affection for her now."

"At least be polite," Siward said with a sigh. "Please. I have enough to do without sorting your quarrels."

"Very well." Alfgiva stood on tiptoes to plant a kiss on her son's still pale cheek. "I shall be polite. For now."

As Alfgiva returned to the hall, Siward gave another wry

smile, knowing how formidable his mother's icy politeness could be. If it was any other woman having to deal with it, he would feel sorry for her. But Oswyth would have to accept it.

He turned away to look again over the fields, trying to think of a way to salvage as much of the produce as possible for themselves.

∞∞∞

Oswyth looked up nervously from her spinning when Alfgiva returned to the hall. Her mother-in-law said nothing as she picked up the spindle, furiously twisting it. The other women in the hall watched curiously. No one broke the awkward silence.

"At least we have plenty of wool," Oswyth said brightly. "There is still another batch of the fleeces sheered in the spring."

Alfgiva did not look at her. "Indeed."

Oswyth cast an imploring glance at the other women. None were meeting her eye and she wondered how much of her conversation with Siward they had overheard. In her rage she had failed to keep her voice low. Until that day everyone on Siward's lands had been so welcoming, it had been easy to feel at home. But these were mostly Siward's people and even those who had come from her grandfather's lands were happy to now owe allegiance to him. In spite of the brightly blazing fire, she shivered. In one burst of temper she had become an outsider. Guessing everyone would follow Alfgiva's lead, she tried in increasing desperation to engage her in conversation until the monosyllabic answers finally drove her to silence.

"Alfgiva," she said later as they took their seats on the dais, either side of the chair where Siward would come to sit. "Please…"

"I have no wish to talk to you, Oswyth."

"Please, listen. I am sorry for what you heard…"

Alfgiva did look at her at that comment. "But you are not

sorry for what you said, are you?"

"I know it is hard. But he did cause the death of my father. You cannot expect me to forget that."

Alfgiva shook her head. "You have no idea what you are talking about."

"But that is between Siward and myself. It has no bearing on us. Please." Oswyth swallowed. She had not realised how much she had come to enjoy Alfgiva fussing over her, just as her own mother might have done. "I truly valued your friendship."

"Well, it is over. I regard you with nothing but contempt."

"But…"

"No. You are a spoilt, spiteful young woman. I wish my son was married to anyone other than you."

Oswyth's eyes filled with tears. Her mother-in-law's voice had risen and she could see others were looking curiously at her. Usually with the noisy bustle of the evening, any such conversation would go unheard but in the subdued atmosphere of that night, her voice had carried.

At that moment Siward entered, pausing at the doorway to exchange a few words with some of the men gathered there and scratch the head of one of the dogs who had lumbered to its feet, its tail wagging.

Alfgiva lowered her voice again. "Listen, Oswyth, Siward does not want us to quarrel."

"No," Oswyth cried eagerly. "It will be best if we are friends."

"We are not friends," Alfgiva said. "I love Siward and I will not make life harder for him as you do. So I will try to control my temper in your presence."

"Thank you. Surely we can become friends again?"

Alfgiva shook her head. Seeing Siward coming towards them, she provocatively filled up his cup, although by rights that was Oswyth's role. "No. I despise you. I shall be polite to you for his sake. But do not mistake such pleasantries for affection. I have none."

Chapter six

O swyth made no further attempts to deceive anyone by standing with Siward as he addressed his people the next day. But as she watched from the side of the hall, a reluctant admiration grew at his confident manner.

Siward was, in fact, feeling very far from confident. He had spent a sleepless night going over everything in his mind, knowing how high the price for failure would be. If the harvest was as successful as it looked to be, all would be well. He repressed a sigh as he faced his expectant people, knowing he was only one bad storm or early frost away from disaster.

"My friends," he said, forcing his tone to sound buoyant. "The demands of the Norman bastard are a grave blow. But it is not one which will finish us."

There were some muffled cheers at this as Siward grinned with an assurance he wished he could feel.

"I thank you all for the efforts you have made so far. Continue with them. We need the harvest to be a success, but with your dedication, I know it will be. Thanks to our efforts in previous years, we are already well stocked. The tributes the churls give to me, will be honoured. I do not forget it is my privilege to feed you in your times of need and there is always a place in my hall for you all." Siward paused as the people murmured their appreciation. "We have also received the stocks of the late Thegn Raedwulf and in your gratitude, I beg you to remember his soul in your prayers."

Oswyth's eyes filled with tears at this comment. It was not

what she had expected. Given her poor relationship with Siward, she was half expecting the people to sneer but instead she saw heads respectfully bow and not just those of the people who had come with her from her grandfather's lands. She bowed her own, muttering a quick prayer herself, wishing her grandfather were still alive to help her settle with these people.

"I intend to increase my efforts in hunting," Siward continued. "Any additional meat will supplement our own livestock. Fishing too will be essential and we are fortunate that the River Severn runs along these lands. While the priority must be the harvest, if any have time to set traps or nets, I beg you to do so." He paused, his expression becoming sober. "My friends, I know I do not need to describe the price of our failure. Too many good Englishman have already been sent into bondage. I know the invaders will not hesitate to do the same to me and my people. Indeed, they are probably hoping to find an excuse. We must not give it to them."

Again there were loud cheers, impressing Oswyth with how inspiring Siward had been. He might be a failure in battle but he certainly knew how to manage the lands and his people.

"This winter will be hard but every effort you make will bring us through it."

"What of poaching or sheep raids?" a man called.

Siward folded his arms, regarding the man with mock sternness. "Naturally, my good Wicrun, I am forbidding any such actions…" There was a long pause until his lips twitched. "To be carried out against good Englishmen."

There was a burst of laughter. All knew where the forests of the Norman lords could be poached. And, of course, Wales was not far away.

Siward grinned, pleased to see spirits so high. "Back to work, my friends. We will survive this. And we will remain true hearted until the rightful king takes his place. God save King Edgar!"

"King Edgar!" the people chorused.

As the people filed out, Alfgiva flung her arms around her son.

"Oh, well done, Siward. All will be well."

Siward wiped his clammy hands on his tunic, relieved the speech was over. "Let us hope so."

Oswyth came forward. "What do you need me to do?" she asked, longing to be fully involved in this effort to thwart the schemes of the invaders.

"You heard the list, Oswyth," Siward said wearily. "You know what you need to do. If you are not certain, be guided by my mother."

Oswyth flushed. As Siward's wife, it was her place to guide the women. But with the pretence now over, the role had evidently returned to his mother.

"You can count on us, my son." Alfgiva hugged Siward again. "Oh, that Norman Duke is a fool in how he has treated you and the other Englishmen. He should have left you all in place. No one knows how to manage the lands as you do."

"I know. So many of the men who now have the lands do not even reside here. They have returned to Normandy, caring nothing for the land or its people. But there is nothing we can do on that for now except ensure these lands remain in my hands." He kissed his mother on the cheek. "I must go. I cannot expect the men to work while I stand idle."

"Siward," Oswyth called as he strode away.

He turned, raising an enquiring eyebrow.

"Thank you for your words on my grandfather. I know how proud he would feel to be helping you."

Siward shook his head. "Yet again you remind me of how much I owe your family."

"No," Oswyth protested. "I did not mean that." But Siward was gone and there was only Alfgiva to look contemptuously at her.

∞∞∞

The following month was an anxious one. Siward felt he was continually looking at the sky, alert for any adverse weather which could ruin the crops. However his fears went unrealised as the harvest was even better than he had hoped. Their fish stocks too had been good. Oswyth and Alfgiva had worked tirelessly to see there was plenty smoked for the winter and he intended to spend the remainder of the autumn hunting, not merely for sport but to provide plenty of meat for their own consumption.

As he tossed a handful of grains in the air to symbolise the completion of the harvest, it was galling to see the rich bounty and know it was to be taken from them. However he ordered a particularly lavish celebration, thinking the people who had worked so tirelessly at least deserved that.

"Is it truly enough?" Alfgiva asked as the musicians started some lively tunes.

Siward nodded. "We shall not live richly this winter but we shall live. Many who have faced the wrath of the invaders are not so fortunate."

"We have managed this year but what of future years?" Alfgiva asked.

Siward shrugged. "Who knows what the situation will be next year? There are rumours of King Edgar's return. The people are surely so tired of the rule of the Bastard, they will rise up. Perhaps by next year we shall be building England anew."

"What will you do to support King Edgar?" Oswyth asked.

Siward sent her a sideways glance. "I shall do what I have done before – rise up in support of him, pledging myself and my men. But until he comes, I live quietly. I am well aware you consider it cowardly to do this but I am content to be a coward in your eyes, if it means these people can eat."

Oswyth bit her lip. She had not even been thinking that. All she had wanted was an excuse to make some sort of conversation in her efforts to fit in, to feel she too was part of the movement to recover England. She tried again. "Siward, the efforts for the harvest have been impressive."

Siward raised his eyebrows. "Praise indeed."

∞∞∞

The moment when the carts rolled away, laden with the tribute the Bastard had claimed, was just as hard as Siward had expected. So much work had gone into the harvest and it was taken from him to feed the invaders. If King Edgar had been on the throne, there would, of course, have still been a tribute but he would not have minded paying dues to his lord, just as his own people paid dues to him. And King Edgar would undoubtedly have been reasonable.

To salve his wounds, he and a small group of men went poaching in the forest on the lands of Turstin Fitz Rolf, returning with boar and deer. There was a grim satisfaction as the antlers of the deer were hung on the wall.

"It is a reminder to us all that we are not powerless," Siward proclaimed. "One day we will prevail."

With the winter upon them, the people kept more to their own dwellings and the hall. Only Father Colman left their lands to journey into Worcester. He returned with news of interest from Bishop Wulfstan.

"It is believed King Edgar will return to Scotland in the spring," he told Siward in a low voice. "We must not proclaim this too loudly. No word must reach the invaders, but be prepared."

Siward nodded. "I shall be. My God, I have been waiting for this news. Let us pray this time his claim will be a successful one."

"It will be hard. The defences these Norman barons have constructed up and down the land will be a challenge to overcome."

"I know but not impossible. It may take time for King Edgar to take back all England but if we can but make a start. Is there any other news?"

Colman nodded. "But this is to be publically known. I shall announce it as we dine."

Siward was curious as he took his place on the dais between

Oswyth and his mother, muttering a polite greeting to Oswyth. Such formal words were the only conversation which now passed between them. He held up his hand for silence, gesturing to Father Colman to speak.

The priest began with the usual evening prayers. "I have also been instructed to impart some grievous news," he said as they finished. "The Atheling, Richard, son of King William and his fair consort has died, killed in a riding accident in the forest of the south the King is commandeering for himself. We are all commanded to pray for his soul."

The response in the hall was one of laughter and jeers. None cared that the Bastard had lost his second son.

Colman shook his head. "Of course we have no love for that family but I am grieved to see the loss of a young life greeted with such glee."

Siward held up his hand. "Father Colman is right. We do not celebrate the loss of a young life. But neither do we grieve for it. How many good Englishmen and women have mourned for their sons in these last years? Far too many. The Bastard and his lady can weep over their son but did they shed a tear, did they care as the men and women of our land wept for their sons?"

At Siward's words Oswyth was consumed by the memory of the news of her father's death arriving at her grandfather's dwelling. The lively conversation had instantly stilled into shocked silence, broken at length by disbelieving whispers. She could almost feel her mother, great with child, pulling her tightly into her arms as the tears sliding down her cheeks soaked into her hair. She remembered how she had clung to her, trying to blot out the news. But nothing could blot out the harsh sobs of her grandfather. His only son, the pride of his heart, taken in one blood-stained day. Overcome with emotion, she sank her head into her hands, her own tears flowing as freely as they had on that day.

All eyes went to her but no one moved. Oswyth wept more bitterly than ever, deprived even of the comfort which had at least been available at the time. A frown crossed Siward's face, convinced her tears were a reproach to him. It was his fault her father had died. He wished he could forget that.

He stared at Oswyth for a moment longer before looking out at the hall again, seeing not the people but those dying eyes accusing him. "So, the boy died in the forest his father created. Good men and women have been forced from their lands to make way for his private hunting ground. Perhaps it will not be the last Norman life that forest will take. Perhaps the land itself is rising up against them as it weeps for the fallen of Hastings, the people driven starving from the soil their people had tilled for generations and the devastation that evil man wreaked in the North. I do not celebrate the loss of a young life but I will celebrate the hope that this land will bring the Bastard and his sons nothing but grief."

Chapter seven

C hristmas was celebrated without the lavish feasts which were the custom, but it was celebrated. Siward was well aware of the need to keep morale high and, although he would have preferred not to have bothered, he gave orders for the traditional music and story-telling.

Oswyth was in a similarly glum mood. She looked at the people, thinking their laughter too seemed false. The musicians' tunes were merry but only a few chose to dance and those in a stilted fashion, a mere pretence of the dances she remembered from her childhood. It was not the paucity of the feast which caused such melancholy, Oswyth realised. It was the mood which had hung over them for more than seven years. Even if there had been the abundance they had initially anticipated, the atmosphere would still have been downcast. As the lady of the household, she knew it was her duty to encourage more levity but she could not. Missing her grandfather and longing for friendship, all she had to offer was her intense loneliness.

Instead it was Alfgiva who engaged in some merrymaking, as both Siward and Oswyth looked on with smiles, stiff and false.

After Candlemas, Siward instructed the people to start preparing the ground for ploughing. Soon it would be time to sow the seeds again and he wondered drearily how much he would be allowed to keep that year. It was also, he remembered, a year since he had married. He glanced at Oswyth, wondering if she had realised it. She looked more downcast than ever so he guessed she probably had.

"Siward," she said one night. "Might I ask a favour?"

Siward raised his eyebrows in surprise. Very little conversation passed between them and it was rare for her to ask him anything. Listening into conversations in a sneaky fashion was much more her style. "What is it?"

"It will soon be a year since my grandfather's death. Could a mass be said for him?"

Siward's impatience died away. He had been thinking of this time as the anniversary of their marriage but little more than a week later was when her grandfather had died. "Of course. He was a fine man. Tell Father Colman of your wishes. Everyone here will attend."

Oswyth bowed her head. "Thank you." Over the last days there had been such a pain in her heart at the thought of her grandfather's grave lying untended so far away. Forgotten or perhaps worse, spat upon by the Norman now occupying his lands. It was good to think of so many paying their respects.

She blinked her eyes free of tears, realising Siward had already left. Alfgiva was staring at her. Awkwardly she patted Oswyth's hand. "Your grandfather's soul is safe with God. He was indeed a fine man."

Oswyth smiled through the lump constricting her throat, the pain easing still further. It had been so long since any showed her affection that even this tentative touch seemed a warm embrace.

Before Lent began they had a few days of dining well as they ate the last of their meat. But after going to the church to be shriven, they settled down to a diet of fish and eels as they prepared for the spring.

It was just a few days later when a visitor arrived late one afternoon. Frebern of Warwick breezed in, sweeping Alfgiva off her feet. She laughed, patting him on the cheek and exclaiming over how long it was since she had last seen him. Oswyth's face broke from the expressionless mask it usually held, into a wide smile. She looked around noticing how everyone's expressions seemed brighter. Truly the exuberant young man was a welcome sight.

He bowed to Oswyth before kissing her on the cheek with a cheerful grin. "Where is Siward? I must speak to him."

Oswyth was delighted by his actions, this friendly greeting very different from the indifference the people held for her. "He is at the church, speaking to Father Colman. Will you take some ale while you wait?"

"I'd be glad of some ale, my lady. But, perhaps I will go to him. Truly it is a matter of some urgency." He took a cup of ale from Alfgiva, downing it almost in one.

Agog with curiosity, Oswyth extended her hand. "Come, I will take you to him."

"How have you fared this winter?" Frebern asked as they walked.

"We have managed," Oswyth replied. "Just. The burden the pretenders placed on us..."

"I heard," Frebern replied. "It does not surprise me. Siward has held out against the Norman rule with a resolve few men have shown. The Bastard would be glad to see him stripped of his lands."

Oswyth glanced at Frebern, her eyes widening in surprise at the respect in his voice. Her impression was that Siward lay low, doing little to obstruct the Norman domination. Questions leapt to her lips but remained unasked. Frebern would expect her to know all that. He would be shocked by her ignorance.

∞∞∞

Siward's look of irritation at the interruption, vanished as he saw Frebern. "My dear friend." He got up to embrace him. "I had no idea we were to expect a visit from you."

Frebern grinned. "It is good to see you. Is all well? Your lady was telling me you have had a tough winter."

Siward glanced at Oswyth, wondering how scathing she had been. "It has been difficult but we have managed."

"I knew you would," Frebern said in a buoyant tone. "I have some news which will cheer you."

Siward folded his arms, a mock frown creasing his face. "I wondered how long you were going to make me wait to find out why you were here. I was certain it was not just for the pleasure of my company."

Frebern laughed, clapping his friend on the shoulder. "No, I have some news of great import. The King is again in Scotland."

Siward caught his breath. "Already? I heard from Father Wulfstan just before Christmas that he was planning to return. I assumed it was still too early in the year to make the crossing."

"I know. He took a risk but it has paid off. He is the honoured guest of his brother-in-law, King Malcolm. From Scotland he will launch his bid to reclaim the crown."

"You know he never got the crown in the first place, don't you?" Siward said, his spirits rising at Frebern's enthusiasm.

Frebern waved away the objection. "But he was chosen king by the Witan and he is of the rightful royal line. You will support him, won't you?"

Siward grinned. "Of course I will, you fool. How can you think otherwise?" He wondered if Oswyth had said something to imply he would not. "I shall march to join him as soon as I can. What of you? You should be mustering your own men, not wasting time riding to me. A messenger would have sufficed."

Frebern frowned. "Perhaps. But I did not want this message falling into the wrong hands. It is believed the King's arrival in Scotland is not yet known to the forces of the Bastard and I want it to remain that way."

"You are right. Besides, it will be good to plan together. We shall join our forces and march north to meet with Bridwin. Does he know of this?"

"Who do you think it was who told me?" Frebern said with a grin.

"Of course." Siward nodded, raising an eyebrow at the smirk on Frebern's face. "Why are you smiling like that?"

"Because I have as yet told you only a small part of the news," Frebern said. "Do you want to hear more?"

"What else can be as fine as the news you have already told me?" Siward asked.

Oswyth too held her breath. She had been listening carefully, hope brimming at the optimism of the men.

"King Sweyn of Denmark is launching his own attack. The pressure on the Bastard in the North will be immense."

"It will," Siward replied. "At least it will if he stands firm this time and does not allow himself to be bought off." His new-found hope faded as he remembered the tragic consequences of the last attack King Sweyn had been involved in.

"Perhaps if he knows he can count on good Englishmen, he will not be so easily bought off," Oswyth suggested.

Siward scowled at her. Trust her to imply the failure was all his fault. "Good Englishmen were ready last time. He was bought off by the lure of gold. Nothing else."

"I know," Oswyth stammered. "I did not mean…"

"He will not want to risk such a strategy this time," Frebern said, looking curiously from Siward to Oswyth. "Not with Scotland supporting King Edgar. He has to choose sides and he hates the Norman bastard."

"Let us hope so." Siward frowned at his friend. "You are still grinning in that foolish fashion. Is there more you have not told me?"

"The King of Francia," Frebern said proudly. "He has disputes with the Bastard in Normandy. He is bestowing some lands on King Edgar in support of his claim. Ha! Now who has a foolish grin?"

Siward laughed. "My God, this is indeed good news. The Bastard will be pressed on all sides. England will rise again. We will build England anew."

Chapter eight

Frebern did not linger long on Siward's lands, returning quickly to muster his men. Siward too threw himself into his preparations. Oswyth looked on as he became a man transformed. No longer did he seem so careworn but instead was focused, determined and endlessly busy. With the smile more readily on his lips, she found her gaze often drawn to him, very aware of how handsome he was.

"Go as soon as you are ready," Alfgiva cried. "We can see to matters here."

"There will be lots to do," Siward warned.

"I know that," Alfgiva replied. "But surely you do not think the women and those men who do not fight cannot see to such matters as the sowing of seeds and the sheering of the flock? Of course we can. With so many away, our work in the household will be lighter in any case."

Siward grinned. "That is true. Well, I shall soon be ready to march. But, prepare well. Remember how heavy the tribute was last year. We may need to meet that burden again."

"Surely King Edgar would not impose such a burden on you," Oswyth said.

"I am sure he will not," Siward replied coldly. "Indeed he is more likely to reward me. But he is not on the throne yet."

Oswyth shook her head, so angered at his tone, she forgot her newfound admiration. "No wonder you are always careless if that is the attitude you take into battle. It is not surprising you have failed so often."

Siward narrowed his eyes, the weary look descending on him once again. Alfgiva stepped closer to him but he did not seem to notice as a sheen of sweat broke out on his brow. "A good commander prepares for all eventualities, Oswyth."

"A good commander, yes," Oswyth replied.

Siward clenched his fists, his face reddening at the inference. "Do not prate on about matters you know nothing about. I trust you will do your part here. It will be hard work. Or are you perhaps too lazy to do what is necessary?"

It was Oswyth's turn to redden. "I always work hard. You know that."

Siward turned away. "Make sure you do."

Oswyth looked after Siward from narrowed eyes before realising Alfgiva was staring at her. Her face turned an even deeper shade of scarlet, aware that in her resentment of Siward she had spoken words she had not intended, especially in front of his mother.

"You stupid, stupid girl," Alfgiva said in a low tone. "How dare you speak to him like that?"

"I am sorry. I don't mean to upset you. But..." Oswyth's eyes filled with tears. "It is because of his foolishness that my father died at Hastings. I cannot forget it. My father, a fine man, might have lived if it were not for him."

Alfgiva shook her head. "Oh, Oswyth. Even you cannot be as stupid as that. Siward is right. You know nothing."

"I do," Oswyth cried, as Alfgiva too walked away. "Or are you implying my father was not a fine man?"

Alfgiva turned back. "Oh, no, he was indeed a fine man. I wonder how he came to have you as a daughter."

Oswyth's tears came faster at that comment but Alfgiva did not look back.

Siward was trying to keep his own tears at bay. "Damn her," he muttered to himself. "Damn her, damn her, damn her." He had felt so hopeful in the last days, confident this would be the occasion which would see an end to rule by conquest. But her words were like knives in his heart, reminding him of the nightmare he so wanted to put to rest. His confidence plummeted, swiftly replaced by the certainty of failure.

"Siward?"

Inwardly Siward cursed as he heard his mother's voice. The last thing he wanted was to worry her. He well remembered his actions when he had returned home for the first time after the defeat at Hastings. For days he had simply lain in his chamber, refusing food and speaking barely a word except to demand more to drink, while snarling at any who questioned that. Alfgiva had been convinced he had sustained some terrible injury in spite of his assurances. At length he came out of his drunken stupor long enough to see how worried she was. He told her everything, weeping in her arms for the loss of England. That was not something he wanted to repeat on this occasion. She needed to concentrate on running the household in his absence, not worrying about him.

"Yes, Mother?" he said with what he hoped was a cheerful smile.

"Oh, Siward. Do not allow that stupid girl to upset you."

Siward shook his head. "Of course not, Mother. I am merely preoccupied with everything I must do."

Alfgiva shook her head, not fooled for an instant. "You know how proud I am of you, do you not? Your dear father too would have been so proud if he had lived to see how hard you have fought."

Siward relaxed. "I hope so. Please do not worry about Oswyth's attitude. I am accustomed to it by now. Do not let it hinder you in working with her while I am away."

"I do not think you are," Alfgiva muttered. "But do not worry. All will run smoothly here. You can rely on me."

"I know I can. I am fortunate in that."

"But, my son." Alfgiva hesitated, tugging at her greying plait as she tried to find the words. "I believe you can be victorious this time. I shall be praying for it, you know that. But whatever happens, whether victory or defeat…"

"What?"

"Bring an end to your marriage. I mean that, Siward. I assume she is still a maid."

"Of course. She's hardly tempted me to change that state, has she?"

"Then it will be an easy matter. Of course it will be easier if you are victorious for then you will gain rich rewards. But even if you are not, we will not depend on her wealth to sustain us. Rid yourself of her. You know no one here would wish it otherwise. She is despised by all."

Siward frowned. "I am sorry to hear that. It is not what I wanted. I promised her grandfather I would look after her. I owe it to her father too. I suppose that is yet another task I have failed at."

"Nonsense. Both of those men would be appalled to see Oswyth behave in such a fashion and you know it. If she enters a convent, she will be cared for perfectly well. You will have fulfilled your obligation."

"I suppose so." Siward sighed. He wondered how Oswyth would fare in a convent. Would her spirit be ground down by the plain clothes, the routine and obedience expected of her? Once she might have risen to high office, her forceful manner well suited to presiding over an abbey. But now such positions were for the most part bestowed on Norman women. "If I am victorious, she may become more amenable."

Alfgiva shook her head. "As a wife she should always be amenable. And more than that, to show you love and respect whatever your circumstances. A wife who honours you only in victory, never supporting you through failure, is no wife at all."

∞∞∞

Siward managed his preparations swiftly, with warriors from all over the Shire of Gloucester soon ready to march. There was little chance that news would not soon reach the Reeve of the Shire or some other loyal to the Bastard, but by acting so quickly he hoped to be well on the way to Scotland before the news could spread any further.

He ran through a long list of instructions to his mother, which she accepted with a good humoured smile and a twinkle in her eye. He grinned ruefully, knowing only too well she was as capable as he.

"Take care of yourself, my son," Alfgiva said as he prepared to depart. She hugged him tightly, the smile on her face so bright, Siward knew it was a false one. "Come safely back."

"I shall do my best." Siward kissed her on the cheek, acutely aware of how many young Englishmen had not returned to their mothers.

He turned to Oswyth, giving a slight bow. "Farewell. When I return, we shall discuss your future. It is time to bring this intolerable situation to an end."

Oswyth flinched. She had been watching Siward bid his mother farewell, touched by the warm affection between them. How she wished there was someone who felt such love for her. She was also conscious of how strong Siward looked, prepared for battle. Handsome too. She had readied a speech to wish him good fortune but at his words that went out of her head. "Good," she retorted. "I shall be glad of that."

Siward gave a grim smile. "I thought you would be. But Oswyth, if I should fall, you will be a widow. As I have no son, these lands will be yours. No doubt you will quickly gain a new husband. A Norman one."

Oswyth prevented herself from flinching again as her heart quailed at that thought. She kept her face in a mask of indifference. "I expect so."

Siward shook his head in disgust, wishing he had not put himself to so much trouble to save her from marriage to a Norman. "In that event, I make one request of you. Take care of my mother. Do not let whichever man takes my lands force her from her home."

Oswyth's face softened. "Of course. I shall do what I can."

Siward bowed again, bestowed one last kiss on his mother's cheek and mounted his horse. With a sharp kick, he urged it into a brisk trot. He did not look back but he could feel the gaze of his mother, probably now full of tears, as he moved swiftly away. He could feel Oswyth's eyes too, cold and scornful. It was a comfort to think that whether he lived or died, he would not have to see much more of her.

Chapter nine

The days after Siward's departure dragged, consumed by the vast amount of work they had to accomplish. It was a relief to Oswyth when at the end of each day, they ate a simple supper and she could at last relax her aching body.

With crops finally sown, the work load eased a little but still there was plenty to do with the livestock and other matters which were usually attended to by the men. There had been no word on how much the Bastard might demand that year, but all assumed, if he was still on the throne, the tribute would be steep. They kept a close watch on food consumption, so although no one went hungry, there was little in the way of luxuries.

The day they sheered the sheep was particularly strenuous as they struggled to handle the large rams of the flock. Oswyth returned to the hall exhausted but proud of the yield. She was confident the men could have done no better. The next task would be the spinning and weaving. These were far from her favourite occupations but at least she would be able to sit.

She entered the hall, knowing there was still more to do to prepare for the evening but unable to resist the temptation to sit down for a moment, pouring herself a cup of ale. Her cheeks, already reddened by the wind, went scarlet in the warmth of the fire. As she set her cup down, one of the churls jostled her, causing half the ale to slop over the cup, soaking her sleeve.

Oswyth looked up in annoyance.

"Forgive me, my lady," the woman muttered, not sounding remotely apologetic.

Oswyth's eyes filled with tears as she sipped at what was left, furious some had been wasted. Since Siward had gone, the household had become more hostile towards her. Alfgiva seemed not to notice how insolently the churls and even the thralls acted, although Oswyth suspected it was more that she simply did not care. Never had she realised how much Siward's presence had shielded her. She closed her eyes, finding herself muttering a prayer for his safe return. Tears brimmed further as, for the first time since his departure, she wondered what he was doing and what state he was in.

She awoke the next morning with even less heart for the work of the day. As she walked into the hall, the vast heaps of wool mocked her with the toil they demanded. All would need to be washed before it was carded, spun and woven into cloth. Alfgiva and several of the other women were already working. Oswyth quickly swallowed some bread and weak ale before moving to join them.

No one so much as looked up, still less gave any greetings. Instead the women continued their chatter among themselves. It was as if Oswyth did not even exist. Her spirit rebelled. If that was the way they wanted it, so be it. They could work without her. With a contemptuous look at the wool, she turned away.

"Where are you going, Oswyth?" Alfgiva called, making it obvious she had known of Oswyth's presence. "Sit down. We have much to do this day."

"No," Oswyth replied.

There was a gasp from the women and Alfgiva got to her feet, the thread tumbling to the floor. "What do you mean?"

"I mean, why should I help? You heard Siward before he departed. I am not to be here much longer. Why should I care if you prosper or not?"

Alfgiva folded her arms, her gaze narrowing to sharp points. "I never knew anyone as selfish as you. Your poor father, your dear mother, how ashamed they would be if they could see you this day."

"Do not use my father against me," Oswyth cried. "He was proud of me. He loved me. You have no idea how hard it is to lose so great a man."

"Your father, your father, your father," Alfgiva snapped. "That is all we hear from you. Do you think you are the only one here to have lost someone at Hastings or in the fights which followed?" She gestured at the women who were staring open-mouthed at them. "Many here lost fathers, husbands, brothers and sons. All were great in their eyes. What makes you and your father so special?"

"My father was killed because of Siward's clumsiness."

"Do not be such a stupid little fool. Stop believing that nonsense. You are not a child now."

Feeling very like the child Alfgiva had accused her of being, Oswyth ran from the hall, her eyes blurred.

"Oswyth, stop," Alfgiva called, following her.

Oswyth sank onto a grassy bank near the hall, her tears flowing. After a shocked moment, Alfgiva sat beside her. "I am sorry if I implied any insult to your father," she said. "Truly he was a fine man. But, my child, you must accept how many others have also faced a loss. My brother was slain. Not at Hastings but at Stamford Bridge. You will find many here to understand your grief."

"They hate me," Oswyth sobbed, letting her loneliness flow out. "All of them."

"Everyone here is devoted to Siward. He has kept them safe these past years, working tirelessly. Many heard your words to him, still more learnt of them. You cannot expect them to love you. If you had treated him with the affection and respect he deserves, it would be a very different story. Everyone here would have adored you." Alfgiva's lips trembled. "As would I."

"Can you not understand how hard it is to know how his actions cost my father his life? Every time I see him, I remember how he is alive and my father is not."

"You have no idea what happens in battle. No doubt you have seen men practise with their weaponry and imagine that you do. But truly you have no idea. Weapons get dropped. Do you think your father never dropped a weapon? Oh, do not look so offended. He was a skilled and brave warrior but the only man who has never made a mistake in battle, is a man who has never fought in one."

"I suppose so."

"Your father did what any brave warrior would do. He took action to defend one of his comrades. And, my God, Oswyth, I think of your father with gratitude every single day. Because of him, I still have my son. Whenever you bleat about this, I am reminded how you wish it was I who lost the one I love."

"No, no, I would never wish that for you."

"Now Siward may be fighting again. Perhaps this very moment he is fighting. Perhaps even now he is injured. Or perhaps even now he is dead. I think of that every day. Every morning I wake, fearing this will be the day I receive the news of his death. And every night I dream I have lost him until I scarce dare sleep at all. And in those dark hours I pray that, if he fights, he fights again beside men who would risk their lives to save his, while I am only too aware he would give his life to save another. I cannot wish it otherwise and I am so proud but it terrifies me. Oswyth, why vent your hatred onto Siward? Why not the man who actually killed your father?"

Oswyth shrugged, puzzled by that question. She realised she barely gave that man a thought. "I know not. I know nothing about him. Not his name. Not even what happened to him."

"What happened to him? I can assure you he did not prosper. Siward killed him. He died before your father did."

"I had no idea," Oswyth breathed.

"And then Siward helped your father from the field, so he might receive the comfort of a priest and secure his salvation. Did you never know all this?"

"My grandfather rarely spoke of Hastings. It was too painful for him," Oswyth replied.

"Siward would have told you if you had asked him."

Oswyth's tears flowed faster, wishing she had spoken to Siward and heard more of her father's last moments.

"You need to grow up, Oswyth. As your father's daughter, your place is to respect the decision he made to risk his own life to save Siward's. Just as you should respect the decisions your husband has made."

"Even though they ended in failure?" Oswyth asked, raising her red-rimmed eyes to look at her mother-in-law.

"It was not Siward's fault. It is the fault of the men he fights for. King Harold, may God have mercy on his soul, made a foolish decision in forcing the men to march so swiftly south to fight the Norman duke before they had recovered from their last fight. He paid dearly for it and died bravely, but he was a fool. Then there was King Sweyn, who deserted the cause Siward was fighting for because of the money the Bastard flung at him." She shook her head. "English blood flowed while King Sweyn sailed away richer."

There was a long silence as both women stared in the direction Siward had ridden. In the bright sunlight Oswyth could see how the lines on Alfgiva's face had deepened since he had gone.

"Now Siward fights for King Edgar but the King is young and untested." Alfgiva's voice was quiet, her thoughts clearly far away. "I do not know how he will fare against a man as experienced as the Bastard. Perhaps if he listens to Siward and other men of good sense and experience like Bridwin of Lichfield, he can triumph. But will he? Far too often kings do not listen to such wisdom." Alfgiva gave a mirthless laugh. "The stupid thing is, that Duke William could probably have won men like Siward to loyalty, if only he had treated them fairly, ruling over them as a noble king instead of plundering their lands for his own men. The Duke too is a fool, for not valuing men like Siward as he should."

Oswyth looked down with no further words to speak. Alfgiva

patted her on the shoulder. "Come back to the hall. We have much work to do. And you need to do it, for Siward."

Oswyth shook her head.

Alfgiva frowned. "Still no, after everything I have said?"

Oswyth swallowed. "I will come back and help, I swear it. But first I must go to the church. There is a confession I should make."

Chapter ten

Siward made good progress with his men, arriving at Frebern's lands near Warwick just three days later. He found his friend in high spirits and ready to depart, allowing them to continue the journey the next day.

"Where are we meeting Bridwin?" Siward asked. "Do we make for Lichfield?"

"With the new Norman bishop in residence?" Frebern shook his head. "No, we need to keep clear of Lichfield. He has been gathering his men to the north of the city. We shall make for his camp."

Siward nodded. "What of the Bastard? Is there any news on his movements?"

"Is he not still in Normandy?" Frebern asked.

"No. He has returned to England."

Frebern cursed. "I was hoping otherwise. It would be easier if he wasn't here."

"I know, but even if we can help King Edgar take back just a bit of the North, it will be a start."

"Yes, it will. Once we have rebuilt one part of England, the rest will surely follow."

Siward urged his horse into a faster trot. "Exactly."

It took another four days before they came to the forest where Bridwin's camp was believed to be.

"How are we supposed to find him in here?" Frebern asked as they started into the trees.

"If he has as many men as we expect, it shouldn't be too hard,"

Siward replied.

But as they rode on, there was no sign a large company of men had passed that way. The path they were on dwindled until they were no longer sure if it even was a path. Siward's horse stumbled, forcing him to cling tighter to the reins until it steadied itself again.

"The woods are too thick here," Frebern said eventually. "We must be going the wrong way."

"I think you are right," Siward replied. "Let us..." His voice broke off abruptly as dark clothed men sprang from behind trees, bows armed and ready.

Siward reined in his horse and was about to order weapons to be raised when he recognised a couple of the men.

"Speak your intentions in these parts," one of the men said.

Siward grinned. "My intentions are no better than your lord's, my good Dunstan. Take me to him. It is Siward of Gloucester and I have Frebern of Warwick with me."

The men instantly lowered their weapons, as Dunstan bowed before him. "Forgive me, my lord. I thought it was you but we are under orders to be careful."

"Very wise. Where is Lord Bridwin?"

"Come this way, my lord."

They trotted beneath trees which had seemed too dense, although this proved to be deceptive. After just a short distance the trees thinned into a stretch of open ground, crammed with tents.

"He has a goodly number of men," Frebern commented.

"He does indeed," Siward replied, feeling more confident than ever. He waved as he saw Bridwin coming towards them, a wide grin spreading over his face. It had been a long time since he had last seen his oldest friend.

Both he and Frebern slid down from their horses, running forward to embrace the man. He was little more than a year younger than Siward and powerfully built, his dark hair loose around his shoulders.

"Greetings! You have made good time. I was sure I would not

see you for another few days," Bridwin said.

"Yes, we have done well. As have you. Look at this force!"

"Loyalty to the true king is strong indeed," Bridwin replied, looking pleased by Siward's words. "So, how are you two faring?"

"Well enough," Frebern replied.

"And what of you?" Bridwin elbowed Siward in the ribs. "I hear you are a married man now. Good for you. Is she pretty?"

Siward had no wish to think of Oswyth and simply nodded.

"She is very pretty," Frebern put in. "A bit strong willed though, I shouldn't wonder."

"Be quiet," Siward snapped, not sure if he was more annoyed at Frebern complimenting Oswyth or criticising her.

There was a tense silence as Frebern looked at the ground. "Sorry. I didn't mean anything to insult her. She is charming. And damned pretty."

Bridwin looked curiously at Siward's expression, but gestured towards the fire. "Come, my friends, let me get you some ale and you can tell me the rest of your news."

Siward nodded, sending an awkward glance at Frebern who was looking as relieved as him to change the subject. "And plan our next move."

After a couple of days' planning they were ready to proceed, moving their men stealthily towards Scotland, trying not to draw too much attention to themselves.

"Keeping the men fed will be the hardest," Siward commented. "I have not been able to bring as much as I would have liked. The Bastard exacted a harsh tribute from me last year."

"I heard," Bridwin said. "But do not worry. I have plenty."

"Thank you, my friend," Siward replied. "I also know of a number of estates and abbeys along the route which are sympathetic to our cause."

"If we are careful, we can always steal from those who are not," Frebern said cheerfully.

Siward laughed, enjoying his friend's optimism. He was younger than him, having barely seen twenty years and had not fought at Hastings. He often speculated that this was why Frebern seemed less affected by the defeat. He had never known how it was when they had managed their lands under a king of the true line.

"I still possess my estate in the North," Bridwin said. "Let us head there. It is not the finest, which is no doubt why I still have it, but it will be a useful base."

Siward nodded. "From there we can send a message to King Edgar, pledging our allegiance."

"And when the storytellers tell of how we retook England, they will tell how it was won from your lands," Frebern said.

"Let us hope so," Siward muttered.

By keeping their men spread into small groups, there were no problems on the journey north. None questioned them, seeing them simply as noblemen travelling with their accustomed entourage. Siward's network of estates and abbeys proved to be useful, particularly during the stretch of poor weather which followed.

All three of the men had a number of scouts which they sent in all directions, to provide information on the movements of King Edgar and for sightings of King Sweyn. They also wanted to keep a close eye on the Bastard, ever alert for any action on his part. But as they moved into the wastelands beyond York, there was still no word of any changes.

Riding through the devastated countryside was a sobering experience, with even Frebern's cheery mood dashed. The charred stretches of land which had once been rich farmland were a warning to them all of the price of failure. Siward was glad they would not need to pass through the lands he had once owned. He remembered it as a thriving estate. The reports of what it had been reduced to were bad enough. He did not need to see it with his own eyes.

Bridwin's estate was a small one, not far from the coast. It was a useful place to base themselves, being just a few day's ride from the border with Scotland, while also in place to aid King Sweyn.

"Let us see who comes first," Siward said, as he watched the messenger depart for Scotland and King Edgar.

"Should we contact the Earl of Northumbria?" Frebern asked.

Bridwin hesitated. "I am not sure. He supported King Edgar's last attempt to claim his throne, but I am not certain where his loyalties lie now."

"He is wed to a kinswoman of the Bastard," Siward said. "For Duke William to allow him to hold the earldom, he must feel confident of his loyalty. I think we should be cautious. Once King Edgar is again in England, we shall know for certain who is with him."

∞∞∞∞

After the hasty march north, they were glad of a respite, all remembering how the late King Harold's failure to allow his men sufficient rest had cost him his crown and his life and them their land. As the days passed they were pleased to see the men becoming restless. They were spoiling for a fight and would be more than ready to retake the North as soon as King Edgar gave the word.

As the days stretched to more than a week since they had dispatched the messenger to King Edgar in Scotland, Siward grew concerned.

"We do not know where in Scotland he is based," Bridwin said. "We are close to the border here but if he is at Scone or even further north, it will take longer to reach him."

"True and the terrain may not be so easy," Siward replied. "The weather too might delay him."

But even so, all three were worried. They had expected their king to respond eagerly. In the end it was one of Siward's scouts to the south who was first to come to them. He was swiftly ushered into the hall, where they greeted him impatiently.

"What news," Bridwin demanded as the exhausted man took the time for a quick mouthful of ale.

"My lords, King William-" the man started.

"Duke William," Siward said sharply. "He is no true king. Let us not forget that."

"Of course, my lord," the man said.

Bridwin put his hand on Siward's shoulder. "Let him speak, Siward."

Siward inclined his head. "Forgive me. Tell us what you know of the Duke."

"The Duke has started a march north," the man said. "It seems he knows something is afoot."

Chapter eleven

Oswyth hesitated at the door to the little wooden church, inhaling the incense scented air. At the altar Father Colman was kneeling, his head bowed before the jewelled crucifix. Unwilling to disturb him, she was careful to make no sound but the priest turned to her.

"How may I help you, my daughter?" he asked.

"I... I need to make a confession."

The priest stared at her tearstained face and gave a gentle smile. "I have been hoping you would, my child. Come. Kneel before the altar."

Oswyth did as she was bidden, staring at the crucifix as she tried to find the words.

"There is no rush, my child. But speak honestly, for God will hear your words and He already knows the truth."

Oswyth wiped her eyes. "I will try, Father."

With an effort she staunched the flow of tears as she began to talk, starting her confession with the anger she had felt from the moment she heard of her father's death, not leaving out the time she had railed against Siward as a child.

"And so you see, Father," she finished, her eyes filling again as they met the compassionate gaze of the priest. "I have behaved in a manner ill befitting a good wife who should always honour her husband. And even worse, I have behaved in a way no true Englishwoman should behave towards one who has worked so tirelessly for our interests."

"Are you truly repentant, my child?"

"Yes, Father. I truly am. I humbly beg God's forgiveness."

"It is granted, my child. Our Father will always forgive those who repent with a pure heart. As to your penance, God requires you to fast for one additional day a week after the end of the Lenten period until Pentecost. You must also dispense additional alms during this period. As food is limited, this can take the form of washing the feet of beggars as Christ himself did."

"Yes, Father." She bowed her head. "It will be done."

"And while your husband is away, I trust you will pray for his success and his safe homecoming."

"Of course. I was doing that in any case."

"Good. There is one more task God will require of you."

"I know what it is," Oswyth said. "I must beg Siward's forgiveness, but..."

"I know you are not yet his true wife. And perhaps you will never be."

"I fear I will not. Siward spoke of his intentions to me before he left. Naturally I shall accept his decision, but that is not my greatest fear. My greatest fear is that I will never be able to beg his forgiveness because he will be..." Oswyth's tears flowed again.

The priest laid a kindly hand on her head. "If such an event were to take place, it would be grievous for us all. But in such circumstances his soul will be beyond all earthly concerns. Your penance may then take a different path, for you will be the heiress to these lands. If this occurs, honour his memory by caring for all who reside here."

"I will, Father but I shall pray it does not come to that."

"As shall we all, my child."

Oswyth wiped her eyes, managing a bright smile at the priest. "And now I have neglected the morning's tasks for too long. I must go."

"God's blessings upon you, my daughter."

They left the church together, Oswyth blinking in the bright spring sunshine. "Thank you, Father."

"Remember, my child, the suffering all in this realm have endured is great indeed, but in this suffering we are being tested."

"And I failed," Oswyth said glumly.

"No, my child. You have been challenged and the loss of both your parents so close together when you were of such tender years is a test for anyone. But now you have freed your heart from the hate and anger, you have succeeded."

Oswyth's smile brightened, her heart indeed feeling lighter. "Thank you, Father. Your guidance and that of Lady Alfgiva has helped me to succeed. I shall pray also for the strength to continue."

Oswyth almost skipped back to the hall, determined to work hard. She had been so certain that she was entitled to the respect of Siward's people but now she knew she would have to earn it. As she drew close to the hall, shocked voices rang out, so different from the usual chatter of the household at work. She quickened her pace, frowning as her eyes adjusted to the dim light of the hall. Everyone was clustered in one area with no one at the looms or spindles.

"What is going on?" she cried. "Why are you not working?"

Some of the women turned. "It is the Lady Alfgiva…"

They parted, allowing Oswyth to see her mother-in-law lying on the ground, several of the women kneeling beside her. She gasped and ran forward, alarmed by the pallor of her face. As she flung herself to her knees beside her, she took her hand, relieved to find it warm and the pulse rapid. For a moment she had feared the worst. But the relief was short lived as the hand lay limply in hers with no reaction on her still face.

"Oh, Alfgiva, you told me just now how you were not sleeping," she murmured. "I should have accompanied you back to the hall instead of indulging myself in a confession. I should have insisted you rest."

"You should not have provoked her this morning," one of the

churls muttered.

Oswyth ignored the comment, afraid she had spoken the truth. "One of you fetch Father Colman. He will know what to do."

There was a moment's hesitation and she looked up impatiently as everyone did nothing but continue to watch her.

"Do it," she snapped. "Unless you consider yourself to have as great a wisdom as Father Colman."

One swiftly left as Oswyth wrapped a blanket around her mother-in-law. Her eyes were still closed.

"What happened?" she asked.

"She was weaving. All seemed well until she rose to collect some more wool. She cried out, her hand clutching her chest before she fell," one replied.

Oswyth shuddered, looking at her pale face, remembering how her grandfather too had felt a chest pain shortly before he died. "She does not need so many standing around her. Everyone back to work."

Again nobody moved.

"Do it," Oswyth cried. "Standing around does not help Lady Alfgiva nor does it help Lord Siward. He is counting on us to keep the estate prospering."

"You never cared about either of them," said another woman. "Do not expect us to obey you now."

Oswyth flushed. "There is a time and a place to discuss that and when Lady Alfgiva is ill, is not the time for it. You know she would order you back to work if she were able, so do it."

"Yes, do it," Father Colman said, entering the hall. "You will all obey Lady Oswyth. I shall be noting any who do not and reporting their names to Lord Siward upon his return."

"They say it will be Lady Oswyth who leaves once Lord Siward returns," one muttered as they reluctantly did as the priest ordered.

Father Colman knelt beside Oswyth, taking Alfgiva's hand and feeling her brow. He gave a kindly smile at Oswyth. "Do not worry, my child. Lord Siward's intentions towards you are not yet clear. Make no assumptions on what will happen when he returns."

"They are clear to me," Oswyth replied. "But I do not blame him. That is not important now. Will Alfgiva live? I do not think I could bear to break the news to Siward of his mother's death."

"These matters lie in God's hands, my child. She shall receive every care and we will beseech God to spare her."

Oswyth's eyes filled with tears. "I know. It is what you said to me just a few moments ago. It is in such times we are tested. But I feel so helpless. What can I do?"

"Keep her comfortable and keep the household at work. You were right in your words. Lord Siward is counting on us and through whatever trials God sends, we must maintain our resolve."

Chapter twelve

Siward, Frebern and Bridwin stared in silence at the messenger before sending nervous glances at each other.

"We knew the Bastard would come," Siward said. "This is not unexpected."

Bridwin gave a helpless shake of his head. "But we hoped he would not come until King Edgar had taken control of at least some of the North."

"Where is King Edgar?" Frebern exclaimed. "We do not even know that."

"What do we do now?" Bridwin asked, running his hand through his hair. "If we do nothing, the Bastard will cut us off from reaching King Edgar. But what is the point of marching north to join him, if we do not know where he is?"

"If the invaders are just starting their march, I think we have a little time," Siward said. "Let us make no hasty decisions. Surely the messenger will return soon."

"I hope so." Bridwin's voice was grim. "Perhaps we should send out another. For all we know, the one we sent might have befallen some accident. King Edgar may not even know we are in position to support him."

"True," Siward agreed. "Yes, let us do that. And let us also send men to watch the roads to the south. The Bastard scuttles as quickly as a spider, we all know that."

"What do we do if he comes before we have heard from King Edgar?" Frebern asked.

"We move our own men north," Siward replied. "Although

we should keep within striking distance of the coast and King Sweyn."

"For the Bastard to be coming this way, he must have some news," Bridwin commented. "He must know King Edgar is about to launch his attack."

Siward nodded, some hope returning. "That is true. Well, let us stand ready." He raised his cup in a salute. "To England! Let it be ours once again."

∞∞∞

They did not have too long to wait for the messenger from Scotland. He arrived, covered in mud, two days later.

"God be praised," Siward said. "We had feared for you, my friend."

"What news of King Edgar?" Frebern cried.

"Forgive me, my lords, for the delay," the man said with a bow. "But when I arrived in Scotland, King Edgar was not there."

"What?" Bridwin said. "I had heard he was there. I am sure my source was a good one."

"Yes, my lord. He had been there but when I arrived, he was there no longer."

"Where the hell was he?" Siward asked in disbelief, wondering if he was to be disappointed in yet another king.

"He was attempting to make it to Francia to ally himself with the Frankish king. King Philip plans to bestow some lands on him."

"We know about the lands, but why is he headed for Francia? My God, are we headed in the wrong direction?" Bridwin asked.

"What possessed him to do it?" Frebern put in. "Why risk a journey like that? Besides, the Frankish king's aim is to increase his reach in Normandy. King Edgar needs to focus on England."

Siward placed his hand on his friend's shoulder. "Hush. I do not think we have gone in the wrong direction. Why else is the Bastard heading this way? Let the man speak."

"Thank you, my lord," the messenger said. "You are right to say the journey was risky. He did not make it to Francia but was blown back to Scotland, shipwrecked on the Scottish coast."

"What a damned fool," Siward muttered. "But at least he is safe, I suppose. Why did he do it?"

"I think he is not as confident of the support of the King of Scots as he would like," the messenger said. "He hoped to claim the support of the Frankish king."

There was silence for a moment as the three considered the wavering support of Scotland.

"King Edgar is King Malcolm's brother by marriage. Why would he not support him?" Frebern asked.

"His son has been kept in England as a guest, if that is the right word, of the Bastard. He will not wish to risk him. Nor does he want to invite trouble into Scotland." Siward sighed. "He is probably being non-committal and will side with whoever he thinks is likely to be the victor. Perhaps King Edgar wasn't such a fool to seek Frankish help."

"At least he is in Scotland now," Bridwin said. "Did you speak to him? Did you assure him of our support?"

"Yes, I did and he is grateful. He requests you move north to join him. He is close to the border, but in the east."

"Perhaps the knowledge of our support will convince the King of Scots to join with us." Siward grinned, trying to appear confident. "Well, my friends, let us march."

Rain hampered their march, leading to soaked cloaks and dampened spirits. That night after lighting fires which spluttered and hissed, they shivered in tents, their drenched clothes never quite getting the chance to dry out. Tempers fractured and their pace seemed agonisingly slow.

"It hardly seems worth moving at all this day," Bridwin commented as they huddled the next morning by a fire, trying to draw what meagre warmth they could.

"Perhaps we should seek out an abbey or residence sympathetic to our cause," Frebern suggested. "The men are not going to be much use in a fight, bedraggled like this."

"I don't know. If the Bastard gets to King Edgar before us…" Siward looked up at the sky, hoping to see a break in the clouds. But instead the bleak greyness stretched on for ever.

"Surely he is a long way back," Frebern said. "He started after us and the weather will be hindering him as well as us."

"I would not be so sure." Siward shrugged. "He will be able to command accommodation in any of the residences and abbeys along the way, as well as all the royal residences he controls. I doubt he has camped as often as us, if at all."

"Faster, fresher… what does this remind you of?" Bridwin said glumly.

"Yes, it is Hastings all over again." Siward shook his head, looking out at the miserable men. They had served him and his friends well, but he knew their spirits must be low. "What is worse, coming to Edgar behind the Bastard or coming first, but exhausted and ill?"

Bridwin swallowed. Despite the weariness on his face and the calm good sense he always displayed, Siward was suddenly reminded his friend had seen little more than twenty-four years. "Siward, you are the oldest and most experienced of us. I think the call has to be yours."

Siward's face remained calm but inwardly his heart was racing as he forced back his protest that he was only a year older. He did not want this responsibility. On every occasion in the past years he had been wrong. Every effort had ended in defeat. He looked again at the men, certain he would be failing them, just as he had failed every man since the death of Oswyth's father.

"We press on," he said, surprised how decisive his voice sounded. "If we arrive first, we will have time to recover and we will be in position. If we do not, the Bastard might kill King Edgar before we even get there. After that the matter would be truly hopeless."

As they ordered the men to pack up the camp and prepare to march on, the rain eased. Occasional breaks in the clouds even brought glimpses of sunshine. Siward's spirits rose as he wondered if God was showing his support for their venture.

"To King Edgar and Scotland," he cried as he mounted his horse.

The echoes of the cry were weary but cheerful. Siward nodded at his friends. It would do for the time being.

With the weather improved, they made better progress, leaving them confident that the next day would bring them to the Scottish border.

"There we will have the border residents to contend with, I assume. I have heard they are a formidable bunch," Siward said with a grin. "How do we convince them we are not invaders?"

"We'll let Frebern deal with them," Bridwin replied. "He can charm anyone."

Frebern's outraged expression only increased their laughter but it was abruptly cut short as a man was spotted riding swiftly towards them, his expression desperate.

Siward reined in his horse, gesturing for everyone to stop as the man's horse almost skidded to a halt in front of them.

"My lords, Duke William has made rapid progress. He is almost on the border."

"Damn him!" Siward ran his hands through his hair. "Can we get there first?"

"I don't know, but I do not think so," the man said.

"How did he manage it so quickly?" Frebern cried.

"He came with a small company from the south," the man said. "He already had men stationed up here, so it was only for the last part that he needed to move a large company of men."

Siward looked at the others. "We need to increase our pace. We have to get there first."

Chapter thirteen

"Return to King Edgar immediately," Siward ordered the messenger. "Beg him to launch his attack, to engage with the Bastard if necessary. We are coming. We will fall on the invaders from behind if we cannot get there first."

Maintaining his calm, he urged his men on. "I think the horsemen must go ahead. Those without horses, come on as quickly as you can."

"Surely it will be hopeless with our men much depleted." Frebern shook his head, his usual cheerful expression deserting him.

"Perhaps not," Siward said. "Fresh men arriving late in the day may prove to be an advantage."

He appointed Wicrun, one of his highest ranking churls, to lead the foot soldiers and urged the horsemen on. The pace could be quicker. They might even still arrive before the Bastard. He muttered a prayer that this would be the case.

Men and horses were exhausted when they finally stopped for the night. "Get a good rest, everyone," Siward ordered. "We will reach the border tomorrow and must be prepared for whatever awaits us."

He ordered fires and good food, but as the weary men settled down, another messenger arrived. "The ships of King Sweyn have been spotted off the coast," the man cried.

Siward looked up. Earlier that day he had become convinced all was lost, but this was truly hopeful news. He grinned. "That is just what we needed to hear."

"Do we still make for Scotland?" Frebern asked.

Siward nodded. "Yes. My loyalties are to King Edgar. He is the one we must fight for. When he faces the Bastard, I wish to be at his side."

"Agreed," Bridwin replied. "But King Sweyn's men will be useful."

"They will indeed." Siward glanced up at the darkening sky. "Remain with us this night, my friend," he said to the messenger. "But in the morning return to the coast. Inform King Sweyn and his men that we are intending to engage the Bastard on the borders of Scotland. Tell him King Edgar is ready and ask him to march to our aid."

"More fresh warriors arriving," Bridwin commented with a grin.

"Exactly," Siward replied. "As long as King Sweyn does not let us down."

As soon as he said those words, he regretted them, seeing the smiles on the faces of Frebern and Bridwin slip. He wished he could forget the failures of the past. At the very least he needed to avoid talking about them and disheartening his men.

"But I am sure he will not," he continued. "He has much more to gain by supporting King Edgar."

Everyone was up when the sky was barely lightening. They dressed themselves for a fight, with mail shirts or tough leather jerkins, stowing helmets, weapons and shields where they could be swiftly retrieved. Breakfast was a hearty one, as all ate with the gusto of men who knew they might never eat another meal. Siward's fears faded as he mounted his horse, wheeling it around to address the men.

"Good Englishmen," he cried. "Our king, our true king needs us this day. These last years have been hard and the resolve of many an Englishman has crumbled. But yours has always held true. All of you here are the pride of England. You are the ones who have remained true to the ideals of our forebears. Did the followers of the mighty King Alfred waver when the land was almost taken by the Heathens? No. They stood firm until glorious victory was achieved and the lands prospered once again. This is now within our grasp. We true Englishmen will fight for King Edgar, we will fight for God and Saint Edmund, we will fight for all England!"

There was a deafening cheer and Siward grinned, surprised to find he had got through that speech without the usual panic assailing him. On either side of him, Frebern and Bridwin wore similarly confident smiles. Not one man displayed any weariness. Victory suddenly seemed assured.

"Let us ride to King Edgar. If we reach him before the Bastard of Normandy, we will stand with him, accompanying him on his return to his realm. If the Norman Duke is already assailing him, we will fall on them from the rear, cutting them down until we have reached the noble King Edgar. God save the King!"

"God save the King!" the men echoed.

Siward gave his horse a sharp kick. "Let us ride!"

At least that day the weather was on their side. They rode swiftly, warmed by the bright spring sunshine which made even the bleak land seem inviting. Moorland birds wheeled through the sky, reminding Siward of days spent hawking. There had been so little time in the last years for simple pleasures such as that and even when he had found the time, he had little heart to enjoy them. How glorious it would be if, with the restoration of King Edgar, he could enjoy such days again, sending his spirit free with the birds into the sky and watching eagerly as they dove suddenly down on their prey. Even better were the nights sat laughing around a fire with friends, while the day's catch of fowl or hare roasted over the flames.

He smiled, thinking this carefree future may yet be within his grasp as he urged his horse up another hill. The men too were in good spirits. Frebern and a few more of the younger ones cantered ahead of him, eager to be the first to reach the top. They suspected that when they arrived, they would be looking into Scotland although none had ever been so far north.

As Frebern and his friends reached the summit, they reined in their horses, pointing and talking among themselves.

"What is it?" Siward called, increasing the pace of his own horse.

"There is a company of men coming towards us," Frebern called back.

Siward and Bridwin urged their horses swiftly up the hill, where they could look down at the men Frebern had spotted.

"No standard," Siward commented. "Who could they be?"

"I don't know. You would expect King Edgar or indeed the Bastard to have a banner," Bridwin replied.

The approaching men were just starting their ascent of the hill, suggesting by their gestures they had noticed Siward and his men. Yet there was no hesitation in their manner. Their actions were not threatening but neither were they friendly.

"Perhaps it is simply a nobleman, travelling for some purpose of his own," Bridwin suggested.

"It may be," Siward replied. "In any case, we have the stronger potion here on this hill. We are also more numerous than they." He turned his horse to speak to the men following. "My friends, we have company. Prepare for defence but there should be no aggression. If this is simply a good Englishman or a visiting Scot or even one of the Normans on his own business, we should not waste our efforts."

The men were well trained, falling easily into position behind him. Siward, Bridwin and Frebern moved their horses to the front, all three silent as they waited. Still the dark clothed men continued steadily up the hill. As they came closer, they could see the men were armed but they displayed no act of aggression and it was normal enough for travellers to keep their weapons handy as a defence against thieves.

"Speak your intentions," Siward called as soon as he judged

the men to be in earshot.

There was no answer. Siward frowned. This was a more hostile act, unless the wind had carried his voice away from them and the men had not heard him. He cupped his hands to call more loudly. "Speak your intentions."

This time he was certain they had heard but still there was no answer. "Prepare for defence," Siward instructed his men. "But hold off from an attack."

He did not look but he could hear the sound of swords and knives drawn from sheaths and bow strings twanged as the archers tested them. He did not need to look to know that every hand would now be grasping an axe, sword or spear. He wondered at the foolishness of the approaching men who must know they were hopelessly outnumbered, as well as vulnerable on the slope of the hill.

The leader of the men held out a hand, bringing the company to a halt a little below them. He pushed back his hood, to reveal the face of a man in his early twenties. His hair was light brown, tied back for travelling very much as his own was. The blue eyes looked into Siward's. There was a gasp from their men and Siward's face lit up into a grin. It might have been a few years since they had seen him but there was no mistaking the man before him. He slid down from his horse, aware that Bridwin and Frebern were doing the same. They knelt on the springy grass, bowing their heads.

"Your Highness," they said. "We pledge ourselves to your service."

"Please rise." Edgar waved his hand. "You do not need to kneel to me."

"But we do, my lord," Siward replied. "It is the privilege of all good Englishmen to kneel before their true king. Soon it will be one enjoyed by every man in the land."

"Truly," Edgar said. "You do not need to kneel. Rise."

There was a waver in the young king's voice which surprised Siward. He raised his head from its respectful bow to direct an enquiring look. Another man had urged his horse forward to take a place next to Edgar. Siward's mouth dropped open, the elation at the sight of his king shattering on the wind. The man's hood was also now back. It was Turstin Fitz Rolf.

"Greetings, Siward of Gloucester," he said. "We meet again." He scanned the men with an amused look. "And I see you do not have your wife to rescue you this time."

Chapter fourteen

Siward and his friends got slowly to their feet, their stunned gaze still fixed on the men before them. Any hope remaining in Siward's heart was chilled at the triumphant gleam in Turstin's eyes.

He looked back at Edgar, noting his pale face and sombre bearing. "My lord, I do not understand. Are you their prisoner?"

As he spoke the words, he already knew they were unlikely to be true. A prisoner of this importance would be better defended. Besides, he still had his sword.

"No," Edgar replied, his voice strong. "I am no prisoner. I have come to an arrangement with the noble King William."

"An arrangement?" Wild thoughts tumbled through Siward's mind. That perhaps Wessex and Mercia were to be ruled separately once again. "What sort of arrangement?"

Edgar glanced at Turstin, who nodded. "Tell Siward of Gloucester everything."

Edgar's smile was obviously false, as he took a deep breath. "Lord Siward, Lord Bridwin, and Lord Frebern, I thank you for your protestations of loyalty and I trust they will now go to the agreement I have made. My noble brother, King Malcolm of Scotland has urged me to an understanding with King William and I have done so."

"What sort of understanding, my lord?" Siward asked, irritated by how long Edgar was taking to get to the point. It did not bode well.

"I have sworn allegiance to the noble King William and re-

144

nounced my own claim."

"Sworn allegiance?" Frebern exclaimed in disbelief.

"But…" Siward's horror was so great, his words stuttered to a halt. There was nothing he could reply to that.

"Your fight against the good King William is over," Turstin said. "I advise you to accept it."

Siward looked again at Edgar, his eyes pleading with the young man to say this was all a ruse, that he had not betrayed the people who had fought for him. Siward thought of the devastated lands they had ridden through, still bearing the scorch marks of the destruction the Bastard had wreaked. Edgar had betrayed all England.

"I too implore you to accept it," Edgar said, his blue eyes fixed on Siward. "King William is God's anointed. It behoves all good Englishman to honour the sacred rite and revere him as God would wish us to."

"King Harold was once God's anointed," Bridwin said. "That did not stop Duke William from overthrowing him."

"King Harold is dead," Edgar replied. "There was no impropriety in King William being crowned after his death." He managed a smile. "I am truly grateful for the allegiance you have shown me. And my last command to you, is to swear loyalty now to King William."

Siward shook his head in disgust. Although he had tried to persuade him otherwise, he had understood Edgar, then a fifteen year old boy, not contesting the succession after Hastings. But there was no excuse for it now. Frebern was younger than him, but he was still willing to fight. His mind drifted to Oswyth, younger still and a maiden at that, yet she too had shown more courage against the Normans than this young man. He thought of the mighty kings the man was descended from – Cerdic, Alfred, the Edmund they called Ironside. Great warriors who had fought and in some cases died, for what was rightly theirs, for the good of England, only for this snivelling wretch to hand it away.

"My good lords," Turstin said in a hearty tone. "I am under

orders to escort you to King William, where you can swear the oath of loyalty. As a favour to his good friend, Lord Edgar, he may be willing to not judge you too harshly."

"Do as he says," Edgar said. "There is no need to fight. England can be at peace again."

Silently Siward mounted his horse, aware that all eyes were on him. If he followed Edgar and Turstin, they too would follow. He lifted the reins.

"I will swear no loyalty," he cried. "William the Bastard will never be my king."

With those words, Siward kicked his horse into action, riding at all speed back the way they had come. There was a loud cheer and from the thud of hooves following him, he knew every man was doing the same.

Frebern had brought his horse alongside his. "Are they pursuing us?" Siward cried.

"I think so," Frebern replied.

"If necessary, we fight them. I do not care if Edgar the traitor is killed in the struggle. We will get away."

"But what can we do now?" Frebern yelled.

"The coast," Bridwin said. "King Sweyn will have landed by now."

"Exactly," Siward called. "I would rather swear allegiance to a Dane than a Norman. His uncle, King Cnut, is said to have ruled us well enough."

He slowed his horse to turn it, pleased his men were streaming down the hillside towards him. On the brow of the hill he could see Edgar and Turstin looking down at them, having decided not to give chase. Siward guessed it was a bitter moment for the erstwhile king, seeing the people who had once revered him, hold him now in such contempt. But it was no less than he deserved.

∞∞∞

They sent a message back to the foot soldiers, telling them of the change of plan. But it was only once they had gone a significant distance from where they had last seen Turstin that they dared stop to rest themselves.

"Before we plan our next move, why don't you two ask me the question I can see you are desperate to ask," Siward said as he sat with his back to a rock, taking a swig of ale.

Frebern grinned, his smile even easing Siward's heart and he knew he was right to lighten the mood before dealing with the more serious matters.

Bridwin too laughed. "Yes, how did your wife rescue you?"

"We were escaping her grandfather's lands when Turstin and his son trapped us. I truly thought it would be the end, for me at least. But she knew those lands well and showed me an escape route which allowed us to lose them."

"Her spirit is certainly an impressive one," Frebern said.

"Yes, it is. If only our erstwhile king could show such spirit," Siward said, guiding them away from the wife he had no wish to think of and into the conversation they needed to have.

Bridwin shrugged. "Everyone has more spirit than him. He has spent the last seven or so years at ease in Scotland or Flanders, yet the spirit is gone from him. While those of us who have had to live with the conquest, are still willing to fight on."

"It sounds as if the King of Scots capitulated as well," Frebern said.

"True," Siward replied. "Not that I had any great hopes of him. Not unless a victory was assured."

"So that leaves us with King Sweyn." Frebern tried to smile but it was a half-hearted attempt.

"Who betrayed us once before." Bridwin gave a gloomy shake of the head as he spoke the words they were all thinking. "Will he do any better this time? Especially when he hears of Edgar's surrender."

"Perhaps he does not need to hear of Edgar's surrender too soon," Siward suggested. "Let us help him land and establish a base. Then we can swear allegiance to him as our king."

"Agreed," Bridwin said. "He might be even more resolute if he knows he will achieve the throne itself."

Siward forced a smile. "We must pray he does."

They rode on until nightfall, but it was a subdued bunch who gathered around the fires with none of the merriment which usually characterised such evenings on the move. The capitulation of Edgar and the failure of the Scots to support them was a grave blow. There would be far fewer men to fight against the formidable forces of the Bastard which had defeated them so many times before.

The next morning they could tell by the downcast expressions on the men's faces that all the night had achieved was to allow the setback to further sink in. But they made a hasty breakfast and mounted their horses, heading resolutely on towards the coast.

At last they came to a cliff top where they were treated to a view of seabirds wheeling through the air and the sun sparkling on an almost empty sea. There were a few fishing boats bobbing up and down on the waves but these were not the boats they had hoped for. Not the boats with the great sails and carved prows of the Danes.

Siward scanned the seas in all directions. "I am certain this was the place the messenger stated."

"Could they have been blown elsewhere?" Frebern asked.

"If this is the right place, they must have done," Siward replied.

"Now what do we do?" Bridwin asked. "We need to find them but I do not want to divide the men."

"I agree. Look." Siward pointed at a man riding towards them. It was the messenger they had sent to greet the Danes. "Where are they?" he called.

The man was almost in tears. "They were here, my lord, not far out to sea. I swear it. But when I returned from delivering the message, they were gone."

Siward gave no sign of the disappointment almost crushing him. "I do not doubt you, my friend. Have you spoken to any on this coast?"

"Yes, my lord. One reported that the boats struggled to land. It was windy a few nights back."

"Then surely they will have tried somewhere else," Bridwin said. "Let us not give up hope just yet. We can send scouts along the coast to locate them."

"Yes," Siward replied. "Let us do that. I pray we locate them quickly."

Chapter fifteen

To Oswyth's relief, Alfgiva's eyes fluttered open. She looked bewildered and simply lay, staring upwards for a moment. She gestured for one of her women to tend to her, while she looked in irritation at the remainder of the household. None of them had done much despite Father Colman's words.

"Everyone listen to me," she said, standing straight to address them all. "I am aware of what you think of me and perhaps you are right to show me little respect. If I were to urge you in any way to act against the Lord Siward's best interests, you would be right indeed to ignore me. But I am not. I am urging you to do, what he would also urge you to do if he were here. He trusts you to maintain the estate, to see the crops and livestock flourish. If you do not do this, it is not me you are failing. It is him and more than that, it is England, for England is depending on men like Lord Siward to have estates which prosper. He is far away, fighting hard for us all. Here it is our duty and our privilege to work just as hard." She looked at the faces watching her, aware of a grudging respect growing. "You are right to say I may not be here much longer. But while I am here, it is my duty to maintain matters as Lord Siward would want them maintained. And while I am here, I will work as hard as anyone to ensure we do not let him down. Will you do any less?"

"No, my lady," they muttered.

To Oswyth's satisfaction, they returned to their tasks with their usual diligence.

"Well done, my daughter," Father Colman said.

"Thank you, Father. What of Alfgiva? They said she clutched her chest. Does that mean her heart is failing?" Oswyth's lip trembled at the thought of breaking the news of such a death to Siward. She could not bear to lose her, especially now she had hopes they could rekindle their friendship.

"Not necessarily, my child. Her pulse is strong. It could be any imbalance in the chest. Even if it is the heart, it does not mean she will die. The strain she is under is not ideal, of course."

"Pray for her, Father," Oswyth begged.

"I will, my child."

Oswyth returned to kneel beside her mother-in-law. She was sitting now, her hands clutched around a cup of warm ale. They were trembling and Oswyth noted the pallor of her face, but she said nothing as Alfgiva finished her drink. At last she set it down and started to rise.

"What are you doing?" Oswyth said. "You must rest."

"Do not be foolish, my child. There is work to be done."

Oswyth smiled at hearing her tone as brisk as ever. "Not for you," she said. "You are ill."

"Nonsense. A momentary dizzy spell. It is warm in here."

Oswyth put her hands firmly on her shoulders, pressing her down. "It is not that warm. You need to rest. We can manage without you for a while."

"Truly there is no need. I am fine. As you just said, and it was well said, my dear, Siward is trusting us to do what is necessary. I will not fail him. Now let me rise."

Oswyth folded her arms. "I will let you rise, if you can tell me honestly, if Siward was here, what would he be commanding you to do?"

Alfgiva's gaze dropped. "He would tell me to rest."

"And are you going to do what he would not want?"

Alfgiva sighed. "No. You are right, my child. I shall hate being useless. My weakness has let Siward down."

Not certain what her reaction would be, Oswyth held her close. "You have never let Siward down. But please rest, so when

Siward returns, he finds you as hale and hearty as ever."

"Well, I will for this morning," Alfgiva said, patting Oswyth's hand, causing her a rush of joy at this return to affection. "But I shall rise later."

"If you are feeling better," Oswyth said, considering Alfgiva's comments a victory. She kissed her lined cheek. "Now, I must go to my work as I have promised I will."

As she went to join the other women with the spinning she was torn between the joy that her friendship with her mother-in-law seemed to be recovering and her fear the older woman might be seriously ailing.

The other women surprised her by greeting her pleasantly as she sat with her spindle. But her burst of happiness was swiftly dampened as she glanced back at Alfgiva. She was reclining again with her eyes closed and Oswyth could only hope she was sleeping.

Alfgiva got her way, re-joining the workers in the afternoon. The women were cheered by her high spirits but Oswyth noticed how slowly she was working compared to her accustomed pace. She suspected her mother-in-law was feeling much worse than she was prepared to admit, yet Oswyth said nothing. It was best for Alfgiva to be occupied than idle with nothing to do but dwell on her fears. That evening she ate little, appearing weary. When Oswyth bade her a good night, she hoped this would mean she should at least sleep well.

Next morning Oswyth was woken from her restless doze by the touch on her shoulder from Alfgiva's favourite thrall.

"My lady, please come to Lady Alfgiva," the woman said.

Instantly anxious, Oswyth swiftly pulled a cloak around herself and did not bother binding her hair before making her way to where her mother-in-law had slept, close to the central hearth. She knelt down, taking her hand. Almost she dropped it again, gasping at the heat. She placed a cool hand against her brow, hoping she was mistaken in the strength of the fever. She was not.

"Perhaps we should move her away from the fire," Oswyth suggested.

"She told me she feels cold," the woman replied.

"Cold? She is burning." Oswyth tried to pull the blankets away, hesitating at how Alfgiva's thin body was shivering.

"I am frozen, my child," she muttered, groping for the blankets without opening her eyes. Reluctantly, Oswyth swathed them around her burning body.

"Are you in any pain?" she asked, taking her hands once again.

"My head aches and my throat stings," Alfgiva said. "I am so tired."

"Well, remain here by the fire today." Oswyth tried to sound cheerful. "Sleep as much as you wish." She gestured to the woman to follow her a short distance away from the fire, lowering her voice as she spoke. "Try to persuade her to drink. Mead or weak ale laced with honey."

"Yes, my lady. What of food?"

"If she will eat, then yes. But I do not think we should force her." Oswyth frowned. "Perhaps we should keep some broth ready. She might manage that."

The woman nodded her agreement and Oswyth knelt back again next to her mother-in-law. In her mind she tried to find the words to pray that all would be well but her eyes filled with tears. Siward's last instruction was to take care of his mother. She had not even managed that.

The days which followed were exhausting as Oswyth divided her time between tending to Alfgiva and managing the work which needed to be done. But she maintained her positive manner, keeping everyone cheerful as she concealed her fears.

Despite the treatments Father Colman prescribed, Alfgiva remained in a poor state. Only the fact that she swallowed the occasional mouthful of broth gave Oswyth any hope. Checking on her was the first act she carried out each morning and the last one each night, frequently inserting a paste of honey and celery seeds into her nostrils in an effort to ease her breathing. At night she took to lying next to her on the hall of the floor, so whenever she woke she could coax some weak ale into her, adding a generous spoonful of honey to each cup, hoping the sweet mixture would give her the energy to struggle on.

After more than a week, Oswyth sat wearily up in the morning, having even less energy than usual for the tasks ahead. The night had done little to revive her, not helped by the fact that several of the thralls had taken the same sickness as Alfgiva, some seeming in an even worse state. It had felt as if every time she had managed to doze off, a harsh cough from one side of the hall or a moan of pain from the other, jolted her awake again. She looked down at her mother-in-law, shocked by how thin she had become. She looked old, her face pale and the lines on it deeper than ever.

"Do not look at me like that, my child. I am not dead yet."

A smile struggled onto Oswyth's face, wondering if she dared feel any hope. "Of course you are not. How are you feeling this morn?"

"Terrible," Alfgiva said. "But at least my head does not ache this day. I just feel so weak." She held up a trembling hand. "Useless."

In spite of Alfgiva's words, Oswyth smiled more, allowing a little hope to trickle in. She seemed so much more herself. "I would be weak and useless if I had eaten as little as you these last days," she said. "Can you eat now?"

Alfgiva nodded, struggling into a sitting position, as Oswyth pressed pillows around her. "I think I can. A little porridge perhaps. And I'll take some ale. But add the honey to the porridge, not the ale. It tastes foul."

Oswyth laughed. Truly she was recovering.

"And now I am sounding ungrateful." Alfgiva patted her hand. "You have cared for me well, my child and I am grateful."

"You do not need to be," Oswyth said. "I am grateful you are recovering." And as a thrall brought over a steaming bowl of porridge, Oswyth was overjoyed as she ate several spoonfuls before exhaustion took over once again and she slept.

Alfgiva grew in strength each day, eventually sitting with the other women and even taking her turn with some of the work. When the worst affected thrall did succumb to the illness, Oswyth wept while feeling an even greater relief at how well her mother-in-law was recovering.

They celebrated Easter in a quiet fashion and enjoyed the warmer weather, often taking their work outside. Despite their fears for the men and Siward in particular, their days were as much filled with light hearted chatter as hard work.

The spring sunshine was warm as one day in a lull in their talk they heard the unmistakable sound of fast hooves on dry earth. Oswyth and Alfgiva exchanged glances. It sounded as if someone was riding hard toward their dwelling. Siward had been away for so long, they knew he must have engaged with the Normans by then and as they were not anticipating any visitors, both were struck by the certainty that this would be the news they were waiting for. Alfgiva clutched Oswyth's hand, not needing to voice her fear that this would be grim tidings as the horse swept up to them. The rider slid down to bow before them.

"Greetings, my ladies. My name is Dunstan. I have news concerning Lord Siward."

Chapter sixteen

They sat in silence on the cliffs, staring at the sea, willing it to fill with the ships they were so desperate to see. The waves, crested in white foam, beat merrily against the shore, while the sea gulls wheeled overhead, their cries a cheerful greeting, breaking hard against glum hearts. Siward had ordered fires to be lit and food served, but they made no attempt to set up a proper camp, knowing or at least hoping they might soon be moving on.

When the first scout returned, the news was not good. He bowed low before Siward and his friends. "It seems the ships of the Danes attempted another landing a little north of here. But locals prevented them from stepping ashore. They soon sailed out again."

"Why would they do that?" Frebern exclaimed. "The Danes are here to liberate them."

"They are frightened," Siward said. "Here in the North they must be even more afraid than the men of the South. Just a short distance away are the wrecks of villages burnt to the ground. Everyone here must have kith or kin who perished for no other crime than living in a region which challenged the Bastard."

They waited uselessly on, not knowing which way to turn, praying there would be good news soon. Scouts had been posted around and Siward sat silently, whispering prayers that soon one would escort a messenger to them, telling them King Sweyn and his men had landed nearby.

"Should we prepare a camp?" Frebern asked as the shadows

lengthened.

Siward looked at the sky. "Not yet. We still have some day-light left."

"My lords," came a voice.

They all turned, hoping this would be the news they had been waiting for. But the man running towards them looked pan-icked.

"My lord, there is a company of men coming our way."

Siward cursed. He was about to order every man to his horse when he saw the group of men, close on the heels of the scout. They were well-armed and numerous. In a swift glance he guessed they were more numerous than his own force. It was just as well his foot soldiers had not yet re-joined them. With only riders present, they had a chance to flee.

"Draw weapons," he commanded. "And keep our horses safe. I do not think we can defeat so many but we can at least give our-selves a chance to escape."

"Flee south along the coast," Bridwin put in. "We are not too far from my estate here. We shall regroup there while we wait for news from King Sweyn."

"Do not mount horses yet," Siward said. "With their numbers they can easily afford to dismount and hack at the horses legs. If that happens, we are doomed. But as soon as I give the order, mount and ride as you have never ridden before." He hesitated. "If I am unable to issue the order, listen to commands from Lord Bridwin and Lord Frebern. We concentrate our efforts at that left flank. If we can break through there, we can escape."

With no further words, he fastened his helmet and drew his sword, waiting for the men to come nearer. He waited as long as he dared before raising his hand. "Archers, be ready." The wind was coming off the sea, which would aid the arrows of his people, while hindering those of his foe. It was a small advan-tage but it was better than none at all.

The horses paused a short distance away and as their leader called out, his voice confirmed what Siward suspected. It was Turstin Fitz Rolf. "Siward of Gloucester, Frebern of Warwick,

Bridwin of Lichfield. You are ordered to surrender yourself to us. I strongly advise you to throw yourself on the mercy of the good King William."

"Now!" Siward cried. He had no idea if Edgar was among their number, but he no longer cared. The man had chosen to side with their enemies and would have to take his chances.

A flurry of arrows arched overhead, through to the company of Normans. They raised their shields but Siward could see they had not all been fast enough. A few men had been struck. He did not know how seriously they had been injured but any pain would slow and distract them. A chorus of whinnies reminded him that the horses had no armour. A few reared up, tossing their riders to the ground in a crash of mail, accompanied by further cries and curses. Siward grinned. For once he had the advantage. Around him the men exclaimed in satisfaction, this initial triumph raising their downcast spirits.

"You will regret that, Siward of Gloucester," Turstin shouted, ordering a retaliation.

But the wind aided them as he had hoped, with many of the arrows falling short. Even those which reached them had lost much of their strength. He heard the thud of arrows hitting shields and mail shirts but there were no cries of pain.

"Shoot!" Siward cried again to the archers. "Remember where to aim." He knew everything counted on putting a dent in the line of men advancing before them, one that he and his men could ride horses through. Their horses were well rested after their fruitless afternoon. If they could get through the line, they had a good chance at outrunning their enemies.

Again their arrows were true. They might not do much damage but they spread uncertainty. And again those arrows which struck the animals caused ever more chaos in the ranks of the foe.

Turstin ordered his men closer, trying to gain some advantage as flurries of arrows went between the groups. Siward eyed the horses of their enemy, pressing his lips together in grim resolution. They were fine beasts. It was a pity to harm them but harm them he must. He needed to force Turstin and his men down from the horses, delaying them as they fled. And if enough of the horses were injured, there would be no possibility of Turstin and his men remounting to give chase.

"Ready the lances," he shouted. "And more arrows."

He could see the surprise on the faces of the Norman men who had expected an easy arrest. They had not bargained on the desperation of Siward and his men. He saw the Norman line weaken exactly where he wanted it to weaken. But as the Normans had edged closer, their arrows too were more forceful. There was a thud as one hit his shield, sticking fast. Siward knew it was only a matter of time before the arrows penetrated the defences of his men.

"Forward!" Siward cried, determined to keep up the surprise. He dashed towards the line, stabbing forward with his spear. He thrust it hard at one of the horses, gleeful as it reared up, throwing its rider to the ground. With difficulty he pulled it back, pushing it at the man on the ground. He screamed as Siward forced it into his leg, crimson spurting from the wound. There were similar cries from all around although Siward did not look to see if they were from his men or the enemy. He concentrated on pressing forward, certain the line ahead was weakening. The weapons crashed relentlessly, but the men before him fell back as Siward edged on.

His voice became hoarse from shouting orders. As man after man either fell before him or were pressed back, he surveyed the enemy. Seeing the gaps in the line and the increasingly frantic attempts from their enemy to regroup, he knew his men had the advantage. It was tempting to stay and finish the foe off completely but he knew that was foolish. At least some of his own men would die and they would achieve little beyond a temporary satisfaction. They had done what they needed to do. Now he needed to get the men to safety.

"Horses!" he cried.

Again the enemy were surprised. They were assuming he would keep pushing forward. This sudden retreat momentarily confused them. And in that confusion, the first of the riders rode at them, still stabbing with lances, swords and axes. To Siward's relief the Norman line weakened further. For the first time he was confident they could get away.

He was almost at his own horse when he saw the man next to him stumble. It was Frebern. Siward did not stop to think. He had always felt protective of his young friend. It had been he who had guided him through his first fight, the futile rebellion at Ely and he would not leave him now. Not when he could see one of the Norman men bearing down on him, his sword raised.

Siward's own sword was in his hand and he clashed it against the Norman's, blocking the blow before it could fall on Frebern. He did not look at Frebern, unsure if he had simply stumbled or if he were injured. Whatever had happened, he needed to stop the man from dealing anything worse.

Several times their swords clashed against each other, each pushing with all their strength, trying to break the deadlock. He smashed his sword down on the man's shield, cracking it, before aiming another strike at his legs. The man was quick, leaping back and raising his sword once again. Knowing he had only a moment to act, Siward thrust forward, aiming another blow. If his next aim was sure, it would finish the man. But as he pulled his arm back to strike, the man pushed his own sword forward, shoving it with brutal strength through Siward's mail shirt.

Siward screamed at the cold slice of metal piercing his arm just below the shoulder. Frantically he forced in his own blow. As the man stepped back, his sword dragged from the wound. The withdrawal hurt even more, tearing at his already tortured flesh and Siward cried out again, louder and more despairing. With his shield arm now completely useless, he knew he was done for, yet he thrust a last blow at the man, determined to take at least one more with him. But with his vision already blurring, his sword fell weakly, not capable of delivering so much as a graze. His legs wobbled beneath him, sending him to his knees, certain death was coming for him. Even as he let out another desperate cry, he caught a glimpse of a sword coming from behind him, a man forcing his way in front, standing over him with his own shield. Again swords clashed but the foe was taken by surprise, his uncertainty proving fatal. The desperate cry which rang out this time, was the Norman's as he fell backwards against the earth.

"Siward!" Frebern yelled, hoisting him back to his feet. "Come, most are already away. We must join them."

Siward forced his vision to clear with an effort. "I cannot ride. You must flee."

Frebern pulled him towards a horse, his sword still outstretched against any of the enemy who might come near. However with most already giving chase there was now little opposition.

"I am not leaving you," Frebern cried. "Can you mount the horse? We will ride pillion."

"I will slow you down." Siward swayed against the horse's body. He would lose consciousness at any moment and he wanted to see his friend away before that happened.

"You are slowing us down by arguing," Frebern said. "Come on. Do not give up."

Siward found himself half shoved from behind as he forced himself to act through the pain. The blood oozing from the mail shirt flowed faster as he somehow scrambled onto the horse, clinging to the reins with one hand. He gripped tightly with his legs, certain he would topple straight off. Only Frebern, swinging up behind him, surrounding him with his arms as he took hold of the reins, kept him on the horse. His vision blurred again, as he slumped against Frebern's arm.

Frebern pushed him upright, his hands gripping tighter to the reins, forming a cage around him. "Siward, there is a skin of ale attached to the saddle. Take some."

Siward did as he was instructed, the drink restoring him to consciousness, reviving him to face the searing pain. In an effort to distract himself from the agony, he surveyed the scene. His men were fleeing south, the Normans in pursuit. But it looked as if the fresher horses had the advantage.

With his good arm still gripping his sword, Siward held it outstretched as Frebern guided the horse through the Normans who were not yet in pursuit. He scanned the ground as they went. He was not sure if any of his men lay among the fallen but he could see no horses remaining. It might mean they had simply bolted, as he assumed his own horse had, but he hoped that most of his men had got away.

He had the satisfaction of bringing one more man down before they escaped from the main body of men. He could tell by the shouts that a few were in pursuit and he worried that with two on the horse, they would be too slow.

"Siward," Frebern cried. "No doing anything heroic like leaping from the horse. I will stop to pick you up, so you will only slow me down even more."

Through the pain and fear, Siward grinned with pride. As a second son, Frebern had not received a warrior's training as a boy yet he had emerged into a truly courageous man. But his smile faded as he heard the thud of hooves coming closer. Frebern deserved better than to end in this way. His friend had trusted him, but it seemed a near certainty that Frebern would simply be the latest man he failed.

He looked ahead, scanning the landscape for anything which could help. They were not far from a wooded area. "Head into the trees. We can lose them."

The plan worked as Frebern took a tortuous route through the low hanging branches. They emerged from the trees with no sound of pursuit.

"I can see some of our men up ahead," Frebern cried. "I am making for them."

Siward nodded, instantly regretting the action as a wave of pain crashed through him.

"God be praised," Bridwin said as they joined him. "I feared you had not got away. I was about to head back to you." He looked anxiously at Siward.

"Do not worry about me," Siward said through gritted teeth. "We must keep going. They may yet find us if we linger too long."

They were able to slow the pace of their horses a little but every hoof fall brought fresh agony. Siward screwed up his eyes, not daring to complain, knowing it would be fatal to stop before nightfall.

"Well, this is to be a fine night," Bridwin commented as he helped Siward dismount at last. His face creased into lines of worry at how heavily Siward was leaning against him. "Just as well the night is a warm one. We have little in the way of shelter or food."

Siward slumped against a tree, breathing heavily as he struggled to manage the pain. "How far to your residence?"

"Not too far," Bridwin replied. "If we start at first light, we will be there by noon."

Siward closed his eyes. "Tell the men that. It will enable them to endure this night better."

Bridwin nodded, exchanging an anxious look with Frebern. "Siward, we need to take this mail shirt off. Your arm needs binding."

Siward thought he had already endured the worst of the pain but it was nothing compared to the agony as Bridwin and Frebern between them, manipulated his arm free of the mail shirt. He could not restrain a scream as his arm was exposed to the stinging air.

Frebern's eyes widened. "He has lost a lot of blood."

"I know," Bridwin replied. "But it is a neat cut. Not too jagged. Steady, Siward. Let me bind it and hopefully the pain will ease."

Siward gritted his teeth so tightly he was afraid they would crack as Bridwin tore a strip of cloth, tying it tightly around the upper arm. Again blackness floated against his eyes, causing a few moments of welcome oblivion. The next sensation was a skin of ale held to his lips, the liquid forcing itself into his mouth. He coughed, tearing his eyes open, just conscious enough to swallow the mouthful. It revived him enough to take another swallow and then another.

"How does that feel?" Bridwin asked.

It felt worse than anything he had ever endured, but Siward managed a smile. "Better, my friend."

"My lords," came an urgent voice. "There is a rider approaching us."

Siward groaned. He had no energy for a further ride that night. He wished he could persuade his friends to leave him there to die if they needed to flee further.

"It is just one rider," Bridwin said. "Capture him, kill him if necessary. He must not take news of us to his masters."

Several men left the shelter of the trees but when they returned, the voices were good humoured.

"It is one of our men, my lord."

Siward looked at the man. It was one of the scouts he had sent to scour the coast for the Danes. Hope surged in him once again. "What news, my friend?" he cried.

The man's face fell at the eagerness in Siward's voice. "Nothing good, my lord. The Danes made a few attempts to land but each time they were beaten back by wind or locals. They were last seen sailing out to sea."

"King Sweyn is gone?" Siward cried, the hope gushing from him even faster than the blood. He slumped back against the tree, the blackness rushing upon him. His body shook. "Then we have failed. England is lost."

Part Three: April – May 1074

Chapter one

Oswyth and Alfgiva stared at the messenger, their hearts thudding as they tried to tell from the man's expression what he was about to say.

"Did Lord Siward send you?" Alfgiva asked in a faltering tone.

"No, my lady. Lord Bridwin of Lichfield sent me. He wishes to inform you that Lord Siward was grievously injured during a skirmish against Turstin Fitz Rolf. They escaped from his clutches but..."

"Is my son alive?" Alfgiva shrieked, clutching so tightly onto Oswyth's hand, her nails dug into her flesh.

"He was when I left, my lady. But his injury is severe. He lies at Lord Bridwin's residence in the north."

Alfgiva slumped down to a stool, putting her head in her hands. "Not my beloved son. Please, Heavenly Father, let him be saved."

"Do you think he will live?" Oswyth asked, her eyes wide as she feared Siward would die without knowing how sorry she was. She put her arms around her mother-in-law as she waited tensely for the man's reply, her mind scrambling for prayers. Even as she did this, she remembered the prayers her mother and grandfather had made for her father. Were all the fine men in her life to be taken from her in this way?

"I cannot say, my lady. The injury to his shoulder was deep and bled extensively but he survived it. However if infection was to set in..."

Dunstan did not need to continue. If infection set in, there would be little anyone could do and Siward would die a slow, painful death. Oswyth's eyes went involuntarily to the burial ground behind the church, the tears welling at the thought a new grave might soon be needed. Siward did not deserve to end that way.

Alfgiva looked up. "What of the fight? Has King Edgar returned?"

"He has returned, my lady, but not as king. Lord Edgar has submitted to King William. He accepts his rule and urges all England to do the same."

Oswyth shook her head, disgust momentarily taking over from the terror. "What of King Sweyn? Has he come ashore?"

"No, my lady. He was unable to bring his boats in and it is believed his ships have returned to their own realm."

Alfgiva's grief returned in a flood of tears. "This will kill Siward even if his injuries do not."

Oswyth looked at the churls surrounding them, seeing the shock on all faces. The struggle for England had been lost. All those claimants for the throne and not one was worthy of Siward's loyalty. He might lose his life because of this and if he didn't, he would likely lose his lands. She wanted to scream at the unfairness of it all.

Alfgiva struggled to her feet. "I must go to him."

"But, my lady," Dunstan said. "It is a long way, far to the north."

"And you have been ill," Oswyth added.

"I do not care," Alfgiva cried. "This is my beloved son. I cannot leave him to die alone."

"He has his friends with him and you are still so weak. You might not survive the journey."

"I do not care."

"Siward would care," Oswyth said softly, putting her arm around her. "If he lives, he will have much to contend with. Do not let your death be one of those."

Alfgiva sank down again. "I hate to think of him lying injured, perhaps dying and I am not with him."

"Then I shall go to him," Oswyth announced.

"You?" Alfgiva looked stunned. "But, my child, I do not think so. He will be in need of comfort. How can you give him that? Matters between you and Siward have never been good and were worse than ever when he left."

"I know and this is my chance to make amends. If I go to him, I shall tell him I am proud of how hard he fought." Oswyth's eyes filled with tears. "I shall tell him how sorry I am that I blamed him for my father's death. If he is dying, I will try to bring comfort to his last moments and if he lives, I shall assure him I will obey whatever commands he makes."

Father Colman laid his hand on Alfgiva's shoulder. "Let Lady Oswyth do this, my daughter. For the sake of her soul, she must make every effort to set matters right with her lord and husband. Besides, she is right to say it would not be sensible for you to make such a journey."

Alfgiva nodded reluctantly. "I suppose you are right. Oh, Heavenly Father, please let him live. We shall bear the rest as God's trial but please not that one."

"We shall pray for him," Father Colman said. "He is young and strong. If anyone can survive such an injury, it is him."

The preparations for Oswyth's departure were swiftly made. Dunstan, the messenger, would form one of her entourage since he alone knew how to find the hall where Siward lay. With the sun shining brightly she prepared to ride, holding her mother-in-law tightly for a moment before mounting her horse.

"Tell Siward how much I love him, how proud I am of him," Alfgiva said, remaining composed with an effort. "Oh, Oswyth, I shall be praying for you too. It is a long journey."

"I know and I shall be praying for you." She forced her features into stern look. "No over exerting yourself once I am not here to remind you to rest. Father Colman, I am charging you with the task of ensuring she takes care of herself."

Father Colman laid his hand on her head in blessing. "I shall certainly do that, my daughter. Now, go to Lord Siward and we shall pray he accompanies you back."

As Oswyth trotted away, she wished she could feel more joy in the bright day. It should be an adventure to ride to the far north but not for her purpose. Although the birds sang merrily and the sky was blue, her heart quailed as she wondered what she would find. She thought of Siward, so young and strong and tried to imagine him a shell of that, a man shaking and sweating as the infection took hold. She shuddered, praying it would not be the case but instead she would find him recovering well and impatient to be home.

At that another thought struck her. Would he even have a home to come back to? If the Bastard knew of Siward's latest attempts, and Oswyth had to assume he did, it would very likely result in the loss of his remaining lands. Resolutely she raised her head. It did not matter. If he lived, she would remain at his side in poverty, if he let her.

Dunstan was familiar with Siward's network of residences and abbeys which were glad to provide shelter for his wife. But the mood in these places was subdued. Word was already spreading that Edgar the Atheling, the one so many had pinned their hopes on, had capitulated and made his peace with the Bastard. In some of these places they witnessed fights break out as the people debated whether to hope for further deliverance or to join him in swearing loyalty to the invader.

Oswyth's disgust with the man she had once considered her king deepened, while her admiration for Siward and his friends grew with every account Dunstan gave. They were men who did not give up. If only one of them had some claim to the throne, the fate of England might be very different.

As they moved further north, the bright weather dampened

and their journey slowed. One afternoon, with the rain beating down on them, causing their horses to slip in the mud every time they tried to increase their pace, it soon became obvious they would not make it to the abbey they had hoped to rest at that night.

"There is a hall over there," Oswyth pointed out, seeing a building through the dripping trees. "Should we beg for shelter?"

"I do not know, my lady." Dunstan looked longingly at the smoke curling from the roof of the hall. "I do not know who lives there. They might be friendly or…"

A young woman had just come out of the hall. She waved at them and Oswyth made a decision. She urged her horse over.

"Greetings," the woman said. "Will you not stop here a while. It is no day to be travelling."

"Thank you." Oswyth gladly slid from her horse. She could smell a rich broth cooking in the hall.

"I am Edith," the woman said. "May I ask who you are?"

"My name is Oswyth. I am travelling north to where my husband lies ill."

"Who is your husband?"

"Lord Siward of Gloucester," Oswyth announced, for the first time overwhelmed with pride to be stating this.

The woman's pale face went whiter. She gripped hold of Oswyth's arm. "Do not say that name. The King's men are looking for him. I think you should ride on." She glanced into the hall. "It may not be safe here."

Chapter two

Oswyth gaped at the woman but before she could say anything, a man with the cropped hair and shorn face of the Normans came to the door. He spoke rapidly to her in his own tongue. She replied before looking back at Oswyth, a warning clear in her gaze.

"Allow me to present my husband, Robert de Croix. I have told him of your husband's illness. He wishes to know more about this."

"My husband fell ill while on the King's business in the North," Oswyth said, thinking this was no lie. Her mind raced for further details. "He is called Drogo de Caen." She picked the first name which came into her head, as well as the only town in Normandy she could remember at that moment.

Robert de Croix could evidently understand English even if he did not speak it. He spoke again to his wife.

"My husband is not acquainted with your husband but he bids you welcome," Edith said. "Although he wishes to know why you have so little command of your husband's language."

"I have not been wed long," Oswyth replied. Her grandfather had refused to even hear the Norman tongue, a view she had wholeheartedly agreed with at the time but at that moment she wished she could have spoken a few words to make her story more convincing. "I am trying to learn but it is hard. I fear I am very foolish and am a great trial to my husband. He has my deep gratitude for his forbearance." Wryly she realised her last words too were no lie.

Robert nodded, his lip curled. Oswyth dug her nails into her hands as she saw his obvious contempt. He had no doubt been in her land for several years and had made little attempt to learn their language. He could hardly cast aspersions on her. She was tempted to make some excuse and ride on despite the poor weather.

Robert cast his eyes over Oswyth's entourage. In a strongly accented voice he addressed them. "You all English also?"

The heads nodded and she could see the puzzlement on Robert's face as he clearly wondered why the good Drogo de Caen had not placed at least some suitable Normans around her to guide her in the language. She was trying to think of an explanation when, to her admiration, Dunstan launched fluently into the Norman tongue.

Oswyth could make no sense of what they were saying, although from the glances Robert was giving her, she guessed it was mostly about her. As Robert laughed, she also suspected the comments were not flattering. She ground her teeth in annoyance as still laughing, Robert turned and led the way into the hall, gesturing to his guests to follow him.

It was warm inside, a fire burning merrily at the centre of a hall hung with tapestries and the spoils of many a hunt. The aroma of broth bubbling over the fire was stronger than ever. Oswyth would have eagerly anticipated the hot food if she had not felt so nervous her deception would be uncovered.

To her relief, Robert left them alone, preferring to sit near the fire with a cup of ale in his hands, talking loudly in his own language to his companions. Oswyth took a seat next to her hostess.

"Thank you for not betraying us," she whispered.

Edith gave her a tight smile. "I am glad to do something."

But after those words she said no more, stitching at a robe while Oswyth sat tensely beside her, wishing she had some stitching of her own to keep herself occupied. The silence was growing awkward when a slight squall brought Edith out of her reticence. Her face suddenly radiant, she took the baby handed to her and brought it to her breast.

"That is a fine infant," Oswyth said. "A boy?"

Edith's face glowed more than ever as she nodded. Oswyth was pleased to see her like this. She had feared her life was a miserable one and was glad to see there was some happiness for her.

"What is he called?"

Edith's radiance dimmed in a flicker of shame. "William."

Oswyth gave a polite smile, realising she should have known he would have a Norman name. She asked no more but guessed Edith's story was much like her own. No doubt her father or brother had died, leaving her the heiress to these lands. But for her there was no wise grandfather to push for marriage to an Englishman.

It was as she took a mouthful of broth that another thought struck her. Edith's fate might yet be her own. If Siward died, she would be the heiress to his lands. She would then quickly gain a new husband and her children too would bear the names of the conquerors. With her appetite dashed by this prospect, it was an effort to empty her bowl. She had always known such a fate was a likely one but seeing it played out before her, made her dread it more than ever.

With the rain continuing to beat heavily, they were urged to spend the night and giving no sign of her reluctance, Oswyth agreed. It was a relief when they awoke the next morning to find the sun shining once again. She hugged Edith farewell, thanking her profusely for her hospitality. She wished she could find something comforting to say. Once she might have believed that liberation would come, that her husband would be sent packing and she could end the marriage. But with Edgar's capitulation and Sweyn's failure to arrive, she knew Edith would have to resign herself to her fate. She only hoped that one day, when little William became a man, he would treat his mother with the respect she deserved.

"You will be in my prayers," she whispered.

Edith's polite smile trembled. "Thank you. But do not worry about me. This was not the life I wanted but it is tolerable enough." She looked swiftly around, lowering her voice. "Robert is not a bad man. He is god fearing and good humoured."

"He is still a Norman who cares nothing for our ways."

Edith nodded. "I know. But we must all adapt to this. There is no other way."

As Robert too came to bid her farewell, Oswyth could see she was right. He was a good man who had welcomed in weary travellers. At least the English customs of hospitality were maintained in these parts. Although, if he had known who her husband truly was, she knew the welcome would have been very different.

As they left, they urged their horses into a brisk trot, at times almost cantering in their wish to leave the hall behind. Oswyth glanced at Dunstan. "Where did you learn to speak their language like that?"

"I have spent some time in Normandy, my lady. In the days of King Edward, I took messages there. And even in recent years I have travelled all over England, sometimes acting as a scout for Lord Bridwin. I have had much contact with Normans and it is not the first time I have pretended to be one."

Oswyth nodded, even more impressed with the man. "May I ask what you said about me?"

Dunstan gave a guilty smile. "I wish you would not, my lady."

Oswyth arched her eyebrows and waited.

"Forgive me, my lady but the man was so puzzled at your husband's failure to teach you his language. I told him you were a lazy slattern and your husband had felt there were other skills you should learn first."

Oswyth laughed, not remotely offended. "You are certainly quick witted. Let us hope we have no more need for such quick wits on the rest of our journey."

∞∞∞

The ride continued for several more days, with Oswyth often worried that if Siward had taken an infection, his chances of surviving this long were remote.

"My lady, we may need to set up a tent for you this night," Dunstan told her one day. "Settlements are fewer here."

Oswyth nodded, assuming he was referring to the remote moorlands they were passing over. They did see occasional settlements but the people simply stared at them suspiciously as they passed, without the cries of greeting Oswyth had been accustomed to further south.

"I think we should stop soon," Dunstan said as the sun hung low in the sky.

The evening was warm but for a reason she could not understand, Oswyth shivered. As her horse turned skittish, she realised she was not the only one who seemed uneasy. Even the birds were silent. She brought her horse to a stop as she noticed some charred ground.

"There has been a fire here." She looked out at the extent of the burnt patch. It seemed to stretch on for a considerable distance. "I suppose some traveller was careless and let a fire burn out of control."

"Perhaps, my lady," Dunstan said solemnly.

Oswyth looked at him, a horrified realisation dawning at his tone. "No, it was not carelessness, was it? This was deliberate."

Dunstan bowed his head. "Yes, my lady."

Oswyth slid from her horse, walking towards the scorched ground. As she drew closer she could clearly see the remains of buildings. She bent down, picking up what appeared to be half a cup. Further on there was a metal platter, warped out of shape by the fire which had raged so fiercely. Oswyth's eyes filled with tears. Once there had been people living there. It would have been a busy settlement of men and women working hard, tending their animals and eking out the crops from the soil. Their life might often have been tough but they would have had merry times. In the summer and autumn, as the harvest was brought in, there would have been laughter and music, while winters would have been spent huddled around fires, busy with repairs and listening to old tales. Babies would have arrived and while not all would have lived, plenty would, bringing gladness to their parents' hearts. Oswyth clutched the platter to her breast, picturing the woman who might have held it, her children clustering around her. Her face would have been all smiles as they reached out with grubby fists to grab the chunks of bread she was dispensing.

And then in one brutal winter, the forces of the Bastard had come, murdering, raping, stealing or slaughtering the animals, burning the rough little huts those people had called home. With her eyes full of tears, the brutal deaths were blurred but she could hear the screams ringing out as the woman of her imaginings tried so desperately to save her children. Oswyth's tears flowed faster as she thought of the fine castles where the Bastard resided. She had heard tales of him strutting around the devastation he had wreaked, still wearing his crown in the ultimate insult to the people from whom he had taken everything.

Oswyth had heard many times of this devastation, the people left to starve or burned alive in their buildings. But witnessing the remains of this horror brought it so vividly to life. Suddenly afraid she might stumble over the charred bones of the people she had imagined living there, Oswyth returned to her entourage. Every face was solemn but Dunstan had tears on his cheeks.

"Are you from these parts?" she asked him.

He nodded, his voice breaking as he spoke. "From a little east of here. The settlement was destroyed as this one was. I never found out what happened to my father and mother or my three brothers and their wives and children. I know not where their bodies lie."

With no words available, Oswyth put her arms around him. Dragged back to his grief, Dunstan did not recoil from such familiarity. In that moment rank was unimportant. They were simply two of the English, mourning for their land, allowing the tears to mingle.

"How can one man carry out such cruelties?" Oswyth asked. "Is life not hard enough? I know there are deaths a plenty in battle but to add all this to the people he was claiming to reign?"

"I know not, my lady," Dunstan said. "There is no explanation for it. And I take comfort from knowing that one day the Bastard will have to account to Our Lord for his actions."

"Yes, he will." Oswyth's eyes narrowed. "One day even he will be on his death bed and I hope then, the memory of your family and all the many thousands of others he killed, return to torment him. It will be no less than he deserves."

"I hope that too, my lady. In that fate, my parents will be avenged."

Oswyth shivered. "Let us ride on a little longer. I do not think I wish to sleep here this night."

They rode on in silence, Oswyth wondering if England could ever recover.

Chapter three

The subdued mood remained upon them for the last couple of days of their ride and became even worse as Oswyth feared what she would find. Each night her dreams were haunted by visions of herself riding beside Siward's coffin as it was born back to his lands for burial. She awoke from those dreams with her heart thudding at the memory of his face, pale and still, yet unable to feel the relief which usually accompanied waking from a bad dream, for she knew it may yet prove to be a true one.

"Journey's end, my lady," Dunstan said, pointing at a small hall with a cluster of buildings around it.

The last day of their journey had been on a track so rough it disappeared in places, with their horses stumbling often on the stony ground. It was easy to see why Siward and his friends had chosen to hole up in that bleak spot, away from their enemies. Even Dunstan, who knew the land well, had at times mistaken the path.

"God be praised." Oswyth dismounted, trying to ignore the sick feeling in her stomach.

"My lady, we do not know what might have happened here since I left," Dunstan continued. "Do not reveal your name unless you are certain it is my good Lord Bridwin who still resides here. I think it best if I keep my distance for now. If the Normans have taken control and any recognise me, I could endanger us all."

Oswyth nodded, wondering what excuse she would offer if

the Normans had located the hall. She would still wish to know where Siward and his friends had been taken. Clouds were amassing around the horizon, bringing an early dimness to the afternoon. She shivered as the wind stirred the grasses in ferocious whirls, praying that Siward was recovering. She could not bear that he die in that desolate spot.

"Greetings, my lady." A roughly dressed man approached her, not hiding his surprise at the visitors. "How may we be of assistance?"

"Greetings." Oswyth tried to smile with assurance. "I wish to speak to the Lord of this place. Is he here?"

"Yes, my lady. Please enter."

She was taken into the almost empty hall, where a fire glowed dully so it would no doubt be ready to build up for the evening. The thrall poured a cup of ale. "Please be seated, my lady. I shall inform my master of your presence."

Oswyth kept her cloak tightly around her as she sipped at the drink, trying to calm her nerves. Her cup was still half full when a young man came into the hall. For a moment she thought his hair was cropped short, but as he looked around, she realised the dark locks were long but simply tied back. His dress too was that of an Englishman. Oswyth got nervously to her feet.

The man's eyes alighted on her, a polite smile curving his lips. He gave a slight bow. "Greetings, my lady. I apologise for the poor welcome. We do not often receive guests here. I am Lord Bridwin of Lichfield. How may I help you? Have you mistaken your path?"

The relief at hearing an English voice was so great, Oswyth could not speak. She stared at him, her frightened mind making sense of his name. This was Siward's friend. The one who had sent the message informing them of his injury.

"My lady?" the man said as Oswyth did not reply.

Oswyth gave a shaky smile. "Forgive me. I am looking for Lord Siward of Gloucester."

The pleasant smile on the man's face slipped into a startled expression. "Siward? What do you want with him?"

Oswyth held her head high. "I am his wife," she said, praying she was not about to become his widow.

Bridwin's mouth dropped further. "His wife? Lady Oswyth?"

Oswyth looked pleadingly at him. "We received your message that he had been injured. Is he here abed somewhere? Can I see him?"

"Abed? No," Bridwin replied, shock still overwhelming him.

Oswyth swallowed. "Does he still live?"

Bridwin's face cleared. "Oh, yes. Forgive me. I did not mean to worry you."

She let out her breath, relaxing her stiff posture. Her face lit into a radiant smile. "Where does he lie? I must go to him."

Bridwin gestured back at her seat, his smile returning at the joy so obvious on Oswyth's face. "He is here. Please, make yourself as comfortable as you can, my lady. I shall inform him of your arrival."

Her legs trembling, Oswyth sank back onto the bench. Siward was alive and he was still there. It was not long before she heard footsteps outside and a few moments later Siward entered. He was plainly dressed in a brown tunic over breeches and his arm was in a sling, but he walked with his usual strength. The only expression on his face was one of annoyance.

"What the hell are you doing here, Oswyth?"

"Siward, you are well. I am so glad," Oswyth exclaimed, his appearance beyond anything she had expected.

"I said, what are you doing here?"

"We… we heard you had been injured. We were worried. Your mother particularly so and she has not been well and…"

"What was wrong with my mother?" Siward demanded.

"We had a sickness. Some died of it but your mother is recovering well."

Siward frowned. "My one instruction to you was to look after my mother. You should not have left her while she was ill."

"She is much better," Oswyth protested. "Truly, I would not have left her if she was still ill. She was so worried when she heard of your injury. I think if I had not said I would go to you, she would have insisted on coming herself."

Siward gave a faint smile. "Yes, she probably would."

Cheered by the softening in Siward's manner, Oswyth smiled back. "She will be so pleased to know you are recovering. As am I."

Siward's smile turned into a sneer. "Are you? Since you are here, you must no doubt have been told how we failed. That King Edgar has crumbled, that King Sweyn did not come. Have you come here to gloat? To tell me what a failure I am yet again?"

"No, truly, Siward, I do not want to do that." Oswyth flushed with distress. "I came out of concern."

Siward shook his head. "Of course you did. Well, I am busy. Sit down and take whatever refreshment you need." He gestured with his good arm towards a door at one end of the hall. "I expect Bridwin will be happy to allow you the bedchamber if you need to rest."

"Yes, of course, thank you," Oswyth stammered. She had expected her reunion with Siward to be very different, imagining herself to be soothing his brow or coaxing hot potage into him.

"But I have much to do. I shall speak to you again later." Siward turned to go, heading back towards the door.

Oswyth stared after him, her eyes blurred with tears. "Siward, can you not spare me just a few moments?"

"No, I cannot. I told you, I have much to do." He frowned. "Of course. I realise now why you are here. You came hoping I was making you a wealthy widow. It would have suited your drama very nicely to have accompanied my coffin, wailing all the way home. Well, I am sorry. As usual I have grossly disappointed you."

He turned away again as Oswyth almost choked on the lump in her throat. "No, Siward," she said as he reached the doorway. "I did not want to be a widow."

He did not stop, striding out the doorway with only an impatient flick of his hand betraying he had heard her.

Oswyth stared at the empty doorway, her voice trailing into a whisper. "I want to be your wife."

Oswyth remained in the hall, barely moving from the bench. Bridwin had sent thralls to serve her, who quickly got the fire blazing and set food on the table. She asked if the men were joining her but was told they were still talking and were taking their meal elsewhere so as not to be disturbed. At that she nodded politely but merely picked at her food, her appetite much diminished.

Even as the household retired for the night, Siward and his friends did not return to the hall. Oswyth sat on, a candle burning beside her as she waited. Her head nodded at times but always it jerked awake again at the sound of nothing more than crackling wood.

Soft voices told her the wait was over as Siward entered the hall accompanied by Bridwin and Frebern. Both of those two bowed politely, Frebern directing a friendly smile at her, but Siward remained unappeased.

"Why you are still awake, Oswyth?" he demanded. "I told you where you could rest."

"Yes, please take the bedchamber," Bridwin said. "I am quite comfortable out here."

"Thank you. But Siward, could we not talk first?" Oswyth looked pleadingly at her husband.

"I am tired," Siward snapped. "I have no wish to talk to you this night. Indeed I have no wish to talk of this matter with you, ever. Yes, I have failed. I do not need to hear your reproaches."

"No, no, I will not," Oswyth said. "Please, Siward."

"It is over. Everything is over including our sham of a marriage." Siward scowled. "Yes, perhaps it is as well you are here. Do you have any preference of which convent you wish to enter?"

"What? No!" Oswyth noticed from the corner of her eye the

shocked look pass between Frebern and Bridwin.

"If it is one of the more prestigious ones, you had better decide quickly. I dare say I shall have nothing soon, so any gifts necessary to endow them will need to be swiftly made."

Oswyth shook her head, afraid to speak, convinced if she opened her mouth, she would burst into tears or scream. All she wanted was a few moments to apologise to her husband but instead it seemed she was to be sent packing without any chance at conversation.

"Well, think about it." Forgetting his injury, Siward went to fold his arms, looking more furious than ever when he could not complete the action. "But make your choice soon. I shall be fit to ride in a few days and I shall escort you to one before returning home. I think it would be best if you did not come back."

Dumbly Oswyth nodded, as she clenched her fists, determined not to disgrace herself by crying.

"But now, go to your rest."

Oswyth nodded again. Somehow she managed to meet her husband's eyes. "Of course. I will bid you good night."

Siward nodded curtly, saying nothing more. Bridwin and Frebern murmured the words in return but both were looking down to avoid her gaze. Oswyth forced herself to calmly pick up the candle and move without running to the chamber door, where her hand shook so much she struggled to open it. The shadows thrown by her candle danced wildly. There was complete silence in the hall as she pushed the door open until it was broken by the gentle thud as it closed behind her.

Chapter four

"Damn her," Siward muttered, sitting on the bench Oswyth had just vacated. He poured himself a cup of ale, taking half of it in one mouthful. "Damn her."

He was furious with Oswyth for arriving that day. It had left him increasingly distracted, until it was impossible to concentrate on the plans he and his friends had been discussing. His arm throbbed, reminding him that he was still unable to ride. He would have no choice but to put up with Oswyth's presence there for several more days. Draining his cup, he instantly refilled it, taking another gulp.

Bridwin and Frebern exchanged glances, hesitantly taking their own places at the table.

"Siward," Bridwin said. "Be reasonable. No matter what arguments you have had with your wife, you cannot simply dump her in a convent. It would not be right."

"She is not truly my wife. The marriage has never been consummated."

"What?" Frebern cried. "Why would you not lie with a wife who looks like that?"

Siward's eyes shot up. "Shut up, you fool."

"Sorry," Frebern muttered, lowering his own eyes.

Siward shook his head, ashamed of being so harsh with his friend. Frebern was young. It was natural he had seen only Oswyth's beauty. It was not as if he had ever been exposed to the harshness of her manner.

"If you had no intention of touching her, what possessed you to marry her?" Bridwin asked.

"Her grandfather begged me to look after her. I owed it to him to do what he asked. How was I to know she was so spoilt? I thought she would become more amenable. But she has not. She is spiteful, selfish, and wilful. I can bear it no longer."

"What of your vow to her grandfather?"

"She will come to no harm in a convent. It will be a dull life for her, perhaps. But not unpleasant."

"It seems a pity," Frebern muttered, earning himself another furious look from Siward.

"You say she is spoilt and spiteful, yet she has made a long and perilous journey to be with you during your injury," Bridwin said.

Siward gave a joyless laugh. "Do not fall for that. She is here to gloat over my failure. Nothing more."

Bridwin frowned. "Are you sure? You did not see her when she arrived here. She was terrified you might be dead."

"It was an act," Siward said. "She would have enjoyed the role of the grieving widow."

"I do not think so," Bridwin replied. "When I told her you were alive, she looked overjoyed."

Siward shrugged and stared morosely into his cup. Everything had gone wrong for both England and himself and the solution they were considering was drastic to say the least. Now all he wanted was to forget everything for a while. This was a night for drinking himself into oblivion, not dealing with the irritation that was his wife.

Bridwin stood up. "Well, I am going to rest." He put his hand on Frebern's shoulder, giving him a meaningful look. He also stood. Bridwin looked back at Siward. "If you want my advice..."

"Which I do not."

"You will talk to your wife. She will find out your plans sooner or later. You might as well discuss it with her now. But it is your choice. I'll bid you goodnight."

As Bridwin and Frebern settled themselves on blankets by the fire, Siward finished his drink. He looked at the jug, still half full on the table. He was not going to get any sleep that night. So, he could either pour himself cup after cup until he found the oblivion he craved. He glanced at the door to the bedchamber. Or he could talk to Oswyth. With a sigh, he pushed back the bench and walked to the door.

He hoped he would find the bedchamber in darkness but as he entered, it was obvious that not only had Oswyth not blown out her candle, she had also lit others. In the tiny space, the light was dazzling. He blinked. Oswyth was sat on the bed, little more than a straw pallet, clad only in her linen underdress, with a blanket over her knees. She was furiously tugging a comb through her hair, her cheeks bright red with what he assumed was anger for she did not look up to display the luminosity of her eyes.

"Look, Oswyth," he said. "The fight for England is over. We have lost. The Normans are here to stay. The Bastard will reign over the realm for as long as he lives and then it will no doubt be ruled by one of his sons. We have done everything we can." He paused but Oswyth gave no response. "For more than seven years I have tried. I have risked everything, lost everything. My lands, kith and kin, my people. Everything. And all for nothing. It is over. I can fight no longer." His voice broke. "I know you will say I am a failure and a coward. I care not. I am so tired of fighting."

To Siward's mortification, he could do nothing other than slump to the bed, his head dropping to his hands as his tears flowed. That morning it had felt as if he had ripped out his own heart when, after days of futile planning, he had blurted out that there was nothing else they could do. For a long time Bridwin and Frebern had avoided his eyes, until they clasped his hand with no words, only able to silently nod their heads, lumps choking all three throats. They had risked all they had and it was all for nothing. England was lost to them. Somehow saying the words again to Oswyth made it more real than ever. The sobs shook his body and he was certain his wife's disgust would be plummeting to new depths.

But he got a shock. Warm arms enclosed him and he found his head drawn against a soft breast. Gentle fingers stroked his hair. "I know you are, Siward. You can stop fighting now."

The shock of that comfort stopped Siward's tears. And it was comforting. He could not deny it. He was tempted to stay there awhile, like a child, blotting out the terrors of the world in a pair of loving arms. But he pulled away, daring to look at his wife. Her expression was gentle, free from the condemnation he was expecting and he could see now the tears filling her eyes. One escaped to trickle down her cheek.

"Oh, Siward, I always thought you emerged unscathed from Hastings but you did not, did you? You were injured just as badly as my father. But unlike him, you have had to live with your pain."

Siward swallowed, only too aware of her arms still lightly touching him. "You have your father's eyes," he said. "Why have I never realised that?"

Oswyth looked confused by that comment as well she might. She had no idea how the memory of those eyes had tormented him. Yet seeing them look on him now with compassion was almost as unsettling as the despair and condemnation of his nightmares.

Oswyth took a deep breath. "About my father..." she started.

Siward stiffened as he withdrew from her arms, thinking he should have guessed this sympathy would not last. "I know. I failed him. I failed him with my carelessness at Hastings. He gave his life for me and all I have done is gone on failing."

Oswyth gave a vehement shake of the head. "No. I know what I have said to you in the past and I have no words to describe how sorry I am. Do not listen to a child's foolish anger." She straightened her back, her voice trembling. "My father was a brave man and he did what brave men do. He risked his life to save that of another, just as you would have done if the positions were reversed. I know my father would be proud to have given his life to save another brave Englishman. You did not fail him, Siward.

I failed him. As his daughter, it was my place to honour his sacrifice. I should have felt pride not anger."

"You have a right to your anger."

"Not my anger at you. As a child, perhaps, it was natural that as you were the one there, you would be the one to receive my anger. But I am no longer a child. All I can do now is beg your forgiveness." She kept her gaze steady as she spoke the words she needed to say to her husband. "You have not gone on failing. You have been truer to England's cause than any of the men claiming to be its king. I am proud to have been your wife, even if it was just for a short time."

Siward gripped her hand with no words. The marriage was over as was the fight but at least this was not ending in the same bitterness.

"What will you do now?" Oswyth asked. "Are you going to swear loyalty to the Bastard?" She wondered how he would bear it and hoped he might keep her with him so she could support him through the bleakest of days.

But Siward lifted his head. "No. Never. That is one thing I have sworn never to do."

"What will you do?"

"I am leaving."

"Leaving?"

Siward nodded. "It is what Frebern, Bridwin and I have been discussing all evening. We are going to amass a fleet. We shall muster as many men as we can, good Englishmen and any others who do not wish to languish under the Norman rule. We are going to sail away from this broken land and we will not stop sailing until we have found a place we may consider to be a new England."

When he had discussed this matter with Bridwin and Frebern, it had seemed a fine, if daunting, plan. But saying the words out loud to Oswyth sounded ridiculous and he rather expected her to laugh. He looked defiantly into her eyes, surprised to see how they were shining.

"Please, Siward," she breathed. "Take me with you."

Chapter five

S iward blinked, shocked by her words. "You want to come?"

Oswyth looked down. "Forgive me. That was a foolish thought. I would be nothing but a nuisance. It is strong men you need, not women."

Siward laughed, buoyed up by her enthusiasm. "Of course I will need women. New England would not last long without good Englishwomen."

Oswyth looked up again. "I can come?"

"It may be dangerous." Siward shook his head. "Why am I saying that when I know you are as brave as any man? Braver than most. Yes, you can come."

Oswyth clasped her hands together, her face lighting up in a smile which took his breath away. "Thank you."

"But, Oswyth..." Aware his plans to leave her in the safety of a convent had been rendered useless, he tried to work out how he felt about that. But as he took hold of her hand, the sight of her fingers entwined with his confused him more than ever. Taking a deep breath, he tried to regain some control over the conversation. "If you come, you come as my wife. And I shall expect a more amenable manner than you have maintained so far."

She nodded eagerly. "Of course. I swear to you, I will be a good wife. Everything will be different. You will never again have cause to complain of me."

"You will need to be my true wife. The marriage must be consummated before we leave."

Oswyth tensed, her heart thudding loudly into her throat. She swallowed, forcing herself to smile through her apprehension. "Of course. Tonight?"

"Perhaps." Siward considered this, remembering the warmth of her arms around him, the softness of her breast against his cheek. It was an enticing prospect to go back into her arms, to forget the difficult day when he had to accept defeat and to lose himself in her body. Watching him gravely, her hair loose around her shoulders and clad just in that thin underdress, she was so beautiful. A night with her would be even better than the drink he had earlier craved, but he wondered if he would be foolish to give in to temptation. That night Oswyth was charming, the sort of wife he had wanted her to be. If only he could be certain her new amiable mood would last. Regretfully he realised he needed to know she would not return to the angry girl he had married before making the marriage a true one.

He squeezed her hand. "Perhaps not this night. You will want time to prepare yourself if you are a maid. I mean you are a maid, aren't you? I mean…" His voice trailed off and he cursed himself for losing his authority over the conversation once again.

Oswyth withdrew her hand. Looking outraged, she folded her arms. "Siward, I think you should stop talking now."

"I think you are very wise."

The meekness in his tone, as he made no attempt to regain control, caused Oswyth to burst into laughter. Siward looked up at that, a rueful grin spreading over his face as he could not help but delight in the joyful sound. With her face so animated, she looked prettier than ever. Forgetting his earlier decision, he leaned forward, bringing his lips to hers.

For Oswyth, who had always assumed that being kissed by a man was likely to be akin to being mauled, the kiss was a shock. Siward's lips were warm and firm and as they tugged gently at hers, her heart fluttered. He had slipped his uninjured arm around her waist and it seemed natural to wind her own arms around his neck, letting her fingers play with his hair. Stunned by the sensations his kisses were sending through her, she became bolder. Her hand drifted to his shoulder, moving down the uninjured arm, for the first time admiring the strength in it.

Siward too was shocked by the desire surging in him at her eager response. He could not remember the last time he had felt so happy. Perhaps it was the night after the battle at Stamford Bridge, when they had slain the Norwegian king and celebrated in the belief they had secured the land. The memory of how brief that happiness had been and the disaster which had followed, acted like a pail of icy water. He withdrew sharply from Oswyth, leaving her staring at him, puzzled by his abrupt reaction. Her heart which had been thudding with excitement, slowed into a dull fear at his rejection.

"No. Not tonight." He shivered. "What am I thinking? If you were to conceive a child and then have to face the dangers of a voyage... It should wait until we are settled."

His face was white as the memories of past disasters flooded his mind. Oswyth forgot her dismay at the kiss ending so suddenly and put her arms around his tense body, more aware than ever of the torments haunting him. He was straining to withdraw from her, yet she could sense his need for the comfort she could offer.

Gently she touched his cheek. "It will be as you wish it to be," she said. "But we do not know how long it will take me to conceive a child. And we do not know how long it will take to find a new England. I do not think we should put off one, while we strive for the other."

The touch of her fingers drove away the memories as his body relaxed again. "You are as wise as you are beautiful."

Oswyth blushed and shook her head. As the strain eased from his features, she feared it was replaced in hers at the thought of what the night would hold. She managed a smile, determined to be the dutiful wife he deserved. "Tonight?"

Siward grinned, no longer fighting the passion consuming his body, as he realised he could that night forget the memories of defeat and his fears for the future. He could give in to the moment. He nodded, kissing her lightly. "Yes, tonight."

With sudden impatience he cast away his shoes, standing to pull off breeches and tunic. Oswyth looked down although he was aware of the surreptitious looks she was sending him. In spite of her efforts, they were not concealing her apprehension. If he was to consider merely his own desires, he would undoubtedly tear the underdress from her that instant, but Siward had always despised men who cared only for their own pleasures, never considering the woman they were with. For all Oswyth's feisty ways, she was still an innocent. He would need to be particularly patient and gentle with her that night. Forcing his body under control, he sat down on the pallet, smiling at her in what he hoped was a reassuring fashion as he flexed the arm he had just released from the sling.

"Are you able to take that off?" she asked.

"Oh, yes. The wound is healing well. I keep it in the sling by day to prevent me using it but I am glad to take it off at night."

Oswyth inspected the mark just below his shoulder, shuddering at the size of it. The skin was puckered around the wound but it was scabbed with no sign of festering. Very gently she ran her hand down his arm, the hairs rough against her fingers, aware how fortunate she was that he was still alive. "Does it hurt?"

At her touch, pain was the last thing on Siward's mind as desire struck him afresh. "It aches but nothing like the pain of the day it happened."

Oswyth nodded and gave a tremulous smile. She shifted over so Siward could come under the covers with her, her mind racing to everything she had been told of the marriage bed. With an affectionate husband, she had been told there could be great joy, but with an indifferent one, there would be discomfort and even pain, while with a cruel man, there would be unspeakable terror. She knew Siward well enough to know he would not be cruel but with everything which had gone between them, she wondered if he could be anything other than indifferent.

Siward cupped her face with tender amusement. "You are looking frightened. I have never seen you look frightened before." Gently he stroked her cheek. "Are you worried I am going to hurt you?"

Oswyth raised her eyes to look at him. "I would not blame you if you did. I have said such words to you, such cruel words. I…" She stopped as Siward put his finger over her lips.

"I have listened to your wisdom," he said. "And now you are going to listen to mine. There have been many words between us. Words spoken in anger, fear, grief and yes, perhaps even in malice. But they are now in the past. They belong in the ruins of old England. We are not taking them to New England."

Oswyth let out her breath, smiling. "It is far better than I deserve. But thank you."

Siward put his arm around her. "Are you sure you do not need more time to prepare yourself? It does not have to be this night."

He was fervently hoping she would not agree with that. The hair brushing his shoulder was soft and all he wanted was to rid himself of the linen between him and her slender body, allowing that hair to flow over them both. It had been so long since he had enjoyed a woman, long since he had even wanted to enjoy one. Casting his eyes over her face, he realised he was not sure if he had ever desired one as much as he desired Oswyth that night. It was a relief when she shook her head, her smile still nervous but her eyes shyly meeting his. "No. I think this night is the right one."

Siward leaned in to kiss her again, his lips more eager than ever. He agreed. It did feel right. The day he had suggested the idea of New England to his friends could also be the day he started anew with his wife. He let his hand drift downwards toward the hem of her dress. As his fingers brushed her stomach he wondered whether that night he might even beget new life in her body.

Her apprehension already fading, Oswyth responded to the kiss, aware of his hands pulling at her underdress. She helped him, tugging it over her head. There was an instant of self-consciousness as she found herself naked with a man but as Siward's eyes ran down her body, his breath quickening, the embarrassment transformed into joy. Never had she felt so beautiful.

Keeping his arms around her, Siward pulled her down, finally giving into the temptation to stroke her body. Her skin was so much softer than he had expected. For a moment he was afraid his calloused hand might be too rough for her, but as their eyes met, he could see the wonder in her face. Her faint gasps were not ones of pain or fear but of joyous surprise.

Every bitter memory of the previous years faded from their minds. Even their dreams for the future were irrelevant. As desire took over, for both all that mattered was that night.

Chapter six

Only smiles passed between Siward and Oswyth as they dressed the next morning but no words until he tossed his sling to her.

"Can you tie this for me?"

Oswyth picked it up, smoothing out the linen. "Was the injury very bad?"

Siward nodded. "I was in a bad way when they got me here. Bridwin and Frebern were worried by how much blood I lost which is, I suppose, why the fools had to worry my mother." He grinned, driving away the memory of the searing agony and the sorrow his friends had so desperately tried to hide from him. "But I can hardly complain of that now, can I?"

Oswyth laughed, standing on tip-toe to loop the fabric around his neck. He bowed his head to make it easier for her, taking advantage of her proximity to press several kisses against her throat. Oswyth lost her grip on the sling and squealed, stepping backwards, laughing more than ever. She was delighted to see this playful side of Siward. This was the young man he should have become, not the careworn one she had known so far. His cares would return, of course. As she considered the task he had set himself, she realised his responsibilities would be greater than ever, but she would make sure he still had times when he could forget those. She forced her features into a stern look.

"Keep still and let me tie this. I shall give you a kiss when I have finished."

Siward grinned and did as he was instructed, enjoying the look of concentration on her face as she tied the knot. He was glad he no longer needed the poultice they had applied to his wound in the first days after he was injured. It had been a foul smelling concoction, which they had told him was mostly chopped earthworms. Their rejuvenating properties would, they said, rejuvenate the flesh of his arm. And so it had but the stench clinging to him for several days had made him permanently nauseous.

"There, it is done," Oswyth said, pressing her lips against his in the promised kiss.

"You do feel well, don't you?" Siward asked anxiously as he pulled away. Holding her now reminded him of how soft and fragile her body had felt lying naked in his arms and how trusting the expression in her eyes. "Are you sure I did not hurt you?"

Oswyth smiled and shook her head, keen to banish the worry from his eyes. Not that there would be any need to lie. At times she had been bewildered by the sensations his lips and hands had aroused in her, but the apprehension she initially felt had swiftly been overwhelmed by exhilaration. "I was not hurt at all. I feel..." She struggled to find a word to describe exactly how she felt, eventually settling on the simplest explanation. "Happy."

"So do I," Siward replied. "It is so long since I felt this way. It almost frightens me."

Oswyth slipped her arms around him again, resting her head against his chest. "Ill fortune has been against us for so long now. Surely it is our turn to enjoy some happy times."

"I hope so."

Oswyth looked up at him, a faint shadow appearing in her eyes. "If I had a wedding night with Ralf Fitz Turstin, I probably would have been hurt, wouldn't I?"

Siward shrugged, surprised to realise she was not such an innocent after all. "It is impossible to say. I have known rough men treat their wives with tenderness and humble ones treat them harshly. But I think it likely. You would be far too spirited for him."

"I know I am. I will try to be less spirited."

Siward caressed her face with his free hand, realising how her bright spark would now light up his life. "No, Oswyth. Do not. I have seen the spirit go from far too many these last years. It has been hard even to maintain it in myself. I do not want it gone from you. If you wish to vomit on the shoes of the invaders or lead them into rivers, do so."

Oswyth laughed. "And may I serve them rough ale?"

Siward joined in. "Absolutely! You may serve them the roughest ale. You can spit in it too, if you wish."

"And may I pretend to be married to a Norman called Drogo de Caen?"

Siward frowned. "No. You may not, even in pretence, be married to any man other than me."

Oswyth rummaged in her pouch for a comb, running it through her hair. "Very well." Her innocent air did not conceal the mischief in her eyes as she guessed her husband was agog with curiosity.

Siward shook his head, just as intrigued as Oswyth had known he would be. "What have you done now?"

As she wrapped her hair, she told him of the journey. Siward laughed, particularly as he heard how Dunstan had described her to his Norman host, and shook his head again. "Oh, Oswyth. Never stop being you. And if it is necessary to keep yourself safe, you can pretend to be wed to this Drogo. The man has my sympathies."

Oswyth threw him a look of mock fury at that comment as she arranged a veil over her hair. But she was unable to maintain it as Siward put his arm around her shoulders. Remembering how she had left the bedchamber on the morning after their wedding, Oswyth was surprised she had fooled anyone then with her happy attitude. It must have appeared so obviously false compared to the radiance she could now feel lighting up her face.

Bridwin nodded to them. "I assume there has been a change of plan concerning your wife."

Siward nodded, guessing how foolish his grin must be but not caring. "Yes, there has. She is coming with us."

Oswyth blushed but smiled, allowing Bridwin to lead her to the food set out on the table, as Siward moved away to talk with a priest. Frebern was already sitting on a bench, a chunk of bread in his hand. He rose to his feet as she drew near, but gave her a cheerful smile instead of the formality of a bow. Oswyth smiled back, realising that not only had she gained the affection of a husband, she had also found new friends.

"I heard how you saved Siward's life," she said to him. "I am so grateful."

Frebern beamed. "I suppose I did but he saved mine first. I had stumbled and he stood between me and one of Turstin's men. That was how he was injured."

Oswyth shot a startled look at Siward, still discussing his injury with the priest who had no doubt treated him. So he had acted to save his friend, just as her father had once acted to save him. She sent a heartfelt prayer of thanks that Siward had not paid the price her father had.

Bridwin sat with them. "I am glad you are coming with us," he said. "I think you are good for Siward. It is a long time since I have seen him in such spirits."

Oswyth turned an even deeper shade of red and quickly changed the subject. "Did you fight with Siward at Hastings?"

Bridwin shook his head. "I should have done but I was injured at Stamford Bridge. It was a trivial matter but I could not manage the fast ride south King Harold insisted on. If he had waited just a few days, I would have been there. Often I have wondered if my presence would have made a difference."

"From what I have heard, waiting a few days would have made a big difference." Oswyth stared sadly into her cup, the memories of all England had lost coming back. "Not only would King Harold have had you and other men who just needed a short recovery but those who did fight would have been so much fresher. He could have had so many more men if only he had waited."

"I know." Bridwin's own smile had faded. "It was a foolish decision of King Harold and we have all payed for it."

Oswyth glanced at Frebern. "I suppose you were too young to fight back then."

Frebern nodded. "I was still a boy. I had barely seen thirteen years. But my older brother and father died there."

"So did mine," Oswyth said, tears filling her eyes.

Siward heard the last comments and shook his head, his confidence dimming. There was still so much grief. Was there really enough spirit left in England for the venture he and his friends were planning? Even if they could escape, he wondered what sort of land New England would be when it was founded on so much bitterness. But even as he watched, Oswyth straightened her back.

"Their sacrifice will not be in vain," she said, laying her hand over Frebern's. "We shall found a New England in their names."

Frebern too brightened. "A land they would be proud of."

"A land we shall all be proud of," Bridwin said, adding his own hand to the pile.

'Good for Oswyth,' Siward thought. Now she was channelling her energies into something other than anger, she was going to be an asset to him. She glanced up, meeting his eyes in a sweet smile. Any last doubts he had about her, vanished in that instant. From that day he was confident she was going to be a great joy.

He sat beside his wife, noting with some amusement the admiration in Frebern's gaze as he looked at her. That would be something he would need to keep an eye on although it was unlikely to be a serious matter. He laid his own hand over all of theirs, silently pledging himself to the success of this venture.

He withdrew his hand to lift a cup of ale in a toast to them all. "To New England! A land where good Englishmen can be free."

Their smiles brimming with a tentative hope, the others picked up their own cups. Raising them to his, they echoed his words. "To New England!"

Part Four: June 1074 – April 1075

Chapter one

Within a few days Siward decided he no longer needed the sling even by day. They had been happy days for Oswyth, listening to the men as they made plans, their enthusiasm for the venture growing ever greater. She and Siward also took the time to be alone, for the first time in their marriage properly getting to know each other. Wandering hand in hand around Bridwin's estate, Oswyth marvelled that she had once considered the spot a desolate one, when now she was convinced no more idyllic place existed. As the days passed she found herself liking her husband ever more, laughing as she had not done in a long time at his dry humour, while endlessly touched at his protective attitude towards her. And every evening she retired with him to the tiny bedchamber where the nights became even more joyous than the days.

When Siward announced he was well enough to ride, they made preparations to return, moving south with Bridwin and Frebern. Even as they rode through the bleak northern lands, the mood was happy, the plans of the men never ending. Oswyth listened intently, rarely contributing but soaking up the knowledge of the adventure awaiting them with increasing eagerness. At nights they mostly camped but with bright fires burning, the merry atmosphere continued.

They rested a few days on Bridwin's estates at Lichfield before they and Frebern prepared to ride on.

"Well, my friend," Siward said as they shared a last jug of ale. "This is not how I thought our campaign would end."

"Nor I," Bridwin replied. "And yet I feel strangely more hopeful than I have in a long time. This is not so much the end as a new beginning."

Siward nodded. "Very true. So, our plan is a firm one. Now comes the hard part. We must spread the word, telling as many as possible without the news falling too soon into the ears of the Normans."

"Can it be kept a secret from them?" Oswyth asked.

"I very much doubt it," Siward said. "The longer it is a secret, the better. However if the fleet we amass is as large as I am expecting, it will be impossible to miss."

"The Bastard has his hands full with Normandy and his trouble with the Frankish king at present," Bridwin said. "That will work to our advantage."

"Are you truly happy for us to gather the fleet in the Severn Sea?" Siward asked. "I would like it there so I can keep an eye on it, but I do not want you to feel as if I am taking over with no regard for your views."

"It makes sense to assemble it close to you," Frebern said. "Your lands are near that coast, while ours, apart from the small estate Bridwin has in the North, are inland."

"And I am not planning on spending much time in the North," Bridwin added. "In any case, the east coast would not be the best spot to launch this venture. If we are to head south, the Severn Sea will be a good starting point. Not as good as the south coast, perhaps but that would be too risky."

"Agreed. For this year we must concentrate on the harvest, so our boats are well stocked," Siward said. "Make sure everyone knows to bring what they can. Is there anything else we have not discussed?"

Oswyth laughed. "There cannot be. You three have discussed nothing else for days."

Frebern and Bridwin exchanged glances. "There is one matter to settle. Bridwin and I have been talking."

Siward raised an eyebrow. "What about?"

"Siward, this venture belongs to us all," Frebern said. "We

three are all leading it but there could be differences of opinion."

"Perhaps," Siward replied. "But we shall work through those."

"I hope we shall but if there is no agreement, a decision will still have to be made." Frebern looked earnestly at his friend. "Although we shall all lead, there needs to be one of us who makes the final decisions if no agreement can be reached. The one who can be considered the true leader."

"We think it should be you," Bridwin stated. "You are the oldest and most experienced of us."

Siward looked steadily at his friends, appearing calm but he clutched tightly onto Oswyth's hand. "Are you sure? I have not been blessed with good fortune in any venture so far." A sweat broke out on his forehead as the memories flooded back. So many had died. Too many.

Bridwin shook his head. "You have always taken those failures too much to heart. They were not your failures. King Harold failed us with his foolish decisions at Hastings, then King Sweyn abandoned us. Finally it was that snivelling fool, King Edgar."

"Not to mention the actions of the Bastard," Frebern added. "I would have accepted him as king if he had treated the Englishmen fairly." He shook his head in disgust. "Four possible kings for us and not one of them any good."

"You are a skilled leader," Bridwin said. "I have thought that many times but it was wasted serving those men. Now you will serve no longer. There will be no king over you to let you down."

Siward gave a half smile. "The responsibility, if it fails, will be solely mine."

"No, not solely yours," Frebern said. "We are in this together. We will support you and advise you. If necessary we will share the responsibility for any failure." He grinned. "Although my plan is to share the credit for our success. You can do this, Siward. There is no one better."

Siward looked at them, noting the admiration, almost worship in both Frebern and Oswyth's eyes. He forced down his panic that he would let them down. They were right. Three leaders, even ones who were as close friends as them, could be disastrous. There did need to be one who was above the others.

"I know you will succeed, Siward," Oswyth said softly.

Siward kissed the top of her head, considering the matter. As Oswyth's belief strengthened him, he grinned in unexpected confidence. "With your support, Oswyth and with you two fools standing firmly with me, yes, I think I can."

∞∞∞∞

They rode on with Frebern to Warwick before making the final stage of the journey to Siward's lands. On the last stretch, Siward marvelled that he could feel so joyful in his return. His march north had been a disaster and yet he returned full of optimism. He glanced at Oswyth. This was partly because of her. With each day he found himself more smitten by her smile and the nights in her arms had driven away all nightmares. The days he had lain abed after a sleepless night, wishing he did not have to rise, were gone. He awoke now gladly, savouring the sight of Oswyth's fair head beside him before he rose, eager to face the challenges of the day.

There was a stab of sorrow as they arrived at the hall. Siward looked at it, his home, the land he had inherited from his father. Soon he would be leaving, never to see it again. But he blinked back the tears, reflecting that it was better he left it of his own choice than be driven away. Oswyth was watching him in concern, guessing at his feelings and Siward smiled back, remembering her grief at leaving her grandfather's hall.

However when they dismounted their horses, the emotion was swept away as Alfgiva ran from the doorway to fling her arms around Siward.

"Oh, my dearest, dearest son. God be praised you are well again."

Siward hugged her tightly. "You should not have worried, Mother. It was the merest scratch."

"I do not think a mere scratch would have prevented you riding for so long." She looked at him critically, the anxiety fading from her expression. "But you do look well." She glanced at Oswyth, her lips twitching. "I suppose that silly girl has something to do with it."

Siward grinned. "Perhaps."

Oswyth laughed and hugged her mother-in-law, delighting Siward as he saw how the affection had already returned between the two women he loved most. "Are you completely well?"

"Of course," Alfgiva replied, a flicker crossing her face. "I am quite strong again."

Siward noticed the expression. "Are you sure? Has everything run smoothly here?"

Again Alfgiva frowned but she nodded. "The animals are fattening and the crops are growing in abundance. Come inside. You must refresh yourselves."

The greetings were many as they went into the hall. Again Siward was impressed at how the attitude of the people towards Oswyth had changed. He hid his laughter as he wondered what would have happened if he had kept to his plan to leave his wife in a convent. Seeing the affection in the smiles, he rather suspected his people would have turned on him.

They sat down, accepting the cups of ale Alfgiva had poured, glad to be back. Father Colman too greeted them, smiling as he saw how closely they nestled together on the bench. Siward knew he would not need to make any formal announcement concerning Oswyth. It was obvious to everyone that matters between them were well. For a moment Siward forgot his imminent departure as he enjoyed the fact he was home, surrounded by everyone he loved. But his cares returned as he noticed some whispered comments between Alfgiva and the priest. Seeing his mother's eyes fill with tears at whatever Father Colman was saying, he set down his cup.

"Mother, I can see everything is not right. Please tell me."

Alfgiva shook her head. "I wanted you to recover a little first."

"Never mind that. Just tell me."

Colman laid a piece of parchment on the table. "The King's messengers have been here. This is the tribute they are expecting this year. My son, it is much worse than last year and even then we barely managed."

Alfgiva pressed her lips tightly together. "The Bastard is punishing you for your loyalty to King Edgar, although Edgar, it seems, is to be rewarded."

Siward picked up the script, his eyes widening as he read. Truly the Bastard was determined to take everything he owned. He began to laugh.

Alfgiva and Father Colman exchanged shocked glances. This was the last reaction they had expected from Siward.

"The Bastard is greedy." Siward took another mouthful of his ale, shaking his head in wry amusement at the list.

"What will you do?" Alfgiva asked.

Siward got up. "With this demand? This." And with those words, he tossed the script onto the fire. "That is what I think of the Bastard and his greedy, thieving ways."

Father Colman stared at the smouldering parchment. "But, my son, in the autumn the King's men will return. They will expect their tribute."

"Then they will be disappointed." Siward looked around to see everyone in the hall watching him from wide eyes. They were depending on him and he would keep them safe. It would not be his people who were sent off to what amounted to slavery in Ireland, like so many had been. "I cannot say much just yet," he told them. "But do not fear. I have a plan."

Chapter two

Alfgiva and Father Colman applauded the plan, both agreeing it would be better to leave the land of their own volition.

"But cheating the Bastard of his tribute," Alfgiva said. "Are you sure about that?"

"The fleet will need supplies, Mother," Siward replied. "We will not be stolen from."

Under Siward's instruction the people worked tirelessly, fattening the animals and tending the crops. Oswyth and Alfgiva turned their attentions to the wool, weaving warm garments and thick blankets and stuffing pillows with feathers. The journey would undoubtedly be a long one and they needed to make it as comfortable as possible. They worked quickly, knowing this needed to be done before the harvest, when they would have to start work on preserving the produce.

Siward found himself endlessly busy as he made tentative enquiries about boats, ever anxious that the Normans would bring his plans to an abrupt halt. Messages passed regularly between him, Frebern and Bridwin, where he found both men cautiously optimistic that all would be well. Nervously Siward knew it was time to let word spread.

"I am riding to Gloucester tomorrow," he told Alfgiva and Oswyth one evening just before the harvest began. "Bishop Wulfstan is at Saint Oswald's Priory. I wish to speak to him."

"Do you think he might come with us?" Oswyth asked, remembering the bishop who had so impressed her. "He would be an inspiration if he came."

"He would be welcome," Siward said. "Although I think it might be too much at his age and he appears to be in no danger of losing his office here. But he is in a good position to help spread the word."

"He certainly is," Alfgiva said. "You have not said where you are heading."

Siward laughed. "That is because I do not know. But south. We leave in the spring and God willing, we shall find somewhere to settle by the following winter."

"And so the conquered will become the conquerors," Alfgiva said.

"Perhaps," Siward replied. "But not necessarily. What I am hoping for is to find a fair minded lord who will truly value the Englishmen in my fleet. We will then pledge our service and request he grant us lands of our own."

"Any king would be fortunate to have you in his service." Alfgiva placed her hand over her son's. "I hope you will find one who is worthy of it."

"So do I," Siward replied. "I am not certain I have ever served a king I can truly revere. Even the good King Edward failed us by not settling the question of the succession before his death."

Alfgiva shook her head. "England has been unfortunate indeed these last years. If only King Edward had begat a son. Or lived a little longer so young Edgar had been a man when he died. Or indeed if Edgar's father had not died so suddenly or…"

"Mother, we cannot dwell on what should have been," Siward said. "Can we, Oswyth?" He glanced at her to see her head drooping. "Oswyth, you are tired. You are working too hard."

Oswyth jerked awake again. "Everyone is working hard," she said. "Why should I not?"

Siward squeezed her hand. "Well, rest yourself now."

Oswyth got up, smiling. "Yes, I think I will. I do feel tired."

Alfgiva gave a misty smile as she noted how Siward's eyes followed his wife. "She is lovely. You are truly happy with her now, are you not?"

Siward leaned back in his chair, a soft smile curving his own lips. "Yes, I truly am. Her grandfather said we would deal well together and by God, he was right."

"I am pleased. It is always a mother's greatest wish for her son to wed someone who gladdens his heart and who truly cares for him in return. It brings me such peace to know she will love you when I am no longer with you."

Siward frowned. "You are not ill, are you, Mother? You seem quite recovered from the sickness you had in the spring."

"Oh, of course I am, my son. But I shall not be here forever."

Siward laughed. "None of us shall. But I am sure you will be with us for some time to come." He kissed his mother's cheek. "I think I too shall go to my rest. I have an early start in the morn."

Riding swiftly along the river, Siward arrived in Gloucester before noon for his meeting with Bishop Wulfstan. After the bustling river bank, busy with boats, the tranquillity of the Priory of Saint Oswald was a welcome change. He knelt for prayers at the altar before wandering around the priory, going over everything he needed to say to the bishop. He paused by one of the graves, that of Aethelflaed, the beloved Lady of the Mercians, who had ruled more than a hundred years before. The daughter of the mighty King Alfred and the sister of another powerful king, she had been a formidable ruler in her own right. Tears prickled Siward's eyes. Those must have been good days to be an Englishman when even the royal women were admirable leaders. Now there was not even a man worthy of the title.

"My son," said a voice from behind him.

Siward turned and bowed to Bishop Wulfstan. "Greetings, Father." He glanced at another man in clerical robes standing behind him.

"May I present Father Leofwine," the Bishop said.

"The Bishop of Lichfield?" Siward asked. "Forgive me, Father, for not recognising you."

"The former bishop," Leofwine said in a gloomy tone. "I have not held the office in some years."

"Few Englishmen have," Siward replied.

Leofwine scowled. "That Norman bishop, Lanfranc, claimed that because I am wed, I am not fit to hold office. But all know it was a trumped up charge to rid themselves of an English bishop."

Wulfstan nodded. "My personal belief is that priests should not be wed, any more than Christ himself was wed. But of course your marriage is a true one and your wife is a god fearing woman who did much for your flock."

"Exactly," Leofwine said.

Wulfstan smiled at Siward. "My son, I think I can guess why you are here. Lord Bridwin of Lichfield has already confided in Father Leofwine."

"And I would like to come with you," Leofwine said.

Siward's eyes widened, wondering how popular this venture would be as he had made his first high ranking recruit without even trying. He smiled warmly at the priest. "I would be glad to have you with us, Father. I know it will offer comfort to the men to receive trusted spiritual guidance."

Wulfstan nodded. "I agree. It would be good."

Siward nodded at Wulfstan. "Might we be able to persuade you to come with us, Father?"

"No, my son. I shall not leave my flock. The people of England need me. I cannot desert them."

"Are you certain the Bastard will allow you to remain in your place?" Siward asked.

Wulfstan gave a gentle smile. "You are assuming my place is to be a bishop. It is true the King may not permit me that office forever, but that is no matter. My place is simply to provide guidance for the English and I shall not leave that, whatever my position. While the people have need of me and God grants me life, I shall be here for them."

Siward frowned. "Do you think I am deserting them? Do you

wish to persuade me not to go?"

"No, my son." Wulfstan laid his hand on Siward's shoulder. "You have fought long for the English but there is nothing more you can do here. I think you are right to save as many as you can from this relentless domination. But my path has never been the fight. My wish has always been to reconcile the English with those who now rule them. I shall remain here to urge the men who now rule to do so fairly, to stop the slavery, in which they confine so many. It is a practice abhorrent to God."

"It is indeed," Siward replied. "I shall pray you are successful. Truly you are a Father for the English. But, Father, you could aid me in another way. You must know of many who, like me, long for freedom even if it is in exile."

"I do, my son. I shall pass on word of your venture. And I shall make such donations as I can to smooth your way. If word spreads to the Normans, I shall intercede for you if necessary. Even King William listens to me on occasion."

"Thank you, Father," Siward replied. "I have no intention of paying my tribute to the Duke this year as I shall need such supplies for myself. I am anticipating trouble on this matter. If I can call on your support, I would be most grateful."

The Bishop nodded. "Certainly. I shall do what I can."

"Not that the Bastard cares if Englishmen starve," he muttered, turning to Leofwine. "I hope to muster a large fleet and we shall need many a priest to administer to them. Naturally my own chaplain will be coming. But if you know of others, particularly ones who have been driven from their sacred office, tell them of the venture."

"I will, my son," Leofwine said. "My wife and I are most grateful to be offered this opportunity. England holds nothing for us now."

"My wife and I feel the same way," Siward replied. "It is grievous to feel this and our future path may be dangerous but I truly feel it is the only one we have."

Chapter three

Oswyth sat very still at the table after Siward left for Gloucester, certain that if she moved she would be sick. She sipped at her ale, hoping it would ease the nausea but the yeasty taste of the liquid had the opposite effect. With her hand clamped over her mouth, she ran from the table. She only just reached the doorway before the bitter mixture rose in her throat and she vomited, splattering it over the ground. Again she retched until nothing more could come. Trembling, she slumped against the doorpost.

"Oswyth?" Alfgiva placed her hand on her shoulder. "Come, sit back down, my child. Take a drink."

Oswyth rested heavily on her mother-in-law as she returned to the table. Her cup was still full of ale, but she grimaced, feeling her gorge rise again. "Not that." Even the bitter remnants of the vomit in her mouth seemed preferable.

Alfgiva poured out some mead, diluting it with hot water. "Try this."

Oswyth took a cautious sip, glad to cleanse her mouth, although not convinced the sweetness of the mead was any better than the ale.

"Some bread might help," Alfgiva suggested, pulling a platter over to her.

Oswyth nibbled, relieved to find her stomach settling. "You can take that smirk off your face, Alfgiva," she said. "I know what you are thinking."

Alfgiva's smile widened. "When a healthy young woman with

a highly attentive young husband starts feeling sick and tired, there is an obvious conclusion. Am I wrong?"

Oswyth gave a reluctant smile. "No, I don't think so. But it is early days yet. I have missed just two moon bleedings."

"Yes, it is too early to be certain." Alfgiva put an arm around her. "But I think you should tell Siward what you suspect. He will see something is amiss and will worry that you are ill."

Oswyth laughed. "And you think he will not worry about me if I am with child? He will be more anxious than ever."

"True but I do not think you can keep it from him."

"Probably not," Oswyth replied. "But if I am with child and all goes well, it will likely be born in the spring. Just when Siward wants to leave. Either I will be great with child and travel will be dangerous, or I will have just given birth and have to travel with a tiny infant."

"The timing is certainly difficult," Alfgiva admitted. "He may have to delay the departure just a little. I doubt he can bring it forward. The winter months are too perilous for sailing."

"And every delay is dangerous," Oswyth sighed, smoothing her hands over her stomach. But she could not help smiling. If there was a child in there and she was certain there was, in spite of her cautious words to Alfgiva, it was a blessing. She prayed all would go well as she imagined Siward cradling his first-born in his arms.

Siward returned from Gloucester in high spirits, the support of the Bishop of Worcester for the venture convincing him more than ever that he had made the right decision. He was also glad to have secured the presence of Father Leofwine. A bishop, even a former one, would confer added credibility on the voyage.

Oswyth waited until they were alone, lying in his arms before she broached the subject of a child.

Siward's first reaction was one of joy. "That is wonderful news,

Oswyth." He rested his hand on her stomach. "I can scarce believe there could be new life growing in there."

Encouraged by this, Oswyth broke the news that if there was a child, it would be likely to arrive in the spring. As the careworn look she had dreaded, returned to Siward's face, she bit her lip, wishing she had allowed him a little longer to enjoy the prospect of a child before burdening him with that.

"I am sorry," she said. "I know how difficult this is."

Siward rolled onto his back. "You should not be sorry. I should be sorry. I knew this was a risk. Damn it, I should have left you untouched a while longer. I wanted you so much and now my selfish desires have endangered both you and the venture."

"No. You must not think like that. I too knew the risks but I wanted you. And do not let this risk the venture. You make such plans as you must and…"

"No, Oswyth. I am not leaving you behind." He held her tightly. "If necessary we keep some boats back. Frebern and Bridwin can go on ahead. I am not leaving you."

"But you are the leader," Oswyth protested.

"Which is why I can take this decision. Hopefully we will already be away before the child comes."

"Perhaps," Oswyth said, thinking how strange it would be to give birth in some foreign port. But as long as she had those she loved with her, it would not matter. "Do not change your plans for now, Siward. I may be wrong about the child and much could change between now and the spring."

Siward took to watching Oswyth anxiously as she was sick each morning, much to her annoyance. Finally, in exasperation, she asked Alfgiva to explain to him how normal it was, since it was obvious her word was not enough.

The harvest was a good one and Oswyth ignored Siward's instructions to rest as she supervised the preserving and pickling of their crops. There was a continuous supply of fish coming in to be smoked or dried and she knew soon the slaughter of their animals would begin, resulting in still more work. Although they would need much in the way of supplies, the fact that Siward was determined to avoid a tribute to the Bastard that year, meant he had no hesitation in encouraging everyone to eat well. The people were bemused at his confidence and Siward knew it was time to make his plans known to them all.

"My people," he said as they prepared to start the harvest celebrations. "I do not need to tell you of the hardships of these last years and I thank you all for your efforts in seeing us through them. In these last months I have come to a difficult decision. I consider our lives here intolerable. I cannot live on, never knowing when I might be driven from my lands. So, in the spring I am leaving."

There was a gasp from the watchers.

Siward held up his hand. "I am not just leaving these lands. I am leaving England in search of new lands. Lands I can truly again call my own. I am aided in these plans by Lord Bridwin of Lichfield and Lord Frebern of Warwick and already I have heard that the number of boats we can command will be huge. I wish to take with me only the finest of Englishmen." He paused and glanced with a smile at Oswyth. "And, of course, the finest of Englishwomen." Stretching out his arms, he grinned at the people. "I know of no finer than those who have served on my lands. Therefore I invite you all to leave with me and my kin, to join me on the noble quest to find for ourselves a new England."

The burst of excited chatter which followed, mingled with a few tears as everyone grasped the implications of such a change. Siward let them talk among themselves for a while before holding up a hand for silence again.

"I do not wish to deceive you. The voyage is likely to be a perilous one. Some may not survive it. Perhaps none will survive it. I am going in spite of the risks for if I die, I wish to die a free Englishman. For those who are unable or who do not wish to come, I shall endeavour to see you safe before I leave. Thralls will be freed from my service, but of course I can make no promises with regards to the status your new lords may force on you."

As the people whispered among themselves again, Siward looked at them, trying to work out which would be coming with him. He smiled as he noticed Wicrun talking in an animated fashion with a number of the younger churls. The enthusiasm was obvious.

Again Siward ordered silence, encouraged by the reaction. "I am aided in my efforts by the Bishop of Worcester who remains, as always, the finest father the English have known. Make no immediate decisions, but consider carefully my words. For now, it remains only for me to thank God for his bounty and you for your efforts. It is the last harvest I shall see here and so it is fitting it has been one of the finest. And, my friends, we shall keep it all. None of this will fatten the bellies of the Bastard and his kin." Siward threw a handful of wheat shafts into the air in the traditional gesture of thanks to the land. "Let there be no sorrow tonight. For this night, let us celebrate!"

The people cheered, helping themselves to ale and clustering around the great fires upon which pigs had been set to roast. Siward watched them, listening as the musicians struck up the same merry tunes he had heard all his life. His eyes filled with tears as he wondered when and where he would next celebrate a harvest.

Oswyth slipped an arm around his waist. "No sorrow tonight, Siward. That is what you said."

Siward smiled, kissing her tenderly. "You are right. It is on nights such as this one, I particularly remember your grandfather. He knew his lands would go to the invaders but he was content knowing you were safe. Well, it is to be the same for me. They will have my lands but it is the people who are most important. You, Mother, Father Colman. All these people. My good friends, Bridwin and Frebern. As long as I keep you all safe, I too must be content."

He slid his hand down to run it over Oswyth's swelling stomach. She was starting to feel faint flutters inside her although they were not yet strong enough for Siward to feel. But even so he smiled. "And most important of all, my child shall be born free."

Chapter four

When the first demand for the yearly tribute came, Siward simply made vague promises. But as the winter came upon them, a second one arrived, far more insistent.

"There has been an unfortunate delay," Siward said smoothly. "It is a trivial matter which I shall soon rectify. Please assure your master the tribute will be sent very soon."

He watched with wry amusement as the messenger rode away.

"Surely they will return," Oswyth said.

"Of course," Siward replied. "But travelling is harder in the winter for them as it is for us. As soon as the weather improves, I shall start moving our produce off the land. Father Wulfstan is arranging abbeys and other such places where we can store it until the boats are ready. I trust him to keep it safe. Those men can return but they will find nothing here. No doubt they will turf me off my lands but as I am leaving anyway, that is of no significance."

Messages continued to pass between Siward, Frebern and Bridwin and shortly before Christmas, Bishop Wulfstan paid them a visit. He had been busy on their behalf, commandeering not only plenty of storage but also another hundred boats.

"But Siward and his friends already had two hundred and fifty," Oswyth exclaimed. "Can we really fill so many?"

Siward nodded. "If the recent communications from Bridwin are anything to go by, yes we shall be glad of these extra boats.

There are so many who have been driven from their lands or fear they will soon be forced away. Once they have brought their kin and entourage, the numbers are vast indeed."

"Can we feed so many?" Oswyth asked. The harvest had seemed fine but in the light of so many, it dwindled considerably.

Siward smiled. "Naturally every man who comes must bring provisions. And on our journey we shall purchase or raid for more. We shall manage."

"I hope so," Oswyth murmured, daunted by this. Never had she dreamed this venture would become so large. She smiled at the bishop. "I suppose we cannot tempt you into coming?"

Wulfstan shook his head. "No, my child. I am far too old for such a venture. But you take my blessings with you."

Alfgiva had stood quietly while they had been speaking but in a lull in the conversation she looked at the bishop. "Father, I wonder if I might have a private word."

"Of course, my daughter. Shall we go to the church?"

"Is something amiss, Mother?" Siward asked.

Alfgiva smiled and shook her head. "A spiritual matter I must discuss. Do not concern yourself."

For their last Christmas in England, Siward ordered the festivities to be lavish. There was music and laughter in the hall, with fine dishes of spiced meat, the best ales and rich wines. Only occasionally did Siward allow his thoughts to drift to where he might be for the next Christmas and swiftly he forced them away again. He looked around the hall, hung with winter greenery and out at the faces of those he had known all his life as well those who had come to him more recently. Slipping an arm around Oswyth's shoulders, he reflected that wherever he went, he had a lot to be thankful for.

After several days of merriments the festivities came to an

end and Siward knew it was time to start packing up everything he intended to take. Oswyth and Alfgiva had been busy all autumn with the produce so they had plenty of smoked, salted and dried meat and fish and great rounds of cheese. Fruits, roots and beans had also been dried or pickled which added to the sacks of grains should sustain them for a considerable time. In the last weeks they would make dry, flat breads which would not easily spoil and brew vast quantities of ale, storing as much as they could in barrels ready for their voyage.

Siward still worried about Oswyth. She was now considerably larger but she insisted she was feeling well. Often he wondered if she would admit to feeling anything less but as she worked with her usual energy, Siward began to hope they would be well away from England before the child arrived.

The day after the final Christmas celebration had been a quiet one with everyone still somewhat bleary eyed from their revels. Siward was glad to take a day of rest, bracing himself for the final burst of activity before departure. It was in the evening that Alfgiva approached him.

"Siward, Oswyth, I need to talk to you both."

"Of course, Mother." Siward gestured to a chair. "What do you wish to say?"

Alfgiva was silent for a long time, wetting her lips nervously as she tried to find the words. "My dearest son, I am not coming with you."

Siward brought his cup down to the table so vehemently that the ale splashed over the sides. "What?"

"But you have to," Oswyth exclaimed. "Where else can you go?"

Alfgiva gripped her hand. "To a convent, my child. To spend my last years seeing to my salvation."

"No, Mother. Do not do this." Siward ran his hands through his hair, trying to think of a solution. "We can have convents in New England. You can found one. You can be the abbess."

Alfgiva smiled and shook her head. "I do not want to be an abbess, my son. I want to spend my days in devotion and peace."

"But, Mother…" Siward's face was white, her words ringing in his ears as if he had just received a blow to the head. He tried to move his lips to make further protests, but nothing would come.

"Please, Siward, try to understand." Alfgiva cupped his face in her hands. "This venture is for the young. You can make a new life for yourselves. But for me, it will not be so. You would be taking me away simply to bury me in foreign soil. I have seen more than half a century now. I shall not be here much longer."

"Mother, why have you never said this before?" Siward cried. "Perhaps I need not have made such plans to leave."

"But you do need to leave," Alfgiva said. "There is nothing here for you now. My dearest boy, is this really so unexpected? You know I first intended to enter a convent when your father died. I wished to wait only until you had settled into his role before I could make my vows. But of course, our lives changed. Just a half year after your father died, the Bastard came. I saw how it affected you and I knew I could not leave you. I planned then to wait until you married." She gave a faint smile. "I might not have waited if I'd known how long it would take for you to wed."

"But I have been married nearly two years," Siward said. "You cannot deny that it is this voyage which is influencing you."

Alfgiva shook her head. "When you and Oswyth wed, I did consider leaving then, indeed I would have done had I not realised how ill matters were between you. I would have felt I was deserting you at a time you needed me more than ever. But now all is different. You and Oswyth are so happy together. You do not need me now."

"A good son is always glad of his mother." Siward choked over his words and Alfgiva cradled him in her arms.

"You are the best son. Oh, Siward, I had almost given up hope of a living child. For almost ten years of marriage I bore children who lived no longer than a month or two and some who did not even survive their birth. Then you were born and somehow I knew straight away you would be different. And so you have been. You grew up so strong, so handsome, the finest son any mother could wish for. It has been my privilege to watch you grow for more than twenty-six years. I never could have stayed with you forever."

As Siward's gaze dropped, tears filling his eyes, Oswyth looked from her husband to her mother-in-law, feeling an intruder on this moment. "But what of our child? Do you not want to see that?" she asked.

Alfgiva smiled gently. "Part of me does," she admitted. "But you two must be away and it is enough for me that I have felt the child stir in you. So many mothers have lost their sons in these last years. I am truly fortunate that I have lived to see mine become happy. Please, Siward. This is what I want. Give me your blessing."

Reluctantly Siward nodded. "Where will you go?"

"In the morn I wish you to accompany me to Gloucester where I shall meet with Father Wulfstan. He is expecting me."

"Tomorrow? Mother, what is the rush?"

"A long goodbye will be unbearable for us both, my son. It is better this way."

"And then where will you go?" Siward asked.

"Father Wulfstan is headed to Canterbury to consult with Bishop Odo, the Bastard's brother. I shall enter a convent there. It seems Bishop Odo is having a hanging made to commemorate the events which brought his brother to the throne. He needs fine needlewomen." Alfgiva looked at some of the hangings on the wall with an air of preening herself. "I am known to be one of the finest."

"You will spend your days making a cloth to glorify the Bastard?" Siward exclaimed, a harsh note he instantly regretted entering his voice.

Alfgiva laughed. "No, my son. Not to glorify. I know we shall have to follow the bishop's instructions but we shall tell the story as it happened and we shall have ways of making our opinions known. We shall show the houses burnt to the ground, so all know what the Bastard did to achieve his victory."

Siward shook his head. In spite of the weight crushing his

heart, he could not help but feel amused at the thought of the widowed and dispossessed women of England in this act of defiance. He suspected it would take a braver man than the bishop to interfere too much in their work.

"And we shall portray the brave Englishmen fighting and dying for their land. As we stitch, we shall remember them, all those good men, like your father, my dear." She squeezed Oswyth's hand. "There will be tears, of course. But into every stitch we shall put our pride."

Oswyth's own tears overflowed and she flung her arms around her mother-in-law, with no words.

Alfgiva's face was serene as she patted her on the shoulder. "Perhaps, my child, one day, when you are settled, you will make your own hanging. One which tells of your escape from the slavery the tyrant imposed on you and how you built England again."

Chapter five

In spite of Alfgiva's instructions, Oswyth shed many tears as she bade farewell to her mother-in-law.

"None of that, my child," she said as Siward prepared the horses. "I want to remember you smiling."

Oswyth wiped her eyes. "Sorry." She tried to force her mouth into a smile. "You have been as a mother to me and it has been so good to have a mother again."

Alfgiva hugged her. "And you have been as a daughter to me. Although perhaps you have been even more than that." She was silent for a moment. "If you bear a son, you will understand."

"What do you mean?"

"When you cradle your son in your arms, you will have so many hopes and dreams for him. And one of them is that he finds a wife who loves him with the same devotion you do. I think now you do."

Oswyth's face broke into the smile Alfgiva had requested. "Oh, I do. I know what a poor wife I was to him in the beginning. But now he has my whole heart."

"Which is why I can leave him with a clear conscience, knowing he will not be alone. You have been the answer to my prayers. Look after him for me, Oswyth."

Oswyth nodded, a lump choking her throat. "I will."

Alfgiva held her close once again. "And look after yourself. I shall be praying for you and your child. I wonder what you will have. Probably I shall never know but that does not matter. I can picture you both, so proud and happy. That is enough for me."

"Are you ready, Mother?" Siward said, leading two saddled horses and a third laden with the belongings Alfgiva would donate to her convent.

"Farewell, my child," Alfgiva said, hugging Oswyth one last time.

"Farewell," Oswyth whispered, still unable to believe she was going.

Alfgiva looked once more at the hall, raising her hand to those who had gathered to see her leave. She had been a kind if eccentric mistress and there were tears on the cheeks of many. Then she turned resolutely away, her own face free of tears and her eyes untroubled.

Siward helped her onto the horse and she did not look back as they trotted briskly away.

∞∞∞

The start of their ride to Gloucester was silent, with mother and son having no words for each other. Siward cursed himself for the waste of their last day but he had no idea what to say. To chat on trivial matters to the mother he soon would never see again seemed pointless, but to say anything more profound would, he was sure, reduce him to tears.

"Really, Siward," Alfgiva said after a while. "I am very glad you will not be around me on my deathbed since this is how you behave simply because I am retiring to a convent."

Siward laughed at that. His mother's life had not been the easiest but her cheerful optimism had never failed, even in the bleakest of times. He would miss it. "What shall we talk about, Mother?"

"Tell me of your voyage. You must have some idea where you will head, otherwise you will simply sail around in circles."

"True. We will head south and enter the Mediterranean Sea. There are lands there in the hands of heathens and Saracens. Perhaps we will take them for ourselves. Or perhaps we will find a god fearing lord we will be proud to serve. I can go anywhere. It is a daunting prospect and yet I feel a curious freedom in it."

Alfgiva smiled. "Perhaps you will go to Rome or even Jerusalem."

"That too is possible," Siward said.

"God will be with you, my son. I know these last years it has felt that God has deserted the English but truly He has not."

∞∞∞

They were welcomed at the priory in Gloucester by Bishop Wulfstan. "I trust this has not been too great a shock for you, my son," the Bishop said as Alfgiva went forward to kneel before the altar.

"It has been a shock and a grief," Siward said frankly. "But I know she has made the right decision. I do not know what I was thinking, wishing to force her from her native land at this time in her life. I am a poor son."

"I heard that, Siward," Alfgiva said, turning away from her devotions.

Siward had to laugh as he hugged his mother. "If you are to reside in a convent, you will need to learn to focus more on your prayers."

Father Wulfstan nodded to him. "I shall give you two a moment together. When you are ready to leave, you will find young Frebern of Warwick in the guest quarters. He wishes to consult with you on some matters before you meet at the Severn Sea so I suggested he come here this day. I thought it might be good for you not to be alone."

Siward smiled his gratitude, relieved he would have company that night. As soon as they were alone, he held his mother tighter than he ever had before.

"Oh, Mother. How am I supposed to walk out of here, knowing I will never see you again?"

"You will do it because there comes a time when every

mother and son must part. For some mothers it is at the time of their child's birth. Others keep them a little longer. But look at Oswyth. She had to part from her mother as a child often."

"That is true," Siward said.

"And Frebern was not much older when his mother died."

"I know," Siward said. "You are reminding me that I am ungrateful. I have had a mother, the finest mother for more than twenty-six years. But one day you will die and I will not even know it. On that day I may be hunting, feasting, laughing as you breathe your last. What sort of son does that make me?"

"Oh, Siward, you have no idea how much I hope that is the case. It will bring me such peace in my final hours to think of you so happy. If you think of me on occasion, tell your children of me, then you are the very best son."

"Mother, you will be in my prayers every night and we will talk of you often. If I am ever blessed with a daughter, she will be named for you."

Alfgiva smiled, smoothing his hair away from his face. "This is the end of my earthly life, Siward. If you feel you must mourn my death, do it now. My life would not have lasted much longer in any case. I have lived long enough to see you become happy and that brings me such joy. Look after Oswyth. She can be a silly girl, but her heart is great. She loves you."

"And I love her," Siward said. "Yes, I am fortunate. I had the finest mother and now I have the finest wife. In the kings he sent, God did not grant me good men to serve but in the women he granted me, he gave me the finest. I hate that I am leaving you under the rule of the Bastard."

Alfgiva kissed his cheek. "You are not. In the convent I shall serve only God. It shall matter not a bit who is the earthly king. Like you, I shall have my freedom at last. Now go, Siward. This will only become harder, the more you linger. Say farewell and go find your freedom."

Siward kept his tears from spilling over as he hugged his mother again. Her body was thin and he knew she was frailer than she had been just a few years before. Yet the expression on her face was tranquil, the smile the same gentle smile which had blessed him his entire life.

"God's blessings on you, my beloved son."

"And on you too, dearest Mother. Farewell."

Planting one last kiss on her cheek and letting his arms slip away from her was the hardest thing he had ever had to do. But he managed it, stumbling away with tears blurring his vision. He paused at the door. Blinking them away, he could not resist one last look.

Alfgiva was watching him, a few tears on her cheeks yet still smiling. In her eyes he could see how peaceful she appeared and he knew she had found her new home. She raised her hand before turning to kneel again before the altar, her body completely relaxed. Siward smiled through his own tears, turning away himself and shutting the door softly behind him.

Outside he could see Frebern watching him. He came slowly forward.

"Greetings, Siward. Do you want to be alone?"

"Alone?" Siward shook his head, his voice breaking. "That is the last thing I want."

Frebern said nothing more, his face uncharacteristically serious as he took his friend into his arms. And Siward, remembering how he had held Frebern after the death of his mother, allowed his tears to flow freely.

Chapter six

Oswyth felt restless after Alfgiva and Siward left. Even before they were out of sight, she found herself missing her mother-in-law. Resolutely she turned back, knowing of the amount of work which still needed to be done. That day they would be slaughtering one of the last remaining cows. Over the next days they would preserve the meat, while the hide would be stitched into packs for their clothing and blankets. The winter's day was bright and clear, but Oswyth gave only one regretful glance around before returning to the hall.

She half smiled at the doleful expressions on the faces of the other women. Everyone would miss how Alfgiva's cheerful chatter helped make the tasks lighter.

"Come," she said, determined to be no less of an inspiration than Alfgiva. "Let us start the brewing of another batch of ale. There is still plenty of grain."

She grimaced at a cramp in her body as she tossed some wood on the fire, coaxing the dull glow into a small blaze. The crisp chill from outside had filtered into the hall and she would be likely to spend much of the day sitting still as they worked. Later it would also be useful for smoking the meat.

Mixing the ale was a pleasant enough task as the warm, yeasty aroma filled the hall. But as she worked she was aware of another cramp in her body, a sharper one. She gave a faint gasp.

"Is all well, my lady?" one of the women asked.

Oswyth smiled. "I have been sitting still for too long."

She got up, feeling the pain ebb away. A faint bellow from

outside told her the cow had just been slaughtered. Once it had been skinned they would bring her the cuts of meat. In the cold weather it would not spoil easily and she decided to keep some back for them to eat fresh. It might be an extravagance to eat beef on an ordinary occasion but she guessed Siward would be in need of cheering when he returned. As thoughts of Alfgiva intruded again, tears rushed to her eyes but she pushed them away, resolved to keep morale high. She was about to issue some further instructions when another pain came.

"Are you sure all is well?" the woman asked, laying her hand on Oswyth's arm.

Oswyth hesitated, looking down at her swollen stomach. "I… I am not sure."

"Perhaps you should rest, my lady," the woman said, urging Oswyth over to a chair.

"I am sure it is nothing." Oswyth looked pleadingly at the woman, ignoring the fear flickering through her.

She gave a reassuring smile. "Well, if it is nothing, there is still no harm in you resting a while, is there?"

Oswyth too smiled, staring uneasily at the fire, praying that would be the last of the pains. But it was a forlorn hope. By noon the pains had come several more times, building up and ebbing away.

"It cannot be the child, can it?" Oswyth said fearfully to the woman. "It should not come for another few months."

"I do not know, my lady. But I think I should summon the midwife to be with you, just in case."

Oswyth clenched her fists, trying to tell herself she was imagining the grave expressions on the faces of all around her. She sat very still, terrified the slightest movement would make everything worse.

When the midwife came, she gently pressed her fingers against Oswyth's stomach, her face not changing at all. "Are you in pain now?" she asked.

"No. It comes and goes. All will be well, won't it?"

"I cannot say at present," the midwife said, keeping her hand against Oswyth's stomach. "Tell me when you feel another pain."

Oswyth continued to sit still, hoping there would be no more pains and the woman would be able to depart. But all too soon another pain built up.

"Your belly tightens with the pain," the woman muttered. "That is not so good."

"But I have felt that tightening for a while now. Alfgiva said it was normal."

"Without the pain it is normal," the midwife said, the sympathy in her gaze frightening Oswyth more than ever.

"The baby cannot come this day," Oswyth cried. "It is too soon. Can you not do something?"

"All we can do is keep you rested," the midwife said. "Put your feet up and relax. This pain is not a good sign but it may not be a bad one. Hopefully it will soon stop."

Far from stopping, the pains became more frequent and harsher, leaving her unable to restrain her cries. The work in the hall ground to a halt as the women stared helplessly at her, their expressions growing more anxious with each one. As a gush of liquid, soaked her kirtle, several cried out themselves, all eyes going to the midwife.

"I am sorry, my lady," the midwife muttered. "There is nothing we can do to stop this now."

"No," Oswyth cried. "It is too soon. The baby cannot survive this."

The midwife squeezed her hand. "I know. You must be brave." She turned to one of the women. "Fetch the priest. Lady Oswyth must be shriven."

When Father Colman came, Oswyth blurted out every sin she could think of. Every flash of anger, every impatient word, every moment of inappropriate levity. She kept talking through the pains, desperate to avoid the night ahead. Almost she wondered if she confessed every sin, God might yet intervene to save her child.

"My daughter," Colman said in a gentle tone as Oswyth voiced the latest triviality. "This is no sin. You have confessed every-thing and all has been forgiven. Now you must let the women look after you. I shall be praying for you."

Oswyth burst into tears as the midwife put an arm around her to lead her to the bedchamber. Frantically her mind scrambled to another possibility. Perhaps she was further along than she thought. She had heard of it happening, with sturdy infants ar-riving almost by surprise. As the women removed her wet kir-tle, she clung onto the impossible hope. The only way she knew to get through the ordeal was to imagine Siward returning the next day to find her with a healthy baby in her arms.

The women were kind, urging drinks of mead on her and rub-bing her body with oils. The pains became ever fiercer, sweep-ing through her with a ferocity Oswyth had never known was possible. Close to her ear the midwife whispered prayers and entreaties in a never ending stream which she barely heard through her own agonised cries.

"I... I need to push," she whispered, clutching onto the mid-wife's hand.

"That is good. It will soon be over," the midwife said, stroking her hair.

Oswyth did not want to push. She wanted to keep the child safely inside her but try as she might, she could not avoid it. She screamed with the pain of it, the pitch reaching a new despair at the look on the faces of the women. She knew they held out no hope.

The pain was never ending as cry after cry tore through her. Her throat grew hoarse from her screams in a way which would normally be painful, but compared to the torment consuming the rest of her body, was scarcely noticeable.

"It will soon be over, my lady," the midwife muttered.

In one of the brief lulls in the pain, Oswyth saw her take up a little pot of water, dipping her fingers in. Another woman held Oswyth close as the fingers probed inside her.

"I baptise thee in the name of God the Father, Son and Holy Spirit," the midwife said.

Oswyth burst into fresh tears as she pushed again. She knew it was only when there was no hope that the midwife would take on a priest's task. One of the older women drew Oswyth's head against her breast for the last moments as the child eased from her.

In the stillness which followed, Oswyth did not dare look up. It was the moment she had so eagerly anticipated, when the baby would let out its first cry. But this one was silent. She kept her face buried in the woman's shoulder, the pain almost non-existent as they dealt with the afterbirth.

"There, it is over," the woman said, trying to smile as they pushed cloths between her legs to staunch the blood she could feel running from her. "You have been very brave. Rest now."

Oswyth looked up, seeing the midwife wrap a white, blood stained object in linen. "What was it?" she asked, her lips stiff.

The midwife hesitated but realising it would be kinder to be honest, she sat back down. "It was a girl. Do you wish to see?"

Oswyth hesitated but she could not reject a glimpse of her daughter. She nodded, afraid of what she would see. The midwife withdrew the cloth and Oswyth looked down at a tiny face. The skin was flaky but that could not obscure the perfection of her features.

"I am sorry," Oswyth whispered, overwhelmed by how small she was. If it were not for the whiteness of the skin, she might have thought it a baby asleep.

The midwife covered the face again, squeezing Oswyth's hand. "I know this is hard but there is no reason to think you will not be more fortunate in the future. She was baptised just before her birth. Her soul is safe with God."

Oswyth slumped back against the pillows. "I know."

As the midwife left, one of the women pushed a cup of hot broth into her hands. Oswyth sipped at it. She didn't really want it but with no energy to argue, it seemed easier just to drink.

"You must rest now, my lady. It will soon be morning."

Oswyth looked around, bewildered that the night had come and almost past without her realising it. Soon the sun would rise on her failure. Some time that day Siward would return to be given the news. She would have to see him grieve, knowing she had failed him. She had tried so hard to be a good wife, but she had not delivered the child he longed for.

Her mind went to Alfgiva, missing her more than ever. She too had lost children and would be one who could truly understand the pain she was feeling. How comforting her loving arms would be at that moment.

But her next thought was to be glad Alfgiva was no longer there. She need never know the grandchild she had been so happy about was now to be placed into the cold earth.

Chapter seven

Siward rode home, his head pounding. The previous night he and Frebern had quickly concluded their discussions and had proceeded to one of the ale houses of the town. There they had drunk without restraint, Siward glad to forget his cares for a night. But as every thud of his horse's hooves juddered through him, he was regretting it now. The crisp winter air was at least soothing. He paused for a moment, taking in some deep breaths and glancing back at the priory he could just glimpse through the trees. He wondered if his mother was still there or if she had already started her journey to Canterbury.

"God speed, Mother," he muttered, turning away.

He did not hurry his journey, letting the fresh air drive away the effects of the drink. He and Frebern had been up almost until dawn, so he was feeling weary as with the winter sun already low in the sky, he eventually arrived home.

As he entered the hall he wondered if he was imagining the emptiness as a hush seemed to fall on the people present. He was assuming it was the absence of his mother which was causing it, but as he tried to smile his greetings, he became unnerved at how everyone was staring at him.

"What is wrong?" he asked. He looked around the hall, disappointed his wife was not there to greet him. Her beautiful smile would do much to take the emptiness away. "Someone tell Lady Oswyth I have returned." He assumed she was in one of the stores but all he wanted at that moment was some food and lacked the energy to look for her himself.

The long silence continued as Siward sat down. No one had moved. "Did you hear me?" he asked. He took in the sombre faces and his heart sped up, although he had no idea why he felt so nervous. "Where is Oswyth?"

Father Colman hurried in. "I thought I saw you return, my son," he said. "It is good you are here."

Siward paused in the act of taking a mouthful of ale to stare at the solemn expression of the priest. "What has happened? Where is Oswyth?"

"Your wife was taken ill shortly after you left yesterday."

"Ill?" Siward dropped his cup, taking no notice as the ale soaked into the rushes on the floor. "What do you mean? Is it the child?"

Father Colman placed his hand over Siward's and nodded. "I am sorry, my son. She delivered a child without breath shortly before dawn this morning."

Siward continued to stare. Dawn. So, at the very moment he and Frebern had been heading merrily to a few hours rest, Oswyth had been in pain, probably afraid and weeping and she had endured it alone.

"What of Oswyth? Where is she? Will she recover? My God, Father, please tell me she is not also dead," Siward cried.

"No. She came through the ordeal. She is in great distress, of course and will need a lot of care but the midwife is hopeful she will recover."

"Where is she?" Siward stared at the door to the bedchamber, realising it was a foolish question. The room where she had lain so often in his arms would be where she had brought forth her dead child. "I must go to her."

"She may be sleeping, my lord," one of the women ventured. "We hope she is, in any case."

"I must see her," Siward said, overcome with the urge to make sure she was still with him. He could feel all eyes following him as he pushed open the door, gently so as not to disturb her if she was at rest.

A single candle lit up the room and he could see Oswyth was

not asleep. She was lying on the bed, staring upwards. She must have felt the draft from the doorway but even as the candle flickered, she did not look in his direction. A woman was sitting beside her and Siward gestured to her, to indicate he wished to be left alone. He sat down in the space she had left, gazing on Oswyth's white face. She turned her head, her blue eyes filled with the despair he remembered so vividly in her father's dying eyes.

"I am so sorry," she whispered.

Siward shook his head, slipping his arm around her. Almost he snatched it away at how different her body felt. The swelling stomach, he had loved to lay his arm gently over, was already gone. She felt small and fragile. He shifted his arm slightly, finding the empty stomach too hard to touch, bringing his lips to her forehead. "Do not say that. This was not your fault."

"Whose fault was it then? All I had to do was grow the child for a little longer. I failed."

"Oh, Oswyth, these matters happen, my love. It is no one's fault. We will be more fortunate in the future, I am sure of it."

Oswyth's eyes filled with tears. "It was a girl."

"She would have been beautiful, just like you," Siward replied

The tears spilled over as she allowed her grief to flow out onto Siward's shoulder. Siward too wept, silently into her hair. Eventually she pulled away, wiping her eyes.

"I am sorry. I have not asked about your mother. Was all well?"

Siward nodded. "Yes. It was the right decision for her. We shall miss her, of course." His voice trailed away as he realised how he would miss her that night as for no other. The loss of the infant awakened in him a wish to sob as a child in his mother's arms, but she was no longer there and he needed to be strong for Oswyth.

"I am glad this happened after she left," Oswyth said, staring at the ceiling again. "After losing so many herself, I would not have wished this to be her last memory of us."

Siward's eyes filled afresh, awed at his wife thinking of another at such a time. He held her close to him once more, wishing he had some words to comfort her. All he could hope was that his presence would somehow help.

"I don't know what to do," Oswyth whispered. "I feel so empty."

Siward stroked her hair. "Just get better. I need you to recover. My mother is gone, my daughter is gone. I cannot cope with losing my beloved wife."

Oswyth closed her eyes, the tears still breaking through, even as a tortured smile flickered over her lips. "I shall try."

∞∞∞

To everyone's relief, Oswyth grew a little stronger each day. With Siward's coaxing, she ate and drank, letting the food nourish her body even if she could barely taste it. The bleeding too eased and the women were confident she would recover. Everyone was adamant she should not shorten the lying in period and Siward too begged her to rest.

"I think I shall leave the bedchamber today," she said to him one morning, three weeks after the birth. The lying in had been tortuous, with nothing to do. The milk had come in to her breasts, causing them to swell and leak with no baby there to suckle. It had been a relief when it had finally dried up and the pain had eased.

"Are you sure?" Siward asked. "You're not yet yourself."

"I need to," she replied. "I cannot keep lying here in the chamber where..." Unable to speak the words, her voice trailed away. She forced a smile. "It will help to be busy again. I can rest easily enough by the fire if I am tired."

Siward nodded his understanding, calling for a woman to bring Oswyth some water to cleanse herself. He waited nearby, knowing she would need his support as she left seclusion to face everybody.

In the brighter light of the hall, Siward had to hide his horror at the whiteness of her skin, broken only by the black shadows in the hollows of her eyes. She looked around in bewilderment, her gaze sliding away from the pity she could see on all faces. Swiftly he put his arm around her, shocked by how thin she felt.

"I have told Father Colman you are rising," he said. "As soon as you feel able, you are to be churched."

Oswyth nodded, wanting to get the ceremony over with. "I am ready now." She had always imagined the churching as a joyful experience, with a lusty infant squalling in Siward's arms.

Siward pulled her closer, keeping his arm around her to make their way slowly to the church. Father Colman greeted her with the same sympathy everyone else was showing and her hands shook as she took the candle, processing forward to kneel before the altar. There all she could do was concentrate on keeping her tears at bay, barely hearing the prayers Father Colman was chanting as he gave thanks for her recovery.

It was a relief when he laid his hand on her head in the final blessing and she could leave the church. Beyond it was the burial ground where Siward's father and other kin lay. It was where all of his siblings had also been placed, close to the eaves of the church so even if a baptism had not been possible, God's own waters would bless them. Oswyth found herself drawn to it, ignoring Siward's protests that she should return to the warmth of the hall.

She stared at the ground with its rough stones, her eyes going to a bare patch of earth where grass had not yet grown. She knew she was looking at the spot where her daughter had been laid to rest.

Her composure broke and she slumped against Siward, the tears flowing faster than ever. He held her tightly with no words, his own cheeks growing wet. The child had been the focus for their hopes but now it was just one more broken dream they would have to leave behind.

Chapter eight

Siward missed his mother more than ever when he realised
that night, he had no idea if it would be right for him to go
to his wife. Probably one of the other women could have
told him but, ashamed of his ignorance, he was not comfortable
questioning them. Oswyth had retired early but was still awake
when he went in.

He sat down beside her. "Is it safe for me to lie with you?"

"Yes," she replied.

"Are you certain?"

She nodded and Siward undressed, sliding into bed next to
her, eager to forget the grief of the last weeks. Gladly he brought
his lips to hers, letting his hand drift lightly down her body, trying to enjoy the soft curves without bittersweet memories of
how beautiful he had found her body when she carried his child.
Oswyth gave no response and Siward pulled away, his brow
creased.

"We do not have to do this tonight," he said.

"I am fine," Oswyth replied. "Do not stop."

Siward tried again, gently stroking her body, alert for any sign
from her. But there was nothing. It had never been like that
between them. From the first time they had lain together, Oswyth's normal style was to welcome him with a kiss and an
inviting smile, unless she was too tired in which case she was
direct in telling him. For her to neither welcome nor reject was
disconcerting.

He moved away again. "Let me just hold you tonight. There is no rush for more."

He put his arms around her, aware of the tension tightening her body. Miserably he wondered if yet again he was doing the wrong thing. "Do you want me to go?" he whispered.

Oswyth's body went limp, slumping against him. She clung tightly to him, breaking into sobs yet again. "No. Do not leave me."

∞∞∞

As they dressed the next morning, he glanced at Oswyth, noticing her drooping posture and the pallor of her face. He continued to watch as she wrapped her hair, remembering how he had once told her how much he loved seeing her comb the long, blonde tresses. Ever since she had carried out that action with a flirtatious smile, while pretending not to look at him. But that morning she did not so much as glance in his direction and her mouth looked as if it would never smile again. His heart ached. The loss of the child seemed to have done what nothing else could – it had broken her spirit.

He was weary himself as he and Oswyth left the chamber, the excitement of the venture ahead swamped by grief and care. His arm was around her shoulders, but he was not sure if she was even aware of it. He poured himself a cup of ale and was sipping at it distractedly as his mind ran over everything he would need to do that day when there was a kerfuffle from the doorway. Wicrun entered, dragging a raggedly dressed boy with him.

"You wait until the good Lord Siward hears about this, my boy," Wicrun said, pushing the boy forward.

"I did not take anything," the boy cried. "I am no thief."

"What is going on?" Siward asked.

"I caught this wretch in one of the stores, my lord. Stealing."

"I was not stealing," the boy said with a defiant look at Siward.

Siward frowned. "What were you doing?"

"Sleeping," the boy replied. "I got here late last night. The hall was bolted. I did not want to disturb you."

Oswyth's curiosity momentarily drove away her grief as she studied the boy. Beggars were not uncommon, but they would not normally sleep in any of the huts without permission. "Were you coming to see us?"

"Yes, my lady," the boy muttered.

"Why?" she asked.

"I have heard you have a great fleet, that you are leaving England to find a land of your own. I want to come," he announced.

Siward raised an eyebrow. "Where are your parents?"

"Dead." There was no apparent distress on the boy's face but he looked down, his fists clenching.

"How old are you?"

"I have seen nearly eleven years, my lord."

Siward cast an eye over the boy's ragged tunic and stick-like limbs. "What possessions do you have?"

The boy shrugged. "Not much."

"I told you, my lord. He is a thief," Wicrun burst in.

Siward shook his head at him before looking back at the boy. "My venture is for strong men with the means to support themselves. I cannot take orphans."

The boy's face fell. "I do not want to stay here where the invaders rule. I want to come with you."

"It is not possible," Siward replied, draining his cup. He got to his feet to start his day's tasks. As he passed him, he ruffled the boy's head, hoping it wasn't as riddled with lice as he suspected. "Talk to my priest. He will know of a household or abbey where you can be safe."

The boy shoved his hand away. "If you do not take me with you, you will be sorry. When I am a man, I shall assemble my own fleet. I will come after you. I shall invade wherever you have settled and take your lands for my own."

Silence descended on the hall and Siward turned with a frown, intending to give the impertinent little brat a good clip around the ear when the stillness was broken by the most beautiful sound. Oswyth had burst out laughing in a proper laugh, which rang through the hall. The boy scowled at her, not happy at his announcement treated with such mirth. His scowl deepened as this only made it harder for her to control her giggles.

Siward folded his arms, his own sense of humour getting the better of him. "I do not even possess the lands of which you speak and yet already you have declared war on me. I am unfortunate indeed to face such a formidable foe. Perhaps I should surrender my lands this day, as I fear you will be harder even than the Bastard to oppose."

The boy directed his scowl at Siward as Oswyth sat down, clutching her sides with tears of laughter rolling down cheeks flushed pink from the hilarity. Others in the hall too started to laugh and Siward grinned. "Do not look so offended. I am not mocking you. Or perhaps I am but you will have to get used to that if you are coming with me."

The boy's scowl vanished and he gaped up at Siward. "I can come?"

Siward smiled. The boy's hazel eyes were so different from Oswyth's blue ones but the excited joy in them was exactly the same as when he had told Oswyth she could come. It seemed every time he thought the heart had gone from England, someone was there to prove him wrong. "What is your name, Boy?"

"Wulfric, my lord."

"And where are you from?"

"Lincoln, my lord."

Oswyth's eyes widened in surprise that the boy had trekked such a distance to join them. Siward too was impressed, thinking that such resourcefulness might well serve them better than any possession. He patted the boy on the head.

"Well, Wulfric of Lincoln, welcome to our venture."

The boy's face broke into a wide grin. "Thank you, my lord. I shall do whatever you command."

Siward nodded. "We do not depart for some weeks yet. I trust you can make yourself useful around here until we leave."

"Yes, my lord. Anything you want."

"Good. I have much to do but I shall talk more to you later. In the meantime behave yourself for my lady. I wish to hear of no cheek when I return."

∞∞∞∞

Siward's belief that the boy would be a useful addition was strengthened when he returned to the hall that afternoon to find him looking considerably cleaner and neatly dressed. He was assisting Oswyth with the preparations for the evening meal, while regaling her with a highly improbable account of his journey across the realm. Siward shook his head but did not interrupt, seeing the amusement on Oswyth's face. He reflected he would take on a dozen of such orphans if it would make Oswyth smile like that again.

It was obvious how much more herself she was when they retired that night. Unlike the previous night, she turned to him directly and put her arms around him. "Siward, I do want you but there is still some pain and…"

Siward stopped further words by brushing a kiss across her lips. "And you know I would never do anything to hurt you." He gave a rueful grin. "I spoke with the midwife this day and she made plain her opinion of husbands who consider it again so soon. I'm sorry. I know so little about these matters."

"I do," Oswyth said. "I knew it was too soon but I feel so empty. I just wanted the hope of being with child again."

Siward held her close. "I know you do and I want it too. But not at such danger to you. Childbearing is dangerous enough. Let us not increase the risks. We will have a child one day, I am sure of it. And when that day comes, I want you alive to enjoy it."

Oswyth nodded. "Will you lie beside me anyway? It helps so much to feel you close."

"Of course I will."

He snuffed out the candles and climbed into bed. Slipping an arm around Oswyth, he was pleased to feel her snuggle against him.

"What do you think of that rascal, Wulfric?" he asked.

Oswyth laughed. "I think he is going to be handful. But I like him."

Siward grinned. "So do I."

Chapter nine

The amount of work they had to do over the next weeks was a blessing for Oswyth as in keeping busy, she was able to keep the bleaker thoughts at bay. Already Siward had started sending the first of their supplies to the stores by the Severn Sea, which Bishop Wulfstan had arranged for them, but there still seemed endless tasks for them to complete.

The lands were strangely empty, mostly free of animals as so many had been slaughtered but Siward was gleeful as he surveyed the amounts of salted and dried meats and fish. Oswyth too felt proud as she turned her attentions to the fleeces from the last of the sheep, weaving it into thick blankets.

The first signs of spring brought a mingling of excitement and fear as they knew how close to departure they had come. Since Siward had sent his vague promises on the tributes he owed, they had heard nothing and he was cautiously hopeful they could be away before the invaders could take any further action.

But that hope was dashed one afternoon when Wulfric raced into the hall where Oswyth was working.

"My lady, there is a company of men approaching. What shall we do?" The boy's eyes were sparkling with excitement. Thanks to the abundance of good food Siward was urging on everyone, he was no longer the scrawny urchin who had arrived a few weeks before.

Oswyth set down the bundles of cloth and hurried to the door. "Oh, no," she cried, seeing who was coming.

"Are they Normans?" Wulfric asked.

"Yes." Oswyth's heart was racing. "That man is named Turstin Fitz Rolf. I have met him before. I was supposed to marry his son but my grandfather married me to Siward instead. He is the most loathsome man."

"We will not let them in," Wulfric cried. "I shall defend the door, my lady. I shall die defending you if necessary."

Oswyth shook her head. This was no time for Wulfric's dramas. "No, Wulfric. Today you must be a man not a fool. We need Lord Siward. You are the fastest of us. Run to him and tell him what is happening."

Wulfric hesitated, his eyes lingering on the approaching company. His fists clenched, betraying his desire to fight.

"I mean this, Wulfric. You cannot fight so many. If you want to save me, you will fetch Lord Siward and the men."

To her relief Wulfric nodded, running from the doorway. Oswyth prayed he would locate Siward quickly, while she desperately considered the best way to stall whatever Turstin had planned.

With a wave of her hand, she summoned those present to stand with her. She cast her eyes over them. Three women, one of whom was with child, two of the older men and four thralls, also well past their prime. She looked grimly back at the armed men now dismounting. Turstin and a young man, about her own age, strode over, their entourage following them.

"Greetings, Lady Oswyth," Turstin said. "Stand aside."

Oswyth did not move. "What are your intentions here?"

"We are here to claim the King's tribute," the other man said. As he spoke, his smile was brisk but not unkind. "Allow me to present myself. I am Roger de Breteuill, Earl of Hereford. Now, my lady, permit us to enter."

"No," Oswyth replied.

Roger's mouth dropped open and Turstin gave a malicious smile. "Force her."

Roger shook his head. "I prefer not to attack women."

"Your gentleness is wasted on this lady. I have had dealings with her before." With those words Turstin shoved her easily to one side, causing her to stumble against one of the thralls. The others were pushed away with a similar brutality.

Roger sent an apologetic look as the men followed Turstin inside, all looking around while their eyes adjusted to the dim light.

Turstin waved his hand, gesturing around the hall. "Take everything of value. It all belongs to the King."

He made his way over to the fine cloths Oswyth had been bundling up. Furious at their hard work taken from them, Oswyth picked up a carving knife. Clutching it firmly, she ran after him, darting between Turstin and the table.

He laughed. "Do not be foolish. Stand aside."

Oswyth brandished the knife, waving it perilously close to his nose. She smiled in triumph as he took a sharp step back.

"All of this is ours," she said. "Go away."

Turstin looked more uncertain, realising the force needed to disarm her would not portray him in a good light.

Roger was watching hesitantly. He had not moved since crossing the threshold and nor had the other men. Oswyth realised in a swift glance around the hall that the churls and thralls had followed her lead and everyone was now brandishing a weapon of some sort. Several more had seized knives, while the pregnant woman was clutching a ladle. Two of the thralls had snatched up cooking pans. She pressed her lips together, wondering if one day she might laugh at this. Of all the skirmishes over the land, this one of women and old men armed with cooking implements must surely be the most ridiculous.

"What will you do now?" Oswyth demanded. "Will you burn the hall with us inside? That is what you barbarians do to the English, is it not?"

"Speaking of burnt halls, I and my son are very much enjoying our new lands in Somerset." Turstin gave a pleasant smile. "They are fine ones and all the finer now they are properly managed."

"Do not say that," Oswyth cried. "My grandfather was the finest of landowners. You are the very poorest of replacements."

Turstin laughed. "Do you know what I and my men did when we arrived on those lands? Our first action? It was to piss into the open grave we found there."

Oswyth's jaw dropped, her heart thundering in her ears as a fury descended on her. The hall faded from her vision. All she could see was the grave where her beloved grandfather, barely cold, lay and this man and his companions standing around, defiling it. As if she was there, the jeers rang loudly.

"How dare you?" she shrieked, her despair echoing in the hall. There was a deathly silence, where time seemed to stand still as she stepped forward, slashing the knife across his shoulder.

Turstin yelped, leaping back. Everyone watched from wide eyes as still furious, Oswyth followed him, raising the knife for a second blow. But before she could strike it, a strong hand gripped her arm. She tried to pull it free as she turned, looking into Roger's face.

"I cannot let you do that, my lady," he said. "Not that I don't sympathise." He looked in disgust at Turstin. "If you truly carried out such an act, the shame is on you."

At this moment Siward sprinted into the hall, his heart thudding and the breath catching in his throat at the speed he had run. His shocked gaze could make little sense of the scene as his eyes focussed on the young man gripping Oswyth. He strode towards him, drawing his own knife.

"Let my wife go," he snapped. "And if I find you have hurt her..."

Roger did as he was asked, favouring Siward with a grim smile. "Trust me. It is not your wife who is hurt."

Siward's eyes widened as he noticed the knife Oswyth was still clutching. He got a further shock as he realised the man standing before her, his face crimson with rage, was Turstin with his hand pressed to a dark stain forming on the shoulder of his tunic. Oswyth met his eyes defiantly.

"Your wife is out of control," Turstin snarled. "In addition to the tribute to the King, you shall also pay me compensation."

"I shall not," Siward said, pulling Oswyth to him. "I do not know what has happened here, but I am certain my wife faced extreme provocation."

It seemed to Siward that the day was to be one shock after another as the man who had held Oswyth gave an almost imperceptible nod. He turned his back on Turstin to address him. "I think we have met before. You are Roger de Breteuill, Earl of Hereford, I believe. Tell me your business here."

Roger straightened his shoulders in his effort to look more commanding. "Siward of Gloucester, you know the tribute due to the King has not been paid. We are here to take it."

"You will not take it. Everything here is mine and I intend to keep it."

"Arrest the man," Turstin said in his own language. "The King will be grateful."

Siward understood enough. "If you try to take me or my property by force, we will retaliate. My people are gathering outside. They will fight you. We have already taken possession of your horses. The two men you left guarding them were no match for my churls. They were easily overpowered."

"That is theft," Turstin cried. "The man is a thief."

"You accuse me of theft? When you are here to take almost everything I possess?"

Roger looked more bewildered than ever, as what he had assumed would be an easy task became increasingly difficult. "What will you gain from your resistance? If you drive us away this day, you know we will return with reinforcements. Be reasonable. You know you have to pay the tribute."

"I will gain time," Siward replied. "Time to escape this land."

"You are leaving?" Roger stroked his chin, his brow creased in speculation. "Bishop Odo has recently been informed that there are a large number of boats gathering in the Severn Sea. Is this something to do with you?"

Inwardly Siward cursed. He had hoped news of his fleet had not yet reached the man who was ruling England on the Bastard's behalf. "It is possible."

"Are you intentions hostile? Do you intend to attack the King?"

Siward looked curiously at Roger. The man sounded interested with no sign of condemnation. He made a swift decision to be honest. "I hate the man you call king as I have hated no man. The cruelties he has inflicted on my countrymen and women are beyond anything I ever thought to see. If I could kill him, I would. But I have spent too many years trying to topple him. I will not waste any more."

"Where are you going?"

Siward shrugged. "Away from here. That is all I can tell you for it is all I know. Many will join me. There are too many of us who cannot bear to live under the tyrant's yoke." He gave a bitter smile. "And once I am gone, the Bastard can have my lands, so he will not be treated of his precious tribute."

Roger looked steadily at him. "I see."

Turstin shook his head, his scowl deepening. "Is that all you can say? This man must be stopped. He cannot be allowed to escape. He has evaded the King's justice too many times. Arrest him now and take everything the King is owed. It is time Siward of Gloucester is dealt with once and for all."

Chapter ten

Siward folded his arms, tossing his head in the direction of the door. "Then you will have to fight. My people are ready and they are numerous. We may well beat you this day. And even if we do not, your losses will be severe."

"We will fight," Turstin spat.

Roger laid a hand on his arm. "I outrank you here, Turstin and I have given no such orders."

"You must. The King will not be pleased to hear you have let this traitor remain free."

Roger raised an eyebrow, his smile taking a malicious turn. "You wish to fight this man? You could not even defend yourself against his wife."

Turstin went crimson again as several of the Normans in the hall sniggered. "Once we have dealt with the men here, she shall be beaten as a punishment."

Siward put his arm around Oswyth, glaring at Turstin from narrowed eyes as all too easily he envisioned the brute standing over her with a stick. "You have not yet told me what you did to so offend my wife. Why not tell me? I suspect I shall be keen to see you punished."

"He spoke of how he defiled my grandfather's grave," Oswyth burst out.

Siward shook his head as he tightened his arm around Oswyth, wishing he could take away the pain slicing through her words. "I thought I could not despise you any more than I already did. You coward. Attacking women is about all you are good for. The only Englishman you dare attack is a dead one."

"Yet we beat you at Hastings and have beaten you ever since," Turstin retorted with a smirk.

Siward's hand flew to his own knife. He took a step towards Turstin, determined to kill the man and put away the shame of his defeat once and for all. The blood was thundering in his ears as his knife slid easily from its sheath. Just as it would easily slide into Turstin's flesh.

"Siward of Gloucester," Roger shouted. "Please do not strike this man. If you do, I will have to kill you and I would prefer not to."

"Then I suggest you remove him from my residence," Siward said through gritted teeth, still clutching the knife. If it wasn't for the people who needed him, he would have struck the blow whatever the consequences.

"I will."

"You are not going to deal with this man?" Turstin cried.

"No," Roger replied. "We are departing."

Everyone in the hall, both Norman and English gaped at him. Siward and Oswyth exchanged shocked glances, wondering if this was some kind of trickery.

"But the King..." Turstin exclaimed.

"I think the King will be glad to see the backs of a number of trouble makers," Roger said. "This way he is rid of them without bloodshed." He turned back to Siward. "When are you departing?"

"As soon as the weather is good for sailing," Siward said. "I hope to leave around Easter tide."

"Then we will return for our tribute after Easter," Roger said with a hint of a smile. "If there is nothing left but the lands themselves, so be it."

Siward nodded, forcing down the bitterness that the Bastard would soon dispose of his lands. He only hoped they were not bestowed onto Turstin. The prospect of any more of his people serving that man would be unbearable.

"I shall also inform Bishop Odo that the boats in the Severn

Sea are of no concern."

"Thank you," Siward replied, relief driving away the bitterness. This was better than he had hoped.

Roger shot a black look at Turstin. "And you should apologise to Lady Oswyth."

"I should apologise to her?" Turstin spluttered with an incredulous glance at the bloodstain on his torn tunic. "I think not."

Roger looked steadily at him. "I do not know if you truly carried out the acts you spoke of or if you merely claimed you did to cause her distress. But either way, it is not fitting conduct towards a lady. I am ordering your apology."

Turstin scowled but muttered something which was presumably his apology.

Oswyth held her head high. "I do not want to forgive you," she said. "But my grandfather had the most generous of hearts. I know he would forgive you so as his granddaughter, it befits me to also do so."

"You are very gracious, my lady," Roger said, bowing over her hand. "We will trouble you no longer. Farewell."

Siward accompanied them to the doorway, keeping his arm around Oswyth. Outside a large crowd of his people were gathered around the horses, bearing the shovels and pitchforks they used to toil the land. Two burly thralls were firmly holding the Norman men who had been left on guard, with Wicrun stood before them, his knife poised to strike at the slightest struggle. Turstin looked more furious than ever but Roger simply directed an enquiring glance in Siward's direction.

"Stand aside," Siward said. "These men are leaving and they pass unhindered."

The crowd edged away, leaving only Wulfric still standing by the horses, clutching a stout stick. Siward shook his head. "Do as you have been ordered, Wulfric."

Wulfric gave him a sulky look but did as he was bidden. There were no further words from the Normans as Roger urged his horse into a brisk trot. Siward kept his eyes sternly on Wulfric, sensing the boy was itching to hurl something at the retreating men. If only he could be sure of the boy's aim, he would probably let him throw something at Turstin. He still looked disgruntled as they finally rode out of range.

Oswyth put her hand on his shoulder. "Well done for fetching Lord Siward so quickly. Truly you saved us."

Siward smiled as the boy grew under her words of praise. "I agree. Well done, my boy. I know you wished to fight them. I have to confess that I did too. But it would have served nothing. It is always best if such incidents can pass without bloodshed." He shot a look of exasperated amusement at Oswyth. "Or almost without bloodshed."

∞∞∞

Over the next days they moved more of their supplies to the port, with Siward more confident now the secret was out.

"Do you trust the Earl of Hereford to stand by his word?" Oswyth asked.

Siward hesitated. The man's father had been the one to crush the spirit in the West in the years after Hastings, yet he had felt a reluctant liking for Roger. "Yes, I do. I hope that does not make me a fool."

"I trust him too," Oswyth replied. "Other than the Bastard and his friends, these Normans are mostly not bad people. There are good and bad ones, just as among our own folk."

The pace of the work increased as the days passed, the amount they still had to do stretching on. They were aware that they should not presume too much on Roger's good will. Bishop Odo too might not be as understanding as Roger had claimed. The worry was never far away so both Siward and Oswyth flinched as they supervised the packing in the hall when the noise of raised voices drifted in from outside.

"Go away," Wulfric's voice rang out. "Leave. You are not coming here."

"Oh, stand aside, you young fool," came an accented voice. "Or I shall ride my horse over you."

"No. I will not let you harm my lord or my lady."

Siward and Oswyth exchanged startled glances. It sounded very like the Normans had returned. Knowing there was no time to waste, Siward seized his sword from its place on the wall. He ran to the doorway, Oswyth just a step behind him, both terrified of what actions the Normans might be planning.

There was an exclamation of pain, which was certainly from Roger. "You little cur," he roared. "You shall pay for that."

Siward almost laughed, his fears vanishing as he reached the door. Roger and a handful of other men were astride their horses with Wulfric standing before them, thrusting his stick at the horses' noses as they paced nervously. He lowered his sword.

"Wulfric, stand aside," he called. "A group this size is no threat to us."

"But…" Wulfric stared at him, agog at those words.

Siward seized him by the neck of his tunic. "Do as you are told, Brat. This is not the day for your heroics."

Roger frowned down at Siward. "Siward of Gloucester, last time I was here I witnessed your wife attacking a man with a carving knife. Now I have had this rascal beating my men with a stick. Do you have any control over those closest to you?"

Siward grinned. "I fear very little."

Roger laughed out loud, sliding down from his horse. "Greetings, Siward."

"Greetings. I apologise for the welcome you have received this day." He sent a reproving look at Wulfric. "Although I do not apologise for the one you received last time. Turstin Fitz Rolf got exactly the hospitality he deserved."

Roger nodded. "That is fair enough. But I assure you this time my intentions are peaceful."

"Then we shall hinder you no further." He cast a swift glance over the other men dismounting. All were armed but only in the way any man would arm himself for a journey. "I trust Turstin was not seriously hurt."

"I think the wound to his pride was far deeper than the cut to his arm," Roger replied.

"Pity," Wulfric muttered. He had retreated to stand beside Oswyth, staring defiantly at the men. Siward shook his head at him.

"He is still furious," Roger added. "I understand this is not the first time he has met your wife."

"No," Siward replied. "She has met him on a few occasions and disliked him more with each one."

Roger laughed again. "Your wife is of a discerning character. From what I understood of his splutterings, I believe she has also bested him on every occasion." He bowed to Oswyth. "My dear lady, you have my sincere admiration."

Oswyth blushed, surprised at the friendly manner. "Truly, you are welcome. But may we ask why you are here?"

"I am here on a matter which may prove advantageous to us all."

Chapter eleven

S iward raised his eyebrows but gestured to the hall. "Since you have no hostile intentions, I too bid you welcome. Please, come inside and take some refreshment."

"Thank you," Roger said, following him in.

Siward cuffed Wulfric around the ear. "Make yourself useful somewhere else." He glanced at Oswyth. "Fetch some ale. Good ale." He emphasised the last couple of words rather suspecting her to have the same attitude as Wulfric.

Oswyth hid her smile as she brought a jug and several fine cups over to the table. She was happy to obey, finding, to her surprise, that she liked Roger. Never had she expected him to side with her against Turstin.

Roger took a mouthful of the ale, exclaiming in satisfaction. "That is very good. Turstin's fool of a son said the ale served here was fit only for swine. But that is excellent."

"Perhaps it was a poor batch that day." Siward grinned. "Or perhaps it was the strong dislike my wife had for him which tainted the ale."

Roger laughed. "My countrymen have not overly impressed you, have they, my lady? It is unfortunate."

Taking a seat beside Siward, Oswyth blushed at the admiration so obvious in Roger's gaze. "In truth, no. But very few have tried to impress me and Ralf Fitz Turstin most certainly did not."

"You say you have a matter to discuss which will benefit us?" Siward said, determined to bring the conversation back to the purpose of the visit, before Oswyth could say too much more. "What can it be?"

Roger gestured to the man seated beside him. "May I present to you my good friend, Drogo. I hope your lady will not find anything to offend her since he is my countryman. He is from a place called Caen."

Oswyth's body gave a sharp twitch, while Siward's mouth dropped open. He gaped at the man. "Drogo of Caen?"

The man's pleasant, round face creased into a frown, as he rested a thick elbow on the table. He leaned forward. "Is there a problem?"

"No, no." Siward recovered himself. He was aware Oswyth had bowed her head but he did not dare look at her directly, knowing it would reduce her to giggles and probably him too. There was a faint tremble in his voice as he spoke. "Forgive me. I thought you were a man I once knew but I see I am mistaken. Welcome."

"I do not think we have met," Drogo replied. "But I thank you for your welcome." He glanced uncertainly at Oswyth, his frown deepening as she avoided his eye, but said nothing more.

"How can we assist you?" Siward asked, keeping the man's focus on him. "Do you reside in these parts?"

"I have some lands in the Shire of Hereford. They are small and not notable," Drogo replied.

"Drogo is keen to increase his lands," Roger said. "Your estate is a fair one. He would like to purchase some or perhaps all of it from you."

"Purchase it?"

Drogo nodded. "I have heard you are leaving England soon. If so, I may be interested in purchasing your lands."

"Drogo is aware you will be taking everything from the land," Roger put in. "Obviously that will be reflected in the price he is prepared to pay. But it will be a fair one."

"What of the tribute?" Siward asked.

Roger laughed. "That is due from you, Siward of Gloucester. But if you are no longer here when we come to collect it, what can we do? Drogo will purchase the lands in good faith. He will have his own dues to pay to the King but he will not be responsible for yours."

"I heard you planned to simply leave your lands," Drogo said. "You will lose nothing by selling them to me. Indeed you will gain some money which will be useful in your venture."

"It certainly would," Siward said. "Forgive me. I had not expected this. I would be happy to gain something for them. What price are you suggesting?" He reflected that anything would be better than the nothing he had expected.

"Perhaps Drogo and I could ride over your lands," Roger suggested. "So he might see the extent of what he might acquire."

"Of course." Siward stood. "Do you currently live on your lands in the Shire of Hereford?"

Drogo nodded. "Yes. I am a third son with no lands in Normandy. My life is now here."

Siward nodded, thinking it would ease the pain of leaving his lands if he was to leave them with a man who would reside there rather than one who simply controlled them from his Normandy estates. Such a man might come to genuinely care for them as he did. "Please, take the time you need. Go wherever you wish and if you like what you see, we shall negotiate a price."

He put his arm around Oswyth as Roger and Drogo mounted their horses and cantered over the fields.

"So," Siward said, squeezing her tightly. "That is my rival to your hand, the unfortunate Drogo de Caen."

Oswyth gave way to the giggles which had been threatening her ever since she had heard the man's name. "Stop it, Siward. How could I have known there would be a man of that name in these parts?"

"Are you taking your people with you when you leave?" Drogo

asked when he and Roger returned from their ride.

"A lot of them," Siward said. "But some are not able or did not wish to leave."

"If you are leaving that urchin who greeted us this day, I shall halve the price I was going to offer," Drogo warned with a smile.

Siward laughed. "Do not fear. I would not foist that brat onto the Bastard himself. Wulfric is coming with me."

"I shall deal fairly with those who are left," Drogo said. "If they are good workers, I will treat them well."

"They are the finest workers." It was as if a burden had been lifted from Siward. He had felt so guilty about the ones he was leaving behind. What a relief it would be, to tell them their new lord was a fair man. "Come this way," Siward said. "There is one more place I should show you."

He kept his arm around Oswyth as he led the way to the burial ground behind the church. "My forefathers lie here," Siward said. "That is my father's grave. His name was Earnsig and under the eaves are those of my siblings who did not survive to adulthood."

Roger looked for a moment at the bare patch of earth, where the first shoots of grass were breaking through. "I think there has also been a more recent loss."

Oswyth's eyes filled with tears at the sympathy in the man's voice. She nodded.

"I ask you to treat the graves of my kin always with respect." Tears had come to Siward's own eyes as he spoke.

"I will," Drogo said. "On the day I take possession of these lands, I shall have a mass said for your father and your other kin. And a mass will be said on the anniversary of that day each year as long as I live."

"Thank you," Siward replied, the pain in his heart easing still further at the man's words.

"What was your grandfather's name, my lady?" Roger asked.

"Raedwulf," Oswyth replied.

Roger nodded at Drogo. "Mention his name in the prayers. His resting place is not being treated with respect but at least his memory can be honoured."

Oswyth's tears rushed over and ineffectually she dabbed at her eyes, forcing a laugh. "Now you have made me cry. You were actually impressing me until then."

Roger's smile remained sympathetic. "So, Siward of Gloucester, are we likely to come to a deal?"

Siward glanced at Drogo. The man named a price. It was not as much as the lands were worth but given that he was stripping them of so much of value, he knew it was a fair offer. He was surprised. There was no attempt to cheat him at all. He took Drogo by the hands. "I accept your offer. Will you come back with us to the hall? My priest can draw up the agreement."

In the hall Oswyth brought out a jug of costly wine, feeling this was a celebration of sorts. The four of them sat at the table as Father Colman got to work, talking over the drinks as if they were old friends, rather than the foes Siward had always considered them. He found himself on such good terms with the men that he explained to Drogo why he and Oswyth had been so startled by his name.

Drogo laughed loudly at this. "If I did not already have a wife, I would be flattered," he said with a wink at Oswyth. "Indeed, she would probably be the first to say that you would be welcome to me."

Oswyth blushed and shook her head, thinking she liked the sound of Drogo's wife. It was not so bad to think of them presiding over this hall after she and Siward were gone.

Siward too laughed. "Why are you doing this?" he said to Roger. "I was just going to leave my lands. You could have had them for nothing."

"I would have had no say in their disposal." Roger's face became solemn. "Besides, my countrymen have taken so much from your people. We have stolen, cheated, raped, starved and slaughtered. I gain no pleasure from this knowledge. You have struck me as a good man, Siward of Gloucester. I am glad not to cheat you."

"You too strike me as a good man," Siward said. "How can you serve a man such as the Bastard?"

Roger shrugged, his eyes no longer meeting Siward's. "He is my kinsman and my king. I serve him as my father did before me, but my loyalty is truly being stretched. Perhaps I will not always support him."

Siward gave a half laugh. "I have tried to make many alliances against the Bastard. With Scots, with Danes, with Franks. It never occurred to me that I might make them with Normans."

"I have heard of your struggles," Roger said. "You are a brave man. I think it is a fault of the King that he did not win you to his side. I wish he had. Your departure is England's loss."

"Could he have ever won your allegiance?" Drogo asked.

Siward hesitated. "I was not happy after Hastings but if he had dealt fairly with the English, perhaps in time I could have been won. But seeing so many stripped of their lands, people driven out to make way for his forest, our bishops, learned, god fearing men, forced from office… no. I could not submit under such circumstances. And after his actions in the North…"

"That is truly a shame on our people, a dark sin to damn all who partook," Roger said. "I too can never forget it, for I know my father was present. Since his death, I have had many a mass said for his soul, but no matter how many are said, I fear it can never be enough."

Siward shook his head. "If more of your countrymen were like you, I do not think I would be leaving. But it gladdens me to know there are men like you who will not forget the English." He clasped Drogo's hand. "I am truly happy to know my lands will be cared for."

Chapter twelve

I t was a strange Easter. Almost everything they were taking with them was already making its way to the ports on the Severn Sea, leaving the hall empty and the stores all but bare. There were few people around. Other than Father Colman and Wulfric, who had refused to leave before they did, everyone who was accompanying them had already departed. Some walking, some riding and others on boats heading down the river. Those who were still on the lands were the ones who would be staying. The people who soon they would never see again.

Siward hardly heard the words of the mass Father Colman was chanting as he looked at the faces, seeing the old men who had helped him saddle up his first pony and the women who had ruffled his head, granting him morsels of the breads they were baking. They had been a presence in his life for as long as he could remember. He had never been aware of feeling any special affection for them until that moment, when he realised that the next day he would be bidding them farewell.

He and Oswyth walked hand in hand through the sun dappled estate to the hall, noticing the flowers springing up, looking more beautiful than the spring flowers had ever done before. Despite the absence of their belongings, the people had done their best with the hall, giving it a festive appearance for the lavish Easter feast Siward had ordered.

"I suppose we do not leave it in too bad shape for Drogo," he commented.

Oswyth squeezed his hand, knowing what a difficult day this was for him. Together they made their way to the dais, taking their places for the last time. Siward's eyes blurred as he carried out the action he had done so many times before. Despite the tempting aromas of roasting meat, he wondered how he was supposed to eat anything.

Oswyth filled his cup with wine. She too was feeling emotional but knew how much harder it was for Siward. She had never expected to live her life there. By the time she had known her marriage would be a permanent one, they had already decided to leave.

He squeezed her hand as he noticed how anxiously she was watching him. "I am fine, Oswyth."

She smiled. "No, you are not. How can you be?"

"Yes, you are right." Siward sighed. "Now I understand how it was for you on the day we left your grandfather's hall. I wish I had been more sympathetic to you that day."

"Oh, Siward, you were always kinder to me than I deserved. Leaving that hall was not as hard as leaving my grandfather. I am eternally grateful I was able to stay with him until the last."

Siward nodded, as always impressed by his wife's way of viewing the situation. "You are right. It is the people who matter, not the walls which surround us." He put an arm around her, pressing his lips against the top of her head. "At least I leave with the one I love most. You had to leave the one you loved most in his grave." He swallowed another mouthful of wine, getting to his feet. He knew he needed to say some words to the people who were still there. They might not be ones he loved as Oswyth loved her grandfather but they were still important to him. He hoped he could say what he needed to say without breaking down.

All eyes went expectantly to Siward and he forced himself to smile cheerfully at them. "Welcome to the Easter celebrations, my friends," he said. "They will be the last celebrations I share with you so let us make them merry ones." He was aware of the unnatural brightness on the faces of all who looked at him. "I wish to thank you all for the service you have given me and the service your fathers and mothers rendered to mine before us. Truly you are the finest of all England."

There was a subdued murmur of appreciation as Siward swallowed the lump in his throat. Desperately he kept his voice steady. "Tomorrow you will have a new lord. Yes, I know that grieves you and yes, he is one of the invaders. But even so, I urge you to serve him well. He has struck me as a fair man and I truly believe he will be a good lord to you. England has changed and our lives with it, but that is always the way of the world. So, as we celebrate the new life of Easter, let us also look forward to our new lives. Yours here, mine in some other part of the world. Wherever we are, we must serve God and know He will always be with us. There will be tears for our farewell but let hope rise in our hearts as surely as Christ rose this day from the dead. My friends, I drink to your good health and prosperity. Accept from me this day, my final blessings."

As he sat down, the tears rushed to his eyes, while the hall erupted into cheers from voices which wobbled. Oswyth put her arms around him and Siward buried his face in her veil until he knew he had his emotion under control.

"Well done, Siward," she whispered.

Siward pulled away, brushing her lips with a kiss. "My God, this day is hard. But as long as I have you with me, I can bear it all."

Siward had given orders for ale, wine and mead to flow freely and everyone took full advantage. So, in spite of the sorrow, the feast managed to be a merry one. Musicians struck up lively tunes, the same ones he had listened to all his life. But as the tears again threatened to overwhelm him, he remembered there would be musicians in his fleet. He could take the tunes with him.

As the sun set, they lit flaming torches, everyone unwilling to bring the night to an end but at last, unsteadily, the people drifted away to their rest.

Oswyth laid her hand on Siward's shoulder. "We too must rest, my love."

"I know. But once I rise from this chair, I shall never sit on it again."

Oswyth put her arms around him. "One day you shall have a new hall and there will be another chair. I do not know where it will be but I do know I shall be sat on the chair beside you."

Siward's eyes filled up once again but he took Oswyth's hand and rose from the chair. Together they made their way to the bedchamber, the place he had been born.

As the door shut behind them, Oswyth again put her arms around him. "It is no longer Lent," she said. "And I am quite recovered now."

Siward's eyes widened, desire shooting through him at the pressure of her body against him. It drove away all other thoughts, as his hands darted to the lacing of her kirtle. "Are you sure?"

Oswyth pressed her lips eagerly to his. "This is our last night here. Let us make it a happy one."

It was an even more difficult moment the next morning as he left the hall, clasping the hands of those who gathered to see him depart. Tears slid down the faces of many. They were tears of sorrow but also of fear as for all Siward's words, they were nervous of changes the new lord would make. Siward knew there was little he could say in reassurance. Changes were inevitable and he could only hope he had been right to trust that Drogo was the good man he had appeared to be.

While the horses were prepared, he looked up at the hall, committing the sight to memory.

Oswyth put her arms around him. "Do you want to set fire to it?"

Siward gave a half laugh. "I did think I might but that was before I sold it. It would be rough on Drogo if he arrived to find the home he was looking forward to, burnt to the ground. He paid a fair price."

"I know." Oswyth held him, wishing there was something she could say to make the moment easier for him.

"How am I supposed to leave?" he asked, his voice shaky. "I was born here. I imagined my children growing up here, fishing in the river and riding among the trees as I did. I thought I would grow old here, with my son to inherit after I was gone. My God, Oswyth, how did this happen? I thought I would tend this land until the day I died."

Oswyth swallowed the lump in her throat. She looked around, seeing a shovel resting against the wall. She dug it deep into the rich soil, shovelling it into a basket.

"What are you doing?" Siward asked.

Oswyth fastened the basket and handed it to him. "We shall take a little of your land with us. And when we settle, wherever that may be, we shall sprinkle this soil to make that land truly our own."

Siward clutched the basket to him, falling to his knees, his tears flowing freely. "Oh, Oswyth, what would I do without you?"

"Come, Siward," Oswyth said softly, as Siward remained down, his shoulders shaking with his sobs. "This moment will only get harder. Let us go."

Siward took a deep breath, pressing his hand one last time against the land which was no longer his.

Oswyth ran her hand gently over his bowed head. "We need to be at the Severn Port by nightfall."

Siward rose, nodding. He wiped his eyes free from tears and put his arm around Oswyth as he turned to the horses. Father Colman stood nearby, his hand resting on Wulfric's shoulder, both of them watching him with solemn expressions.

"Let us depart," he said, helping Oswyth onto her horse.

Father Colman mounted his, but as Wulfric prepared to trudge alongside, Siward gestured him over. "Come, Brat. You had better ride with me."

Wulfric's face lit up into a grin as Siward helped him mount, swinging himself up behind the boy. He ruffled his head, reminding himself of why he was leaving. It was so boys like Wulfric could grow up as free Englishmen. With Oswyth on one side of him and Father Colman on the other, he urged his horse into a brisk trot, waving his hand at the people who lined his way. No more tears flowed and not once did any of them look back.

Chapter thirteen

Oswyth reined in her horse with a gasp as they looked down at Brygstow, the port where the River Severn met the Severn Sea. It was always a busy harbour, full of boats laden with wares arriving from all over Christendom, as well as the grimmer departures of men sent in bondage to Ireland. But even for that port the scene was spectacular. The sea was crammed with boats, their brightly woven sails bobbing up and down on the waves. "Are all of those ours?" she asked.

Overwhelmed with pride, Siward nodded. "This is only some of our fleet. We have so many boats, they are spread over a number of ports along the coast. Keep still, Brat," he said to Wulfric who was bouncing up and down in his excitement.

"With so many boats, could we not invade England and drive the Bastard away?" Wulfric cried.

"We could invade but I am not sure it would be a success. The forces of the Bastard have proved too formidable for us on too many occasions. I fear it would be a waste of this effort." Siward shrugged, wondering if the bitterness of this knowledge would ever completely leave him. "Besides, even if we were successful, who would we place on the throne?"

"Is there no one left of the true royal line?" Wulfric asked.

Siward looked down at the port. "Strangely, the woman who holds these lands is of the true royal line."

"Who is she?" Wulfric cried. "I would be happy to fight for a lady of the true line."

Siward gave a wry smile. "She is Matilda, Duchess of Normandy and wife of the Bastard. Her line goes back to our mighty King Alfred."

Wulfric looked crestfallen. "Oh. I suppose she would not welcome such an invasion. But one day her sons might rule this land."

"Perhaps," Siward said. "But although the blood of Alfred flows in their veins, their ways are not ours. I am not staying here to see if they deal more fairly with the English than their father."

"If this land belongs to the Bastard's wife, is it safe for our boats to be based here?" Oswyth asked.

Siward nodded. "Bishop Wulfstan has assured me they are. Roger too has promised we will leave unhindered. Besides, the Lady Matilda, like her husband, bases herself for the most part in Normandy. I doubt she either knows or cares about our actions here."

Colman looked over the boats, quickly losing count as he tried to calculate their number. "Are there enough Englishmen to fill all these boats, my son?"

"Yes and not just Englishmen. There are also plenty of Danes who once considered England their home but can now do so no longer." Siward laughed. "Who knows? We may even be able to count some Normans among our number. Ones who were tempted over here before finding the new life was not as good as had been promised. Come, let us head down."

As they cantered down to the port, they caught sight of Frebern waving to them. "Siward!" he cried, running towards their horses.

Siward slid down, flinging his arms around his friend. "It is good to see you. Is Bridwin here yet?"

Frebern shook his head. "I am expecting him tomorrow or the next day."

Siward helped Oswyth dismount, leaving Wulfric to slide down on his own. Frebern shot a startled glance at Oswyth's stomach, which Siward hoped she did not notice. He had forgotten that merry night in Gloucester when he had rambled on about his child, not knowing the infant had been lost. There was certainly no sign she had as she planted a kiss on Frebern's cheek. His face turned a bright crimson shade at that, but he grinned at her as they exchanged greetings. "Who is this?" Frebern asked, not disguising his curiosity at the boy by Siward's horse.

Siward ruffled Wulfric's head. "This is New England's first enemy. He declared war on me so I am taking him with us as my prisoner."

"Just as well." Frebern laughed. "I hear you were able to sell your lands. I was too. The Earl of Hereford was most helpful. He is here."

"Is he?" Siward looked around, surprised to see Roger in the doorway to an ale house.

"Oswyth, did you really attack that wretch, Turstin with a carving knife?" Frebern whispered in admiring tones.

Oswyth blushed, suspecting it would be an incident she would never be allowed to forget.

"Greetings, Roger," Siward called as the young man came towards them. "I trust you are not here to stop us. I would hate to think I had been lured into a trap."

Roger clapped him on the shoulder. "Not at all. I am just checking you leave as promised. I hope it will be soon. I have a number of other matters to attend to." He looked around and lowered his voice. "I am forming an alliance, using the marriage of my sister, with the Earl of Norfolk. If the King does not like it..."

Siward raised his eyebrows. "Rebellion?"

"There would be a place for you, if you choose to stay," Roger said with a sideways glance.

Siward was silent for a long time, looking into the eager eyes of the Earl. He hated the thought that the Bastard had beaten him. Might one last attempt topple him at last? But feeling Oswyth watching him, he shook his head. "If you mentioned this before I sold my lands, I might have been tempted," he said. "But not now. These people are depending on me to lead them."

"I suspected you would say that," Roger said. "But it is a shame. With your help, my chance of success would be greater."

Siward shrugged, half wishing he could be part of it, but knowing his decision to be the right one. "Would you care for my interests or those of my countrymen? If you cared for that, where were you last year, during our own attempt to topple the Bastard?"

"A fair point," Roger conceded. "In truth, I did not expect you to change your mind. So, Siward of Gloucester, all that remains is for me to wish you Godspeed."

"Thank you. I shall not forget how you have helped me in this and wherever I reside, I would always welcome you," Siward replied. Under different circumstances he could so easily have considered Roger a friend. Sympathy flared in him as he looked at him, this young man so determined to take on the Bastard, just as he had once done. He too had enjoyed that bright eyed confidence until the relentless defeats had broken it. But all he could do was hope that Roger would fare better. It was his struggle no longer. "I shall pray for your success in whatever action you take. I certainly wish nothing but misery on the Bastard and his line."

∞∞∞

Bridwin swept in with the last of his entourage the next day, including Leofwine, the former bishop of Lichfield and accompanied by Bishop Wulfstan.

He was in high spirits as he pulled Siward and Frebern into an embrace. "My God, I knew we had a lot of boats but I could scarce believe the sight as I came over the hill."

"I know," Siward replied. "It is glorious indeed."

"Greetings, my son," Wulfstan said, taking Siward by the hands. He smiled. "I left your mother in good spirits at Canterbury. There are several other women there who she remembers very fondly from her days at King Edward's court. She will be well and among friends. If I see her again, I shall be glad to report your successful departure."

Tears had rushed to Siward's eyes at that comment but he was glad to hear such pleasing news. "Father, if you see her, she may ask about my child." He took a moment to compose himself. "Alas, we have no such good tidings on that but I would prefer it if she did not know this. I do not wish to ask you to lie, however I do want her last knowledge of us to be happy."

Father Wulfstan smiled gently. "She spoke of the child but I understood that if all had gone well, the infant would likely not have yet arrived. So, if I tell her you have not yet welcomed your firstborn, that would not be a lie."

Siward nodded. "Thank you, Father. Just tell her Oswyth and I are well and happy. That too is not a lie."

They both looked over at Oswyth laughing at whatever outrageous comment Wulfric had just made and Wulfstan smiled. "I can see that."

Noticing their gaze, Oswyth came over, smiling her greetings to them all. She was delighted to see Dunstan among Bridwin's entourage. Having developed a deep respect for the man during her trek north, she had been hoping he would be coming.

"Greetings, my daughter. I was just telling Siward that I left the Lady Alfgiva well and contented in her new life."

"I am glad," Oswyth said. "I wonder if she has started work on that hanging for the Bishop of Bayeux yet."

Siward half laughed. It was good to picture his mother engaged in an activity she had always loved. "She is probably busy stitching herself into the story."

Bishop Wulfstan's lips twitched. "I would not put it past her."

There followed several days of planning. They organised the throngs of people into groups and divided their supplies, sending them to the required ports ready for loading. Father Colman,

Father Leofwine and the other priests who were accompanying them had the lengthy task of taking from every man an oath of loyalty before assigning them to a boat.

Siward, Bridwin and Frebern appointed thegns and other high ranking men to be in charge of each boat, dividing the fleet into three with one of them leading each section.

"I shall lead the boats out of Brygstow," Siward said. "If you take command of the groups further up the coast.

"Agreed," Bridwin replied. "As we see you pass, we too shall sail out of port."

"So, my friends, this is it." Siward put an arm around each of them as they stared at the mass of boats bobbing up and down in the smooth harbour waters. "We are really going."

Father Colman came over. "Every man has sworn an oath of loyalty to you and this venture. Will you now swear your own oath?"

All three nodded, stepping into a circle of thegns to take their places beside Bishop Wulfstan. Siward glanced around, recognising the expression on the faces staring back. It was the same look of hope and fear he knew frequented his own face.

Frebern was the first to take the cross from the Bishop, holding it aloft. "I, Frebern of Warwick, do swear by almighty God to lead well these men under my command. I pledge my obedience to the final decisions of Siward of Gloucester. Wherever we travel, I shall serve God and while there is life in my body, I shall not give up the quest for New England."

He handed the cross to Bridwin who repeated the words, before finally passing it to Siward. His hand became clammy as he realised how everyone there was depending on him.

He took a deep breath. "I, Siward of Gloucester, do swear by almighty God to lead well these men under my command. I pledge my obedience and eternal service to God wherever I go. And while there is life in my body, I shall not give up the quest for New England."

Siward felt a weight lift from him at those words. He was committed. There was to be no more agonising over his decision.

As the circle of thegns dispersed, Oswyth came to put an arm around his waist.

"I half expected you to be tempted by Roger's offer," she said.

Siward tightened his arm around her. "I think I was, in a fashion. But then I remembered how it felt when Bridwin, Frebern and I took the decision to fight the Bastard no longer. It was the bitterest decision I have ever made and yet there was relief in it. I don't want to be dragged back to that desperate, hopeless struggle." He brought his lips to hers, letting them linger as the optimism she always inspired took hold. "I want to look to the future even though I do not know what it will hold. I just hope I can always keep you safe. Do you ever regret marrying me?"

Oswyth tilted her head to one side, pretending to consider the matter. "Let me see. I suppose I could have been enjoying an idyllic life of married bliss with that odious son of Turstin…"

Siward grinned. "Very true."

Oswyth's mood turned solemn as she took a cross from under her kirtle. "You have not asked for a pledge of obedience from the women but I give it to you anyway. I, Oswyth, wife of Siward, daughter of Raedwulf and granddaughter of the noble thegn who also bore that name, pledge my loyalty to you, Siward, Eorl of Gloucester, to be maintained wherever God takes us."

Chapter fourteen

On the morning of their departure, Siward and Oswyth were up before it was light. Most people were already on board the vessels, waiting for their departure but they had spent the night on land, making the most of their last night in a proper bed. They were both dressed in thick woollen clothes, with their warmest cloaks clasped around their shoulders. As they left the chamber, they stepped over Wulfric who was curled up by the door. He had ignored Siward's instructions to go to the boat, maintaining his determination to stay wherever they were.

Siward prodded him with his foot but the boy barely stirred. "It would serve the brat right if we sailed away without him."

Oswyth put her arm around Siward's waist. "You cannot fool me. I think you are becoming most attached to him."

Siward grinned. "I think you are."

"I know." Oswyth hesitated. "It felt strange that as we were grieving for our own child, a child who had need of us, entered our lives. Almost as if God had sent him."

Siward rolled his eyes. "You think this unholy little imp is sent from God?"

Oswyth laughed, bending over Wulfric to wake him. He grumbled for a few moments before opening his eyes to stare up at them.

"Come along, my boy. A warrior cannot sleep when there are lands to be won," Siward said, pulling the boy up.

They walked into the cool air, breathing in the harbour smells of rancid fish and stale sweat. The sky was a pale shade of grey, dimmed by the torches which lit their path. Before them were the boats, just dark shapes in the water, their sails looming over them, fluttering in the breeze as they strained to break free. Lights burning on board, hinted at the activity taking place, accompanied by the calls and occasional curses as the sailors prepared to depart.

Father Wulfstan came towards them, his cross raised in blessing. He laid his hand on their heads. "I shall be praying for you, my son. I wish you every success."

"Thank you, Father." Siward smiled at the kindly face of the Bishop, thinking how he would miss him. "Take good care of England."

The Bishop nodded. "I will. And you, my son, take good care of the English."

With no further words, he and Oswyth walked hand in hand to the boat, Wulfric scampering ahead of them. Around them people had risen early to watch curiously, eager for a last glimpse of the man who had so defied their conqueror. As Wulfric reached their boat, hands reached down to haul him on board, but Siward and Oswyth paused. Looking back at the town, the smell of smoke rising from dwellings suggested people had just risen to start their day. It was an ordinary scene. One which had taken place there every morning for longer than anyone could remember and which would continue every day as life would go on. England was changed for all time, yet somehow still the same.

"I can hardly believe these are our last steps in England," Oswyth whispered. "It feels so strange."

"It does," Siward agreed as they reached the boat. "But, Oswyth, there must be no regrets."

Oswyth pressed her lips briefly to Siward's. "No, my love. There are no regrets."

"Come then, let us do this together."

They clambered onto the boat, Father Colman putting out a steadying hand to help Oswyth on board.

"Prepare to cast off," Siward cried.

From the nearby boats he could hear the sound of his order being relayed as behind them the sky had lightened a little further.

Thord, a short, sinewy man who was regarded as one of the finest sailors alive, stood with Siward. "There's a good wind out there, my lord, and a smooth sea. Perfect sailing conditions. We should make good progress out of the Severn Sea."

"I pray we shall," Siward replied. He was still nervous there might be a pursuit. He knew he could not completely relax until they were safely away from the English coast.

Oswyth looked out, seeing the ropes untied and flung to the boat. She leaned back against Siward, glad to have his arms around her at such a momentous time. Almost overcome with excitement at the activity, Wulfric came to stand with them. The boy's wide grin helped. It was impossible for them to feel overly emotional in the face of such enthusiasm. Siward gave a wry smile, resting one hand on his shoulder. Perhaps the boy had been sent by God to them after all.

The men pulled on the oars, easing the boat towards the harbour mouth. The boat glided smoothly along, cries of farewell drifting over the still air. Many on the boat returned the calls, the shrill noises echoing as the first seagulls awoke to wheel raucously overhead.

Beyond the harbour the waves picked up and wind stirred into the sails. Oswyth gasped as already the boat gained speed. She eyed the waves suspiciously, wondering, if this was a smooth sea, what a fierce one would be. As they made their way into the Severn Sea, she and Siward looked back to see the other boats streaming out behind them, their bright sails lit up by the first light.

Siward grinned in triumph, imagining what the sight looked like for those watching. Bishop Wulfstan, perhaps Roger and many another, both Norman and English, would be stood on the shore and the surrounding hills, witnessing this last glorious act of defiance on the behalf of the English as they made plain to all they would not live under the Norman domination. Any along the coast would have quite a sight to see.

They had not been sailing long when they heard a great rumble of drums and the voices of many men shouting. Siward looked towards the shore, the sky light enough to clearly see the boats sailing out of another harbour to join them. It was the boats under Frebern's command and in the one at the head, they could see their friend waving at them as the wind brought him out to join them.

"We are really going to manage it, aren't we?" Oswyth cried, her cheeks already pink from the brisk wind.

"I think so," Siward said. "We are not away yet, but who could possibly stop us now?"

They swept on up the coast to where another huge group waited, the boats skimming over the waves to greet them.

"What took you so long?" Bridwin had cupped his hands to shout at the top of his voice yet the sound only just reached them.

Siward laughed. Even now the sun was barely over the hills. "Let me see if you can keep up," he shouted back.

The day passed slowly, with Siward keeping a constant eye on the coast as first Somerset and then Devon slipped past. Occasionally they encountered boats but it was obvious that these were simply engaged in fishing or the transportation of goods and there was no danger.

It was well into the afternoon before Thord informed them they were now along the coast of Cornwall.

"We are just passing Tintagel," he said.

"We are making good progress," Siward commented. He stared at the stronghold on the rocky outcrop, overlooking the sea. He wondered who was in residence there and if they knew what was going on. He could just about make out a group of men pointing at them. Siward shook his head. He had been busy worrying about the possibility of pursuit but it suddenly occurred to him that this enormous fleet, skipping over the waves, was a terrifying sight to those who had no knowledge of their purpose.

"Is all well, Oswyth?" he asked, seeing her seated in subdued fashion.

"These waves are not doing my stomach any favours," she said with a rueful smile.

Siward grinned. "Take some bread. It will settle you. But you will have to get used to this. We are going to be on a boat for a long time yet."

"I do not know if I can ever become accustomed to this," Oswyth replied, trying for what seemed to be the hundredth time that day to smooth her hair back under its veil, only for the wind to whip it again into her face. "Never have I travelled at such a speed."

The sun was setting ahead of them when Thord announced they had reached the tip of Cornwall. There was a burst of frantic action as they guided the boats away from treacherous looking rocks. Siward was glad they had reached this point in daylight as he looked back anxiously at the boats following him. But on every one were trained sailors, many of Danish origin, who confidently navigated the peninsula, allowing their boats out into the open sea.

"We have done it," Siward cried. "We have cleared the coast of England."

Oswyth looked back. The setting sun lit up the land of her birth in a golden haze. Tears slid slowly down her cheeks as she gazed at the coast retreating behind them. She would never look on it again. By the time the sun rose, it would be gone.

Siward put his arms around her. "Do not weep."

She clung to him. "How can I help it? We are leaving so much behind. Your mother, our people, the graves of our kin, the realm our fathers and grandfathers served. I do not know if I can bear it."

Siward had no words. He thought of the home he had grown up in, where his father had presided before him. So clearly he could see the hall, beautiful in the twilight with the first torches lit as the night drew in. Now Drogo was there, resting in the chair he had once sat in, calling for ale just as he had once done. A crushing pain swelled in his chest and he too wondered if he would be able to bear it.

He looked around, seeing similar expressions on many as they looked back at the land they had once called home. Even Wulfric's shoulders had slumped, his gaze now fixed on the deck. He shook himself. This was no way to start a voyage. And all these people were depending on him. There was now no king to either serve or defy. The success of this venture was up to him.

He wiped the tears from his eyes and turned away from the sight of England basking in the evening light. Pulling Oswyth with him, they lurched as the boat pitched on the sea but made it safely to the centre of the boat. He climbed perilously onto a chest, clutching at the mast to steady himself.

"Be of good cheer, my friends," he cried, taking one last look at England. "That land back there is but rock and dirt. It has no meaning beyond that. The true essence of England is in our hearts and we shall take it with us wherever we go. I know what you have left behind, for I have left it too. Homes, possessions, kith and kin. But look around. Take the hand of the one beside you, for we shall now be kin to each other. And we are free, my friends. There can be no greater possession than that. From this moment we are no longer under the Bastard's control. We are free Englishmen and women."

There was a loud cheer, the faces brightening. He looked out at the other boats. They could not hear his words but they would see the change in mood. He extended his hand to Oswyth. She too was smiling, her eyes looking up at him in love.

He had lost so much in the last years but it was nothing compared to what he had gained. She took his hand, stepping onto the chest with him, allowing their lips to meet. At this the cheers rang out louder than ever.

Siward grinned, keeping Oswyth tightly to him as he gestured to where the prow of the boat skipped along. "Look back no longer. Instead look to the home ahead. Somewhere out there is New England. No matter how long it takes, we are going to find it."

Characters

The leaders of this expedition are named in the sources as Standardus, Brithniathus and Frebern with the first two names Latinised. They are described as earls, but as Gloucester, Lichfield and Warwick are not known to have had earls pre-conquest, it is not clear exactly who they were. It has been suggested that Siward was Siward Barnes, a key rebel against William the Conqueror, who is known to have had lands in Gloucestershire. However, if this migration did indeed take place in the 1070s, it cannot be him, as he was imprisoned at the time.

Other names recorded as being part of this venture include Coleman, who in this has found his way to becoming Siward's chaplain, Father Colman, Dunnigt who here is called Dunstan and Wicredus who I have called Wicrun.

Bishop Wulfstan of Worcester was the last English bishop and Turstin Fitz Rolf was a Norman who fought at Hastings, receiving many lands in the years after. He is believed to have had a son named Ralf. Roger de Breteuill was the Earl of Hereford who took part in the failed Revolt of the Earls in the year this books ends. However the part all these men played in this story is my own invention. Leofwine was the Bishop of Lichfield, who resigned from office after the conquest due to his marriage. It is not known for certain what he did after that, although retirement in an abbey is the most likely possibility. Wulfric too is based on a real person, although his character, background and how he came to be on the voyage, if indeed he was on the voyage, is fiction. All other characters are fictional, although a Drogo is mentioned in the Doomsday Book in possession of lands in Gloucestershire near the River Severn beside one of the estates of Turstin Fitz Rolf, with the owner in the reign of Edward the Confessor named as Earnsig, the name I have given to Siward's father. It is a complete invention (although not impossible!) to suggest that between these two might be a man named Siward who had inherited the lands after the death of Edward the Confessor, but was there no longer by the time the Doomsday book was compiled.

Edgar the Atheling and King Sweyn of Denmark were rival claimants to the throne, with Edgar being the last of the Wessex line and King Sweyn a relative of King Cnut. The man known mostly here as the Bastard, whose dark presence looms over the book, I am sure needs no introduction!

Available now

in ebook (paperback coming soon)

Quest for New England

Book 2

Peril & Plunder

The English exiles, under the command of Siward of Glouces-ter, sail into the Mediterranean, where they find wonders await-ing them and treasures ripe for the taking. Braving storms and Saracens, they sail on undaunted, their spirits higher than ever.

But as they settle on the island of Sicily, they find their old enemies, the Normans are already there and discover the wounds of the past are not as healed as they had hoped. When Siward realises the ghosts he thought he had left in England are waiting for him on the island, his fear of failure returns with a vengeance.

Consumed by terror, he struggles to maintain authority over his men, finding even his old friends, Bridwin and Frebern no longer support him. With his behaviour spiralling out of con-trol, Oswyth tries desperately to help her husband until their love too is stretched to breaking point. With Siward no longer appearing to care if he drives everyone away, she is left broken hearted, convinced her marriage is in tatters.

As it seems Siward will lose both the leadership and everyone he loves, he draws strength from a surprising source. But with

Bridwin preparing to take command, has that help come too late to save either his marriage or his friendships?

And as the Norman threat lingers, will Siward's quest for New England end as just one more broken dream?

I hope you have enjoyed reading Rising from the Ruins. The Norman Conquest is one of the best known events in English history, but all too often it is told from the view of the victors. Good reviews are critical to a book's success, so please take a moment to leave your review on the platform where you bought the book. I look forward to hearing from you!

For more news, offers, upcoming releases and all things medieval please get in touch via

My Facebook Page
https://www.facebook.com/darkagevoices/
Check out my blog:
https://darkagevoices.wordpress.com/
Follow me on Twitter: https://twitter.com/anna_chant
And Instagram:
https://www.instagram.com/annachant_darkagevoices/

Also by Anna Chant

Women of the Dark Ages

More than a thousand years before today was a fabulous period where history and legend collided to form what is often known as the Dark Ages. Peering through the mists of time figures emerge, often insubstantially becoming as much legend as history. And if the men are hard to see, the women are even harder with dates and even names left unrecorded. Each of the books in the Women on the Dark Ages series tells the stories of the forgotten or uncelebrated, but very remarkable women who lived through these tumultuous times.

Kenneth's Queen: The tale of the unknown wife of Scottish king, Kenneth Mac Alpin.

The Girl from Brittia: The curious tale of a sixth century warrior princess, known only as The Island Girl.

Three Times the Lady: A Frankish princess, a Wessex queen – the exciting true story of Judith of Flanders.

The Saxon Marriage: The story of Eadgyth of Wessex and her marriage to Otto, the young Hope of Saxony.

God's Maidservant: Treachery, tragedy and triumph – the story of Adelaide of Italy, one of the tenth century's most remarkable women.

Dawn of the Franks: Bitter betrayal, forbidden love and the visions sent by the Gods as Queen Basina of Thuringia seeks her destiny.

About the author

Anna Chant was born and spent her childhood in Essex. She studied history at the University of Sheffield, before qualifying as a primary teacher. She currently lives in Devon with her husband and three sons. In her spare time she enjoys reading, sewing and camping. 'Rising from the Ruins' is her seventh novel and the first in the 'Quest for New England' series.

Printed in Great
Britain
by Amazon